Annmarie,

FAMINE'S FEAST

CLUB APOCALYPSE

BOOK THREE

RAISA GREYWOOD

Happy reading !

Raisa Greywood

Cover art by Wicked Smart Designs.
Editing provided by Amy Briggs.

Ebook ISBN: 978-1-952596-31-5
Print ISBN: 978-1-952596-20-9

Playlist

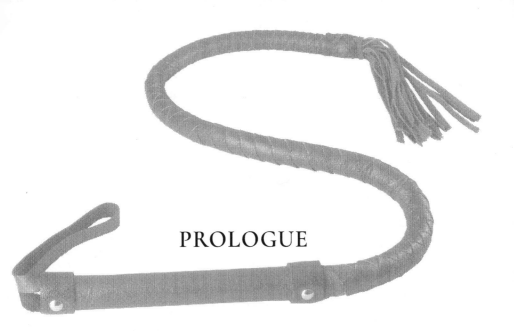

PROLOGUE

Ryan thought he was being sneaky, but Jake McBride knew his pantry. There was no way he was going to miss three hundred dollars' worth of caviar going missing the morning after Ryan finally claimed his wife. He'd also nicked a bottle of their best champagne. Asshole.

Still, he couldn't muster up much irritation. Ryan and Carrie were perfect for each other. He just wished they could find a little fucking space to do the honeymoon thing.

But no. Although now defunct, the Shepherds of the Coming Peace were still trying to fuck them without lube. And because Carrie opened her big mouth, she was a social media heroine with women all over the world giving her a fist-pump. Her face was on memes now, and that shit never died.

Granted, he loved everything about that impromptu video. She'd been badass as fuck. Even more so than Kendra, their vice-president of operations.

He let out a breath, then focused his attention on Olivia Rivera, his new sous chef. She'd been mentally absent and distracted for almost a week, and nothing he'd tried had managed to grab her attention.

What the fuck was she doing? She was in no danger of losing her job, but he'd have thought an ex-con still on parole would have pulled her shit together now that she was safe.

She kept looking out the windows and cowered every time a motorcycle went by. They were on Route 66, for fuck's sake. Most days, there was nothing but motorcycles on the two-lane stretch of highway fronting Club Apocalypse.

"Fish course," he snapped, liking the way she jumped. "You have two hours to create a recipe without looking something up on the internet. I suggest you don't disappoint me."

"May I ask what the rest of the meal will be?"

"It'll depend on what you come up with."

"Yes, sir."

Leaning against one of the worktables, he smirked as she gathered supplies. She probably thought he didn't understand her litany of Spanish curses, but he caught every word. With mortar and pestle, she pounded a flame roasted cayenne pepper, toasted cilantro seeds, and weirdly, a dusting of grated allspice berry into a paste, then sauteed it.

The savory fragrance filled the air and his mouth watered. Lime zest went into crema fresca along with a few fresh cilantro leaves, and one very carefully tempered and flash-chilled yolk from a duck egg. It was a somewhat unusual choice he'd have never considered, but Olivia had an incredible gift for sauces.

He'd have sworn she could barely use a can opener when she started working for him. Although he had taught her what she'd need to do her job, she always tried to go further. More than once, he'd caught her experimenting with his recipes when she thought he wasn't looking.

And that annoyed the fuck out of him because some of what she came up with was better than the original. It was just one of the many things that didn't make sense about Olivia.

He didn't like or trust things that appeared too good to be true. Olivia's sauce skills fell into that category, and no matter how much he wracked his brain, he couldn't figure out her game.

His gut was telling him something was wrong about her, and it got worse every day. He almost wished he could have her parole officer find her another work release position, but he had no justification or even the thinnest shred of evidence. It was also possible he was wrong. If so, he'd be acting without cause.

Her whisk flew as she blended the ingredients into a creamy yellow sauce. To his irritation, she never used electric appliances unless he forced her. After tasting it, she tapped in a pinch of salt, along with an additional scant teaspoon of the cayenne paste and a squeeze of lime juice.

He waited until the additions were incorporated, then grabbed a spoon. "The moment of truth," he said, nudging her out of the way before she could taste it again. She never needed a second taste for her sauces to be perfect, the brat.

Her expression rearranged itself, her round face moving from spitting rage to a blandly innocuous smile. "Of course, sir. If it pleases you, let the flavors meld and taste it again in a few hours."

He let the sauce dribble on his tongue, noting the bite of cayenne soothed with crema fresca. Rich from the egg yolk with a vibrant Caribbean-influenced flavor profile, it would be sublime after it had time to rest.

There was no fucking way he'd tell her that though.

"Adequate," he finally said, tossing the spoon at her. "Barely. Are you planning a carb or a vegetable?"

She caught the spoon out of the air, then inclined her head. "Thank you, sir. I was thinking slaw of Napa cabbage with sweet vinaigrette if it's a starter, or fried plantains with Hungarian peppers and spring onions if it's a main."

"And your choice of fish?"

"Seared red snapper fillets. There's a whole one in the walk-in that should be—"

"Use tuna." It wouldn't work with the delicate sauce she'd created or any of the sides she mentioned, but he wanted to see what she'd say. Would she have the balls to disagree when they both knew the snapper had been the right choice?

A vein pulsed in her neck, and he wanted to rub his hands together in anticipation of her outburst. Instead of exploding, she gave him a sweet smile that belied the fury boiling in her huge brown eyes. "In that case, I'd like to do tuna tartare with shredded fennel dressed with black truffle oil, fresh garlic croutons, and a dust of Parmigiano-Reggiano. It's something I've never—"

"Sloppy, Ms. Rivera. Did you forget the wine pairing?"

"No sir." Her cheek dimpled as if she bit down on the inside. "You didn't ask for a wine pairing, but for the snapper, I like the pinot gris. For the tuna, I think the shiraz might work better."

Even though her pairings weren't quite on point, they were close. He clamped his lips tight on the praise he wanted to give her for remembering what was fresh and ready to use in the coolers. Both the snapper and fennel would need to be put on the menu in the next day or two before they went bad. Unfortunately, the fennel was too strong for the tuna dish she described and would overpower the earthy truffle oil. Served with arugula or baby spinach, he'd write it on the specials board in a heartbeat.

"Too much going on." Hoping it would send her into a

meltdown, he dumped her sauce into the waste bucket even though he wanted to sob at the loss of such culinary brilliance. "Try harder if you want to reach the bare minimum of competence."

"Yes, sir. Thank you." Her hands shook, but she obediently washed the empty bowl he left in the sink.

Smirking, he turned, but didn't make it two steps away before she opened her deliciously filthy mouth.

"I'm going to shove that fucking tuna straight up his ass."

"Sorry?" He turned and crossed his arms over his chest, the urge to tell her he understood Spanish nearly making him let go of his secret.

"Nothing, sir." She met his gaze steadily, then added, "However, it would create less waste if you gave me the caveats before I start the sauce."

"Are you telling me how to run my kitchen, Ms. Rivera?"

"Of course not, sir."

Lovely. She was nearly shaking with rage. Her hand inched toward her fish knife, but she folded her arms behind her back before she touched the handle of a blade he'd personally commissioned to fit her small hand. She treated it, and the others he'd had made, like her children.

That was yet another thing he'd never tell her. She thought she was using off-the-rack department store cutlery, and he loved how she treasured them anyway.

The unconsciously submissive pose nearly dropped him

to his knees. With her chin tilted up, she'd never looked more beautiful, but she said not a single word in her own defense.

That wouldn't do at all. Silently, he begged her to take a shot. Just one. It would give him the excuse he needed to punish her generously curved ass, then he could tell her how amazing she was.

There were only two problems with that.

Kendra would kill him for laying a hand on an employee, and they'd never find his dismembered corpse. There were some people in the world with whom one did not fuck, and she was at the top of the list—even for a dominant who demanded unquestioning obedience from a slave who willingly put themselves under his mastery.

Olivia also understood what it meant to be on parole, and if there was one thing he'd come to learn about her, it was that she would do nothing that might risk a return to prison.

Even to her own detriment—no matter how many times they told her she and her continued employment were safe.

And that gave him a powerful anger.

He left the kitchen, still wishing she'd given him something. Just one fucking bone to let him know she wouldn't roll over for abuse. Fuck knew he'd tried to make her stand up for herself.

Then again, she was cursing him in Spanish. He just wished she had the nerve to say the words in English.

Six goddamned weeks and she still took everything he dished out. Still took every insult, every abuse, every word denigrating her skills, which made him wonder things he didn't have time to think about.

There was still a mess to clean up with the Shepherds—especially after the perplexing murders of the two leaders. Gaelic curses still echoed from Gabby's office as she tried to stop multiple cyber-attacks a day, and they hadn't yet figured out her connection with the Italian mob. Carrie's friend Valentina would need help and a safe place to go—whether she liked it or not, and now they had Ian Paxton back in town to add his own brand of crazy. Yet Jake couldn't stop himself from wondering.

What scared Olivia Rivera?

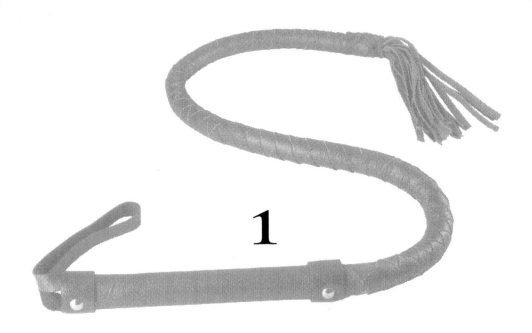

1

OLIVIA

Her running shoes beat a steady rhythm on the hard-packed earth, matching the thumping bass coming through the earbuds she probably shouldn't have been wearing while jogging in the desert by herself.

Of course, two hours before dawn, the only thing out here was her, and maybe a mountain lion or two. The morning chill would keep the snakes and scorpions snug in their dens. She didn't mind the animals though. They were less dangerous than what had lived at her last address, but none of that would follow her.

At least, she hoped not.

These were her only moments of peace. Too soon, she'd

have to be fresh-faced, smiling, and ready for her spot at the omelet station for the breakfast buffet—which would then be followed by eight hours of Jake McBride—AKA the kitchen troll—looming over her shoulder like a fucking vulture.

She got a four-hour break for lunch and personal time. If she hadn't had a daily chance to decompress, she'd have knifed him already.

He didn't speak Spanish, thank God. Otherwise, she'd have been fired after the first week. Several of the kitchen staff did, but oddly enough, they never told on her.

There were no words to adequately convey how much she despised him. With all the fires of a burning sun, she loathed his rich baritone voice, the astringent scent of his herbal soap reeking of rosemary and sage, and the measured squeak of his nonskid shoes on the tiled kitchen floor. Everything about him abraded her senses, leaving them jangling and out of sync until she could barely concentrate.

He reminded her of drain cleaner. It was as if he was specifically designed to dissolve people into sludge. His caustic commentary on her food ate at her very bones. The steady gaze of his poisonous blue eyes did the same thing to her soul.

Was he better than prison? She'd thought so at first.

Worse, she kept trying to please him. Every step she made in his kitchen was thought out, carefully calculated in a vain attempt to receive a word of praise. Just one would have made everything she did worthwhile.

Fuck my life. He said I was adequate, and it about stopped my heart with pleasure.

And why the hell was such a gorgeous man so damned toxic?

There were worse places to spend her parole though. Aside from Jake, she got along with her coworkers. The guests were usually kind and pleasant. Club Apocalypse was safe and secure, and most importantly, clean.

She could have gotten stuck in the recycling center where things would smell a lot worse than a commercial kitchen. She shuddered inwardly.

With every step, she tried to come up with something positive about her life. She'd aged out of foster care, so no more swapping houses when people got tired of dealing with her. Aside from Jake, nobody was bullying her, stealing her lunch money, or making fun of her wiry curls. She also didn't have to trade favors to keep herself safe like she had in jail.

Altruism truly didn't exist in her world, but she'd make the best of what she had.

Cooking wasn't so bad either. If she had a different boss, she might have been happy someday, but her happiness didn't matter anymore. Her old life was gone. She could finish her degree and probably receive CPA certification but didn't see anyone hiring an accountant who had served time for drug trafficking.

As she approached the best part of her morning run, she pushed Jake and her stupid praise kink out of her head. She might have to spend too many hours with him, but this was her time. Slowing to a walk, she approached the small escarpment and sighed happily. After a few swallows from her water bottle, she slid her earbuds into her pocket, then stuffed her shoes, socks, and jacket into her pack. Wearing only a sports bra and shorts, she taped her fingers and began her free climb.

This far out in the desert, there was no light pollution to diffuse illumination from the stars and lowering moon. Her handholds, memorized after weeks, were visible and it felt as if they almost reached for her.

You belong here, the cliff said. *This place is yours.*

The rock face was a personal challenge between her body and all the forces that had sought to drag her down for so many years. Every time she reached the top, it meant another triumph.

Another day where she lifted herself from her past with callused fingers.

And if Karma or some deity with nothing better to do decided to yank her off her cliff someday? That was okay too.

It wouldn't be today.

Muscles burning, she reached the top and...breathed. Sweat cooled on her body, making her shiver, but it felt too good to reach for her jacket. Although she was less than a hundred feet up, the air felt different somehow, like it welcomed her to the rarified heights where only she could go. It was sanctified in silence.

It was the one place she didn't have to listen to Jake McBride. There were no guests in the hallways, no incessant chatter of housekeepers or servers...

There was only the sound of the desert.

Granted, there was a relatively easy trail on the other side, but she only used it for the trip down. She might be crazy enough to free climb in the dark on the way up, but she didn't have a death wish. Bare toes gripping the edge of the cliff, she relaxed her muscles as she watched false dawn come and go.

With her mind at rest, she sighed, filling herself with as much calm as her secret place could give her. It was almost time to head back and clean up for work.

"Rivera, your cooking isn't that bad."

Fuck's sake! Could she get no peace from the man?

"I'll give you a reference to McDonalds if you can't handle it here, but don't splatter cute Latina all over my desert. I don't have time for the paperwork."

Holding a curse inside, she tried to turn, but her toe caught on the edge and made her fall backward. Screaming, she windmilled her arms in a desperate attempt to keep her balance. Her feet found nothing to stand on and all she could think about was that Jake called her cute.

Karma was a cast-iron bitch.

Without warning, something grabbed her wrist hard, then yanked her away from the edge. The motion sent her sprawling at Jake's feet.

"Are you okay?"

Hauling in a deep breath, she looked up at him, but the darkness prevented her from seeing his expression. Slowly, she got to her hands and knees, then stood. Her shoulder throbbed, both from Jake's violent pull on her arm and her fall, but she was fine otherwise.

Sure she'd heard a note of concern in his voice, she smiled. "Yes, sir. Thank you for—"

"Since your attempt at suicide was just as inept as your poached salmon, I trust you won't be late to work?"

Hate him. Fires of a burning sun. Drain cleaner. Jail was definitely better than this bullshit.

"No, sir."

———

JAKE

His heart pounded, both from the desperate race to the top of the cliff when he saw her standing on the edge, and from her mishap.

She'd have been killed.

He made a note never to buy another lottery ticket. He'd

used a lifetime of luck. It had been sheer chance that he'd seen her from the road. Hell, it was incredible coincidence in the first place, considering the only reason he was out at this ungodly hour at all was to pick up some hardware from the Walmart in Winslow for a plumbing issue in one of the guest suites.

If he hadn't been... He stopped the thought in its tracks.

As he tried to get his shit together so he could speak without wanting to beat her ass, she retrieved a fleece jacket from her pack and put it on before her socks and shoes.

Without a word, she got to her feet and jogged down the trail, forcing him to hurry to catch up.

"Where's the fire, Rivera?" he called out.

She quickened her pace. "You told me not to be late, sir."

"God damned fucking runners." Bearing down, he caught up, then cut in front to force her to stop. "Why were you going to kill yourself?"

"I wasn't. I—"

"I saw you, Olivia. You made your imminent swan dive abundantly clear."

Her jaw worked and a vein pulsed in her forehead. "Sir, am I off the clock?"

"What the hell kind of question is that?"

"Am. I. Off. The. Clock? Will you fire me if I answer truthfully?"

The fear left his body but was replaced by another kind of tension. Would she finally say all the words she'd hidden behind Spanish curses? He wasn't sure how he wanted to respond, but his cock shot hard at the thought of what she might tell him.

"Nobody is going to fire you for telling the truth."

"Good." She took a step back, then looked up at him, her eyes sparkling with furious tears. "You're a fucking asshole, Jake McBride. I hate you. I hate your tasteless food with too much pepper and not enough salt. I hate that you can't even smell it when you fuck up, and that you don't believe me when I try to say something."

Mess up one steak and never hear the end of it.

Was it possible she suffered from hyperosmia? It would explain her gift with sauces and flavor profiles, even with such limited experience. Damn. If he'd even guessed at something like that...

And now...he was jealous.

"Go on," he finally said, enjoying the way her tentative, halting speech smoothed into a delicious accent that made his cock stand to attention.

"I hate that you can't make a decent omelet to save your life. I hate your constant criticism when you know I'm doing a good job, and I especially hate that it's worse when I do something better than you."

"Is that all?" he asked, hiding a smile. It might have taken a near-death experience, but he was delighted she was finally saying what he'd needed to hear.

The moonlight was nearly gone, meaning he couldn't see

her very well, but one last shard of silvery light caught her face. Her dark hair hung to the middle of her back in loose spiral curls from a ponytail at the base of her neck, and her brown eyes sparkled. A faint sheen of sweat on her face made her glisten, and she'd never looked more glorious.

"No." She jammed a finger into his chest, making him move back a step. "I absolutely cannot stand that I still want to hear you tell me I did a good job. Just one time."

Interesting. If he'd realized Olivia had a praise kink, he might have handled things differently. Then again, maybe that wasn't a good choice, considering they were coworkers. Too bad his dick thought it was an excellent idea.

"Anything else?"

"Yes." She took a deep breath and scrubbed a hand over her eyes. "I'm walking on fucking eggshells every day because of you. I hate that my nerves misfire and it feels like ants are crawling all over me every time you speak or move. I hate the way your shoes sound like dog whistles. I hate your stupid soap because it makes everything smell wrong, and I hate that you're too nose-blind to recognize it. And I really hate that I'm thinking about breaking parole so they'll send me back to jail, just so I can get away from your arrogant ass!"

"No," he replied softly, taking a step toward her. "You're not going to be doing that."

She snorted and turned away. "You have no idea how close you are to a carving knife between your ribs every time you open your mouth. I wouldn't lose a minute's sleep, and best of all, they'd send me to Perryville instead of Navajo County Detention."

"What's so great about Perryville?"

"It's further away from you." She stepped around him, then took off down the trail.

"Tell me how you really feel," he murmured.

Instead of chasing her, he let her go and thought about everything she'd said. Unfortunately, it left him with more questions than answers.

Why hadn't she blown up earlier? With as much as she'd obviously held inside, she should have set him down weeks ago. At the very least, she should have complained to Kendra.

Thankfully, she hadn't. He wanted Olivia close where he could watch her. Something inside him needed to have her nearby, and Kendra would have moved her to another position in a heartbeat.

The closer he got to his truck, the more he worried. He didn't understand why he made her feel like ants were crawling on her, but that couldn't continue.

Making her work for praise, yes, that was well within what he was willing to do. Physically or emotionally harming her wasn't on his agenda.

There was another problem too. She hadn't given him the one answer he really wanted.

Why had she been on that cliff?

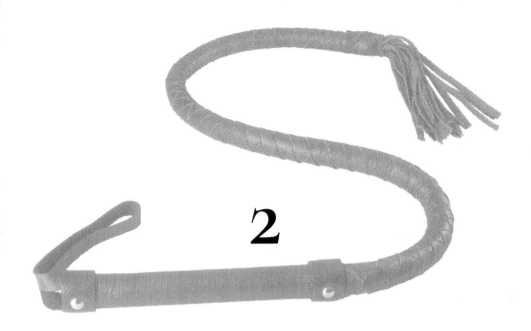

2

OLIVIA

The awful scene with Jake wouldn't leave her head and she expected to be fired at any second. Going back to jail didn't bother her as much as losing her private space on the cliff. Jake McBride had spoiled it forever.

"Miss Olivia, *mo chridhe*, is there any chance I can beg for a full English? It was a long night, and I'm a bit hung."

Okay, so there were a few nice things about Club Apocalypse. Dr. Gabby Knox smelled like candied ginger. Although Olivia hated food scents on people, the spicy perfume seemed to fit her, and she was sweeter than Tia Jozefina's *alfajores* filled with *dulce de leche*.

"Of course, but we're out of black pudding. It should come in with today's delivery. Is that okay?"

"There are beans, right?"

"I wouldn't forget those." Olivia dredged up a smile and finished cleaning up the omelet station. "They're simmering right now."

"Ohhh, yes." Dr. Knox shivered with delight and hugged herself. "You make the most fabulous beans. Proper ones too, instead of the revolting mess these silly Americans make."

"Yes, ma'am."

It might not be coming from the kitchen troll, but she basked in the praise. It felt like a soft blanket around her shoulders on a cold day. She'd be seated by the wood fired stove while Tia stirred *pulique* fragrant with peppercorns and epazote, and...

"Olivia..." Dr. Knox waved a finger in her face and tapped a foot covered in a pale turquoise Doc Marten boot. "What's it going to cost me to make you call me Gabby?"

"I'm sorry. I'll try harder." She set her skillet in a bus pan along with the empty bowls which once held omelet fillings. The portable cooktop went on the lower shelf of her cart. Although the buffet would stay open for another hour, her work was done.

She didn't mind doing omelets. They made people happy, and it meant she could talk to one guest at a time and create the exact perfect meal for them.

"Ma'am makes me feel like someone's grandmother."

"Sorry. Is twenty minutes okay? We have the Welsh dragon sausages you like, so I'll add an extra to make up for the pudding."

"Perfect. You're a love." Dr. Knox gave her a dimpled smile and skipped from the restaurant.

Although guests were encouraged to eat at the buffet, she liked making Dr. Knox's breakfast, and nobody else seemed to want to do it. She figured it was on account of the black pudding.

Dr. Knox was right. Americans were weird. There was nothing wrong with blood sausage. It was delicious. The pennyroyal that shouldn't have worked but did gave her nose a wonderful tingle every time she smelled it.

Her shoulder aching from the mishap with Jake and two hours of flipping omelets, she pushed the cart into the kitchen, deciding she'd make Dr. Knox's breakfast before she had to deal with him for yet another day of what he called remedial lessons.

Although there were many skills she hadn't known until she came to Club Apocalypse, she wasn't completely useless. Too bad the kitchen troll didn't recognize it. He didn't give two shits about what she could do and only focused on what she couldn't.

Still lost in her own head, she left the cart near the industrial dishwashers, then went to the cooler to fetch what she'd need for a full English. She considered the supplies, then grabbed a few loaves of bread left over from table service, plus eggs, mushrooms, a tomato, sausage, and thick-cut British bacon, then trudged back to the kitchen.

To her horror, Jake stood over the stove and dipped a spoon into her pot of beans. Her heart almost fell out of her chest when he tasted it and grimaced.

"Are we living *Orange is the New Black?*" he asked, carrying the pot to the waste bucket. "Don't serve prison food to my guests, Ms. Rivera."

"Please...don't." She reached for the pot but yanked her hand back. She couldn't stop it if he was determined. That was a hard-learned lesson she'd never forget.

"Why not?"

He stood over the bucket and met her gaze with eyes like pools of radioactive waste, daring her to protest. On any other day, she would have kept silent, but not when she'd promised the contents of that pot to a guest.

"The beans are for Dr. Knox's full English breakfast."

"Ah. I see. That would explain what you're carrying from the coolers. I suppose you can play short order cook for that."

Maybe she wouldn't lose her job. Not today, at least. "Yes, sir."

Trying to ignore his gaze boring into her back, she went to the grill to start the sausages and bacon, praying he'd return her pot of beans to the cooktop so they'd stay warm.

Finally, he obeyed her unspoken wish, and even turned the burner on. "Where's the pudding?"

"It was supposed to get here yesterday. I added an extra sausage to make up for it."

Thankfully, he didn't say anything. She'd added black pudding to the list, and it wasn't her job to order stock for the restaurant, but she was sure he'd find some way to make it her fault.

Behind her, she heard Kendra walk toward the kitchen. The sound of her heels was both comforting and irritating. Olivia liked Kendra's no-nonsense attitude. She didn't put up with shit from any of the Horsemen—including the kitchen troll.

"Hey, Jake, there's a staff meeting in my—ooh! I smell real baked beans! Are you making someone a full English, Olivia?"

"Yes, ma'am. It's for Dr. Knox."

Kendra leaned over the pot and inhaled greedily. "Oh, shit. These aren't from a can, are they?"

"No, ma'am."

"Please tell me there isn't enough for two."

That was another thing she liked about Kendra. Although she tried to stick to a healthy diet, she was easy to tempt.

Olivia slid the rest of the sausages and bacon to the grill. "Unfortunately, there's no black pudding."

Kendra's smile disappeared. "Where's the pudding? Why is there no pudding?"

"It got missed in yesterday's delivery, but—"

"Jake, tell the supplier they're done if they fuck up again." Kendra grabbed a spoon and dipped it into the pot. Her eyes closed and she moaned as she licked the spoon clean. "Hello, treadmill, my old friend. When will it be ready?"

"Fifteen minutes?"

"Perfect." As she walked toward the door, she added, "Jake, I asked Gabby to attend the staff meeting. Bring our breakfast with you, and if you steal a single bite, I'll take you outside and—"

He rolled his eyes and scowled. "I know, you'll hunt me for sport."

It probably wasn't a good idea to enjoy his disgruntled expression so much, but Olivia couldn't help it. This might be the last meal she made here, so she decided to get some fun out of it.

Besides, when he wasn't paying attention to her, she liked looking at his face. The man's cheekbones would make a supermodel weep, and she loved the way his hair fell over his forehead. Although touching him would be just as stupid as what she'd done to get herself thrown in jail, her fingers itched to straighten the waves into order.

Thankfully, he left her alone, allowing her to relax and turn the sausages. When they were browned, she moved them aside to finish at a lower temperature. Humming under her breath, she flipped the bacon. The rich odors of cooking meat let her fall into the memory of watching Tia Jozefina perform the same task over a griddle made from the steel lid of a fifty-five-gallon drum. The sizzle and scrape of her spatula were almost identical, even if the food wasn't.

"Rivera, is there any hope you'll stop staring at that grill and prep the mushrooms sometime today?"

She flinched and spun around, finding him bare inches away from her. "I—"

"Now would be good," he snapped. "We don't have all day."

Olivia scurried to the worktable and began quartering mushrooms, then nearly sliced off her thumb when she realized she'd never heard him approach with the additional ingredients. A quick glance at his feet revealed sneakers instead of his usual nonskid shoes, and the only thing she could smell aside from the food was plain, unscented soap.

———

JAKE

"Stupid fucking kitchen troll."

He pressed his lips together and tried not to laugh at her creative insult. Sooner or later, when he decided to share his secret understanding of Spanish, he might have his old CO

Zach Stratton make up a wooden sign for the space above
the door.

El troll de la cocina exige un peaje.

Zach's wife Jolene would love it.

Instead of sparring with Olivia, he stepped back to let
her work, his focus intent as he watched her pull together
the relatively simple meal.

She counted things.

Each sausage got three turns, while the bacon got four.
The sizzling mushrooms were scraped and moved in a
strangely hypnotic geometric pattern, and she placed the
tomato halves at precise cardinal compass points around
them. He thought it was weird at first, then understood
what she was doing when she spooned fragrant tomato juice
over the mushrooms, creating a decadent sauce with a scant
tablespoon of unsalted butter.

She never, ever used salted butter if she could help it,
and she could tell the difference by scent.

The food was plated like she was measuring the fucking
angles too. Even the fried eggs were laid just so next to the
sausages, with the grilled bread arranged on the side to hold
the beans in a perfect ring.

With every movement, some gracefully economical and
others awkward, his belly grew tighter. The signs had all
been there, but he'd never noticed them because he'd been
too damned busy picking her apart until she burst open.

He felt like the worst asshole ever—especially after

threatening to throw away the beans he'd known perfectly well Gabby wanted. Hell, he didn't even know why he'd done it, and it went well beyond forcing Olivia to stand up to him into outright cruelty.

Her neurodiversity wasn't the problem and never would be. Her unwillingness to ask for what she needed was a big fucking issue, and the minute he got back from telling Kendra he was blowing off the staff meeting, they were going to fix it—whether Olivia liked it or not.

Thankfully, the breakfast service was almost done, meaning they'd have plenty of time for their conversation. He had less than zero interest in finding her on top of that escarpment ever again.

"Everything looks delicious," he finally said. "Good job."

To his surprise, she stilled and shivered. Her shoulders dropped, and she let out a slow breath. "Thank you, sir. Do you want me to deliver them?"

"No." He grabbed a room service cart, then set the plates on it along with a coffee service, flatware, and napkins. "Go ahead and start cleaning up. I'll be back to help you in a few."

When he reached Kendra's office, he pushed the cart inside. "Sorry, I have things to do. Someone take notes for me."

"Hey, wait!"

Ignoring Kendra's surprised shout, he walked out, then headed back to the kitchen. Instead of sneaking up on Olivia as he might have done before, he made noise before he pushed the door open.

She hadn't touched the mess. Instead, she sat on a stool and carefully honed her knives. All of them—not just the chef's blade she'd used for the mushrooms and tomatoes. It had irritated him at first, but he was coming to recognize it was necessary.

Olivia couldn't move forward until she'd cared for her tools.

Content to watch, he grabbed a cup of coffee and waited until she laid them in their leather case and covered them with a piece of soft flannel, then closed it.

"Sorry," she murmured, hopping down from her stool. "I'll clean up now."

"No, leave it. I want to talk. Grab some coffee and come sit with me."

"Yes, sir." She scurried to the industrial carafe and filled a cup, then added a touch of cream. Carrying her coffee, she returned, but didn't sit.

"Have a seat first."

Her posture communicating her wariness, she set her coffee down and stole a peek at him before looking away. She drummed her fingers on her thigh for several seconds before sitting across from him. "I'm sorry for this morning, sir."

"Don't be. I've been riding your ass for weeks, and I deserved every word you said. We'll talk about how best to work with your sensory needs later. Right now, I want to tell you I've set up an appointment for you with our on-call therapist this afternoon. Until then, you're not to leave the building without an escort."

"Um...why?"

Carefully, he reached across the table to touch her shoulder, but didn't force her to look at him. "I owe you an apology. I've been an absolute ass to you, but I never want to see you up on that cliff again. Suicide isn't the answer to problems."

Olivia flinched, then parted her lips as her eyes widened with surprise. "Wait! I—"

The blare of a fire alarm cut off what she'd been about to say. Jake stood, then let out a vicious curse. Taking her arm, he hustled her to the emergency exit and pushed her outside. "We'll finish our conversation later. Go to the evacuation point on the other side of the pool. Make sure to check in with security and stay put until I come get you."

3

OLIVIA

Before she could say a word, Jake slammed the door in her face, leaving her stunned and off balance.

"When did someone replace the kitchen troll with a real human?"

She'd unloaded all her frustration and anger on the cliff, which explained his comments about her sensory issues, but how did that end up being an attempted suicide? Olivia also had no idea if he was being kind because he thought she might harm herself, or because he thought she might sue him for ADA violations.

It was one of the two. Jake wouldn't go out of his way to be nice to her otherwise.

Grumbling under her breath, she trudged across the

property to the pool and joined the small group of house-keepers and maintenance workers.

"Hi, Olivia." Isabelle, one of the security guards, gave her a smile and made a note on her clipboard. "Are you okay?"

"Yes, I'm fine. What happened?"

"Some asshole threw a bunch of Molotov cocktails into the lobby. We're waiting to make sure the fire is out before we let everyone back in."

"On a Monday morning? Aren't there security cameras?" She wandered around the side of the building, expecting to see tour buses carrying protesters, then remembered the Shepherds of the Coming Peace religious cult was supposed to have been disbanded. Aside from that, they'd never attempted to damage the property.

Isabelle frowned and shook her head. "The cameras were—"

"Let me go, you bloody wanker!"

Olivia turned and blinked in surprise as Sean Franklin carried a struggling Dr. Knox over one shoulder. His face was set in a thunderous scowl, and he delivered a blistering spank to her backside.

"Watch your language, little girl."

Still swearing, she pounded on his back. "Piss off, asshole! Someone turned my firewall into rubble and the entire system is shut down, including the cameras. Let me go so I can fix it!"

A muscle twitched in his jaw, and he set her gently on

her feet. "Gabby, please. Let us make sure the fire is out. The computers aren't as important as your safety."

"I—"

"Shh." Cupping her cheeks, he kissed her forehead, then took a step back. "Be a good girl."

Without waiting for her to answer, he took off at a run and soon disappeared into the building.

Frowning, Olivia cocked her head. Sean's behavior seemed off somehow. Didn't he and Gabby dislike each other? She shook the thought away. It was absolutely none of her business, and she had enough trouble without borrowing more.

"The idiot didn't even let me bring my laptop." Huffing out a breath, Dr. Knox sat on a lounger and crossed her arms over her chest. "Heaven only knows what will happen while that lot wastes my time."

"Who would have done such a thing?" one of the house-keepers asked. "The Shepherds are gone."

"Did anyone see anything?" Isabelle asked. "We probably won't get footage from the cameras, so anything you could tell us would be helpful."

No one offered any information, but that wasn't too surprising. Housekeeping would have been busy in the dungeon, which didn't have any windows, and the guests would have been either eating breakfast or in their rooms.

It sounded like something her cousin Berto would have done, but he was in California with the rest of his gang of thugs. He'd come to Arizona once to watch her trial and make sure she didn't implicate him or the Wolves, then again when she'd been released to remind her to keep quiet.

She wouldn't have said anything anyway. Although they'd grown apart, she and Berto had been close when they were kids. Nobody had forced her to take that package from him or drive it to Arizona without asking what was in it. That was all on her, but he was on his own the next time he wanted a drug mule.

Maybe she was judging him too harshly. He had eliminated Carlos after he and his friends had tried to assault her and Kendra. He'd always protected her—just not necessarily from himself.

Aside from that, she doubted Berto would have wasted the time or resources burning a building so far out of his territory and unless he'd found someone good with computers, shutting down a security system wasn't in his skillset.

"Where are the guests?" she asked, forcing herself to pay attention.

"They're being questioned in the employee parking lot for now, but I expect they'll be moved here shortly," Isabelle replied.

That made sense. The emergency exit from that wing led to the parking lot. When she heard the wail of sirens in the distance, she sat in the shade of a deck umbrella and watched the sunlight flicker on the pool water. The staff chatted with each other, but she didn't join them aside from thanking Isabelle for a bottle of water.

Her English was good, but it didn't matter what language she spoke. Conversations always ended in awkward silences and discomfort for everyone, so it was better when she didn't open her mouth at all.

Hi! I'm Olivia Rivera and I just got out of jail. My only living relative is a drug dealer. Oh, and my boss thinks I tried to commit suicide this morning, but I really didn't.

Such delightful small talk over cocktails. She rubbed her sore shoulder as a sudden chill coursed down her spine despite the heat.

A large group of people, led by Sierra, rounded the building, and walked toward the pool. Everyone seemed in good spirits, which would make things more pleasant if they were going to be stuck outside for any length of time.

"Drinks are on the house until we can go back inside," Sierra called.

As the guests applauded, someone asked, "What happened to the two-drink maximum?"

She smiled and opened the poolside concession stand. "The dungeon is closed, and I'm sure we can all be grownups, right?"

The tone of her voice would do more to remind everyone of the rules than anything else.

As the guests found places to sit, Olivia slunk away to huddle in the shade behind the utility shed containing pool supplies. Her throat tightened and she struggled for air at the thought of being forced to speak to guests when it didn't involve their breakfast. They would soon start laughing and talking and...

She needed a quieter place to hide. It crossed her mind to escape to her cliff, but it wasn't safe anymore. With luck, nobody would notice her until they were allowed back inside. Of course, Jake would want to talk, and would probably force her to see the counselor.

Then again, the counselor would likely be the only person on the property who wouldn't judge her for her past —at least not to her face. Maybe it wouldn't be a bad idea to talk to a professional.

———————

JAKE

He glared at the red spray paint dripping down the wall next to the main entrance. It had been over five years since they'd chased away the last gang who thought they could use Club Apocalypse as a hideout, and it hadn't been a gang as much as a bunch of squatters looking for somewhere to cook meth.

The single fire truck was already gone, but had left a mess of chemical foam, water, smoke, and charred furnishings in the lobby. He cursed under his breath, then reminded himself they'd planned to remodel anyway. It meant moving the timetable up by months, but at least insurance would cover part of it.

It was a dumbass silver lining, but he'd take it.

"*Los Lobos de la Muerte*." Officer Walt Thompson said, tucking his phone in his pocket. "They're based out of southern California. It's a small gang and usually nonviolent, but they're suspected of transporting several million in illegal narcotics every year."

"What are they doing this far east?" Sean asked, snapping photos of the stylized wolf head gang tag and the fire damage.

"Good question. Did anyone see anything?"

"Not that I'm aware of," Kendra replied. "Most of the guests were still picking at the breakfast buffet, and housekeeping was in the dungeon. Sierra, Mark, Dr. Knox, Sean, and I were in my office for a staff meeting. Jake was in the kitchen."

Walt tipped his hat to Kendra, who looked mad enough to spit nails. "I'll get the police report to you later this afternoon. I'm also going to do some research and see if I can figure out what they're after."

"Thanks." Sean shook Walt's hand. "Let us know when you find something."

"Will do." Giving them a wave, Walt returned to his cruiser and drove away.

"Fucking gangs," Kendra muttered. Her heels clicked on the asphalt as she walked toward the lobby. "I'm going to call the insurance company and get the paperwork started. Jake, help Mark and Sean cordon off the lobby. We'll use the pool entrance until we can get this mess cleaned up."

"I need to bring Gabby back in so she can get started on the computer systems," Sean said.

"Good idea. Can you do that first, please?"

"On it." Sean hurried away.

Her ever-present legal pad in hand, Kendra strode into the building, muttered curses singeing the air in her wake.

Jake stretched caution tape across the main entrance, then went inside to help Mark secure the area, but he couldn't stop thinking of Olivia.

He'd read the transcript from her trial. She'd refused a plea deal for trafficking narcotics, but as a first-time offender with no prior criminal record, her sentence had been fairly light. It had been clear to anyone with half a fucking brain she hadn't acted alone and was likely terrified of retribution.

She'd also been driving a car with California plates and her driver's license listed a San Diego address.

It didn't mean anything. Lots of people lived there. Hell, he didn't know if there was a connection between her and *Los Lobos de la Muerte* to begin with. It might have been coincidence, but it seemed strange a gang known for transporting drugs would show up so soon after she'd started working for him.

He reminded himself she, along with Kendra, had been assaulted after her first shift in his kitchen. Kendra had filed a police report, but their attackers were never found, and Olivia had sworn she only knew the men's first names.

With some effort, Jake calmed his breathing and heartrate. Coincidence wasn't proof of guilt, and there was no evidence she had anything to do with the vandals.

It would take careful handling to get to the truth, and he needed to keep his rage in check if he had any hope of helping Olivia trust him enough to share her secrets. He didn't want to terminate her employment, but he'd be forced to if she was still in contact with the gang.

"You look like you swallowed a lemon," Mark said, blocking the guest wing with caution tape. "What's on your mind?"

"Just thinking. It's been years since we've had trouble with vandals. Why now?"

"I think a better question is who managed to break Gabby's security and turn the cameras off."

"Good point. I'd also like to know why we're having so many issues all of the sudden." Jake wrapped the roll of caution tape around a post to secure the entrance leading toward the atrium. "I mean, we've been open going on six years now. First, it was the Shepherds, and now gang tags? What gives?"

"No idea." Grimacing, Mark studied the front desk. "Wonder if any of the computers still work."

"Doesn't matter. Do you think anyone's going to stay where they might get firebombed?"

"Thanks. I was trying not to think about that."

"Same." Jake finished stringing tape around a broken window. "Good thing is we're low on food in the kitchen. I'll just cancel tomorrow's produce order."

"We still have to eat, you know."

"There's plenty for live-in staff. Besides, you go home with Kendra."

"Neither of us cook." Mark pinched his brow, then sighed. "I guess I'll start hunting up a contractor to get this cleaned up. At least we already have the design for the new lobby planned."

"Fixtures are picked out too. You going to use the same folks who did the restaurant?" Jake asked.

"I'm going to try. Cross your fingers Sadie can do it quickly."

"We should call Ryan and Carrie."

"No, let them enjoy what's left of their honeymoon," Mark replied.

"He's going to be pissed when he finds out we kept this from him."

"Shit, that's true. With the heat still on Carrie, he might do the smart thing and stay put." Mark tossed the empty roll of caution tape toward a wastebasket. "Anyway, I'll try to get a contractor, then come back to help clean up."

"I'll call for a dumpster."

"Good idea." Picking his way around a puddle, Mark walked toward his office behind the dungeon.

After arranging for the dumpster, Jake decided to commandeer the housekeeping staff to get the cleanup started.

By the time he reached the pool area, everyone was gone. Despite telling her to wait for him, he didn't see Olivia. Hopefully, she hadn't gone back to that damned cliff. Pasting a smile on his face, he found Sierra cleaning up the poolside concession stand.

"Where did everyone go?"

"The night auditor delivered the folios before I got here, so everyone checked out and went to find rooms in Winslow. Sean sent the staff back to work."

"Just as well," he muttered. "I wanted to see if I could grab a few people to help in the lobby."

"How bad is it?"

"Bad enough we're doing the remodel early."

"Ouch." She scowled, then added, "If I ever catch those losers... Do we know who did it?"

"Walt identified the gang tag as belonging to *Los Lobos de la Muerte* from California."

"Why would they come so far east?"

"Good question. He's going to do some research and get back to us. Anyway, is Olivia around?"

Still frowning, Sierra shook her head. "She was earlier. Maybe she went back inside with everyone else."

A tinge of worry built. Had she gone back to that damned cliff? "I told her to wait for me."

"I'm here." He heard her voice before she crept from behind the utility shed. "I didn't want to take a seat from a guest."

She didn't seem to be in any distress, but her fingers drummed rapidly on her thighs, and she wouldn't meet his gaze. Maybe the surprise of the fire and all the people had set her off.

He really needed to sit down with her and learn how to accommodate her needs, but it would have to wait until after they got the lobby cleaned out.

Instead of asking why she'd stayed hidden, he nodded. "Thank you for waiting for me."

"Um...you're welcome. Should I go back to the kitchen?"

"No. I'm going to need your help cleaning up the lobby. I'll walk you to your room so you can get changed into something you don't care about."

4

OLIVIA

It took every bit of her courage to stay calm while she walked, and all she wanted to do was hide under her bed before she lost it completely.

"Are you okay?" Jake asked, studying her with piercing blue eyes that seemed to see everything as they walked back to the building.

"Yes, thank you."

She wanted to tell Jake about the Wolves. The secret was burning her from the inside out, but she'd promised Berto she wouldn't.

She couldn't tell him—not without risking her job and her parole.

But she could call Berto and...

What? He was going to run his gang the way he wanted. Nothing she said would change anything, but he must have had a reason to attack Club Apocalypse. He wouldn't have come all this way just to set some fires.

The emergency exit slammed behind them, and she hid her flinch. Judging by the way Jake looked at her, she hadn't been successful.

She kept her pace steady until she reached her room. "I'll...um... I'll be just a few minutes," she finally said, trying to force the words through numb lips as she fumbled for her key card.

"Let me." Using his master key, he unlocked the door, then held it open for her.

"Thank you."

To her surprise, he followed her into the room. Thank goodness she kept it tidy, as she was unwilling to bother housekeeping to pick up after her. Aside from that, she didn't have that much stuff to make a mess with.

At least she didn't have to share with anyone, and there was no danger of her having to move. The room she'd been assigned was on the schedule to be remodeled, so they wouldn't have put guests in it anyway.

Maybe she should have been worried about being alone with Jake, but she wasn't. He was shouty and mean, but he'd never once laid a hand on her—even when they were jostling for space in the kitchen.

The only time he'd ever touched her was to save her from

falling from her cliff. Aside from that, he wasn't shouting or saying nasty things to her.

Ice trickled down her spine as she realized what he must have wanted to talk about. Somehow, he'd learned about her connection to the Wolves, and he wanted to fire her in private. Maybe he wanted to make sure she didn't steal anything when he threw her out.

"I—"

He frowned and jumped to his feet, then helped her to a chair. "Sit, please. You look like you're about to faint, but I promise I'm not going to hurt you, okay?"

"Um...yes, sir."

"Jake is fine. You don't need to call me sir." He strode into the bathroom, then returned quickly with a glass of water. "Drink this. You're probably dehydrated."

Her hand shook as she took the glass, and to her shock, he helped her hold it while she drank. The cold water soothed her throat and made it easier to breathe.

"Better?"

"Thank you, yes."

"Good." He sat on the couch, putting space between them. "I was going to take care of the lobby first, but I need you to relax for a few minutes. I want to talk about what I can do to make things easier for you."

"I don't understand."

"Well, I've already figured out you have hyperosmia, and you're sensitive to sound."

Frowning, she tried to think if she'd heard the term before. "I don't know that word."

"It means you have a very sensitive nose, which explains why your sauces are so good, and why my soap bothered you. I stole a bar of unscented soap from Sean. Is it better?"

"It was the rosemary." She sipped her water, praying she could keep her hands still. No one had ever done anything so thoughtful for her, and his praise over her sauces made her want to melt into a puddle at his feet.

Not once in her life had anyone ever accommodated her sensitivities without being asked, and she had no idea what to do. The tightness in her chest eased and she took a full, relieved breath to let go of her worry about the Wolves.

"I like rosemary. It reminds me of my grandmother's roasted chicken."

"A little is good," she finally said, hoping she didn't offend him. "A lot is...loud. No, not loud. I can't think of the right word."

He grinned at her, making something odd dance in her belly. "Too strong, you mean?"

That smile probably had women all over Arizona throwing their panties at him, and she wasn't immune either. Despite how badly he'd treated her, he was one of the most gorgeous men she'd ever met. Knowing there was a kind person under the asshole just made it worse.

"Yes, I'm sorry, but it overpowered everything, and I..." She glanced at him, then quickly looked away. "Thank you."

"No problem. And don't worry about looking at me when we're talking. I can see it bothers you. What else will make your life easier?"

"I don't..." She swallowed and drummed her fingers on her thigh, unable to keep her hands still any longer. "I don't like when you shout. You're out of tune."

"I'm not sure I understand what that means, but I'm sorry." He gave her another smile, changing the planes of his face until she thought he looked kind. "Kitchens are loud. I can't promise it won't happen, but I'll try not to shout at you."

"Did you...did you mean what you said about my sauces?"

"Every word. And I'm really fucking jealous of you."

Olivia giggled, then slapped a hand over her mouth. "Sorry, I shouldn't have laughed."

"No, it's funny." He leaned back and crossed an ankle over his knee. "I promise to give you more space to create your own recipes, but I need you to meet me halfway on that."

"What do you mean?"

"I mean, we can't put your food on the menu if we can't reproduce it. You don't measure ingredients, and it might not always be you making a dish."

"I measure things."

"With your hands. If I'm lucky, you use a soup spoon. I

need you to use measuring tools or a scale before we can serve it to customers."

The thought of Jake featuring her food after all the weeks of telling her she wasn't good enough...

It was almost too much, and she didn't deserve it—not when she was hiding such an awful secret from him. She could give him something though. She could take away the worry that she might hurt herself.

"I...okay, I can do that." She peeked at him, then jerked her gaze away from his face. "I also need to tell you something."

"Are my shoes still irritating? I'm not sure I can fix that for you. They have to be at least somewhat nonskid to be safe in a commercial kitchen."

"No, but thank you for thinking of it." She stood and went to the window. "I wasn't trying to kill myself this morning."

"It's okay." He joined her, then squeezed her hand. "I already set up an appointment with our counselor, and I promise we'll get you the help you need."

"I don't mind talking to someone if you think I should, but I'm not suicidal. I run five miles every morning before breakfast. At the halfway point, I free climb the cliff, then... I don't know. It's my private place, and I go there because it makes me happy."

He went deadly silent and stilled. The utter absence of sound was the most terrifying thing he'd ever done.

———

JAKE

He couldn't decide whether to kiss Olivia or turn her over his knee.

Although he was happy to know she hadn't been trying to hurt herself, the thought of her doing something so dangerous... He took a deep breath and tried to push his anger aside.

"I'm trying very hard not to shout right now, but you need to tell me you're not free climbing in the fucking dark without a spotter."

She bit her lip and her fingers drummed even faster against her thigh. "I've been doing it since I started working here. I know where the handholds are."

"Weeks. You've been tempting death for weeks?" he asked softly. The urge to yell at her grew with every passing second until he thought he might explode, but he'd promised he wouldn't shout.

"It's my quiet place." She moved out of reach, then crossed her arms over her chest. "It used to be anyway. Until today, I've never been in any danger there."

"You and I have very different definitions of danger."

She went to the dresser and pulled out a pair of worn jeans and a T-shirt. "Excuse me."

Before he could stop her, she went into the bathroom and closed the door. A few moments later, she returned.

He rubbed his face, then let out a long-suffering sigh. "You're not going to stop climbing that cliff, are you?"

"No, sir."

"Even if I forbid it?"

Her lips quirked into a sexy, naughty grin and she met his eyes for longer than he'd expected. "Still no. You don't get a say in what I do with my free time."

There she was.

One meltdown and a little bit of kindness brought out the woman he knew had been lurking inside. He'd been dying to see her, and fuck, it was glorious. Smiles were a good look on her, and he wanted to trace that cute gap between her front teeth with his tongue.

"Fair enough," he finally said, reminding himself Olivia was an employee and Kendra would kill him if he tried anything. "But you're getting a running buddy from now on."

Frowning, she sat and put on a pair of battered sneakers. Hoping they weren't the ones she wore for running, he made a note to replace them. Work boots would have been a better choice for cleaning the lobby, but he doubted she had any and his wouldn't fit her small feet.

"No. I go there because it's quiet and I can be by myself."

"What if I promise not to talk?"

She graced him with another beautiful smile, then

glanced at his face for a split second before standing. "I don't think you're capable of not talking."

"Ouch!" He laid a hand over his heart, then staggered. "Are you saying I'm loud?"

"I—" As if realizing she'd kept up her end of a pleasant conversation, she paled and looked down, then scurried to the door. "Sorry. We better go."

He cursed under his breath and nodded. She was right, but he didn't want their banter to end. Then again, maybe it was better. She needed time to digest the changes in their relationship and pushing her out of her comfort zone would put him right back where he started.

That didn't mean he'd let her run by herself again. It just meant he'd keep his distance to give her the illusion of solitude. The cliff wasn't the only danger in the desert—especially with the threat of a gang. It wasn't a big step to imagine them moving from property damage to assault.

Or worse.

Reminding himself to be patient, he followed her to the lobby. Mark and Sean were already there, along with several people from housekeeping and maintenance.

Without a word, Olivia joined another woman to help her carry an armchair out through the broken glass doors.

"Olivia," Sean called, holding up a pair of work gloves, "wear these before you do anything else. Gabby will be upset if I let anything happen to the provider of her breakfasts."

She put down her end of the chair, then took the gloves and put them on. "Thank you, sir."

"My pleasure. Don't lift anything too heavy without help, okay?"

"Yes, sir."

"Maybe we should put her back in her room for safe-keeping so she can keep making those full English breakfasts," Mark said, smiling at Olivia. "Kendra actually cleaned her plate this morning. She stabbed me with her fork for trying to steal her last sausage."

"She told me she'd hunt me for sport. You got off lucky," Jake said, studying Olivia to gauge her reaction.

Her cheeks darkened with a flush, turning her golden complexion ruddy with color as a faint smile ghosted across her plump lips.

"Don't steal food from a hungry woman," she murmured. "You'll live longer." Her blush deepened when everyone within earshot laughed.

Once he'd managed to stifle his chuckles, Jake said, "Hey! What am I? Chopped liver?"

"I bet her chopped liver is better than yours too," Sean said.

"Considering I've never made it, you're probably right."

He tuned out the conversation and kept an eye on Olivia while she helped haul debris from the lobby. When the dumpster arrived, she worked her cute butt off to help fill it while he and Mark broke apart the larger pieces for hauling out.

"I'm going to the lumber yard for plywood," Sean said, pointing at the busted windows and front doors.

"Sounds good," Jake said, grabbing a broom to sweep up the broken glass. "Mark, did you manage to get Sadie to come in?"

"Yeah, her crew will be here tomorrow. She said it would be about two weeks."

"That's always a contractor's answer," Sean said. "We should probably plan for a month, but I'm glad Sadie was available."

"She's willing to wait for our insurance company to pay out before she bills us and knows we'll be hiring her for the spa if we ever manage to get it built."

Leaning on his broom, Jake gazed around the lobby and sighed. Scorch marks covered the floor and walls, and everything reeked of smoke. Without the front desk and furnishings, it looked barren.

It was as if they were starting all over with a condemned motel, a few promises, and little else but dreams.

5

OLIVIA

Jake looked so defeated. It hurt her heart seeing him like that. He and the Horsemen had worked so hard on Club Apocalypse.

And now it was ruined because of her worthless cousin.

She understood defeat. Her whole life had been a constant struggle of one step forward and two steps back. She trusted too easily, and the people who should have had her back never came through—at least not when it counted.

Exhaling through her nose, she gave herself time to calm her frustration before she went to him. Forcibly stilling her hand, she laid it on his shoulder.

"I'm sorry."

He gave her a brief smile, then patted her hand and gave it a quick squeeze before removing it. "It's not your fault. I guess we'll be remodeling sooner than we planned is all. Anyway, we've done about all we can do here."

He was wrong. Maybe it wasn't her fault directly, but Berto was her cousin.

"Okay. I'll start cleaning up from the buffet. I'm sure it didn't get done."

"No. You already did the omelet station. The bus staff do the buffet."

She shook her head and started walking to the kitchen. "They already went home, remember? It's at least two hours past their normal quitting time, and they were helping clean up the lobby."

"Shit." He rubbed his face and followed her. "I hate that you're right, but I don't like making you work during your free time."

Olivia would give him that. Even when he was being nasty to her, he always chased her from the kitchen after the breakfast service, then told her not to be late for supper prep.

"It's okay. We'll call it a special occasion."

He laughed softly, then hooked his arm through hers. "Sure. Why not? I'll make sandwiches for lunch."

"Or I can make my Tia's *pupusas*."

The minute the words came out, Olivia wanted to kick herself. Jake would have no interest in what she'd grown up eating, but it was too late to take it back. With luck he'd refuse once she told him what they were.

"I don't know what that is."

"It's kind of like a hand pie filled with cheese. Parents make them for children when they won't eat anything else."

Squeezing her eyes shut, she tried not to lose herself in the memory of her and Berto sitting at Tia Jozefina's table. Tia used to sing while she cooked.

"The Guatemalan version of a grilled cheese?"

With some effort she forced herself to focus. "Yes, something like that, but they're popular all over Central America."

His chuckle faded and he sighed when he pushed open the kitchen door. "Fuck."

The odor of spoiling food and filth assailed her nose, and she reeled back. Full bus carts were strewn everywhere, parked haphazardly near the sinks and industrial dishwasher. The floor was nasty with the detritus of a hurried cleanup.

Logically, she knew the food hadn't been there long enough to spoil, but even a few hours without refrigeration made the pungent odor more powerful.

"Huh." He scanned the room and pushed a cart toward the sink. "I'm almost afraid to see what the dining room looks like."

"Maybe not so bad." Swallowing hard, she gathered her courage and unloaded one of the carts into the dishwasher. "If the mess is in here, it might not be there, yes?"

Without warning, he grabbed her arm and spun her around, then marched her into the dining room and pushed her into a chair. "Sit your cute ass right there, young lady."

"But the kitchen—"

"You turned green. You still look pale." He went to the bar and filled a tumbler with ginger ale from the fountain, then set it in front of her. "No puking in my restaurant."

"I'm fine. We'll get it cleaned in no time if we work together."

To her shock, he leaned down and tapped her nose with a gentle fingertip. "Nope. I need to protect that perfect sniffer. You can come back in once I get rid of the waste from the buffet."

Before he moved away, she filled her lungs with his clean, masculine scent, unpolluted by chemical perfumes. The faint tinge of smoke from the fire only added to the appeal.

"I...yes, sir."

He smiled and took a step back. "Finish your drink. I'll let you know when you can come back in."

He walked away, leaving her alone.

"*Ay coño.*"

She drank her ginger ale, then rose to her feet and scanned the dining room for a private place where she could call Berto. When she told him she was working at Club Apocalypse, maybe he'd leave it alone. At the very least, she needed to know why he'd come all this way to attack a property so far out of his territory, so she could tell Jake. It would mean breaking her promise, but Berto could have killed someone with his stupid stunt.

Unfortunately, Jake would hate her after that, and she'd definitely lose her job. If she could keep someone from getting hurt, it would be worth it.

After risking a quick peek at the kitchen door, she raced for the bathroom on the other side of the restaurant, then shut herself in a stall. Hands shaking, she stabbed a finger on Berto's contact, then waited for it to ring through.

"*Hola, muñequita.*"

Switching to Spanish, she asked, "Been to Arizona lately? Maybe you've seen some mangy wolves too far from home?"

He went silent for several seconds and she heard the sound of a motorcycle in the background. Her heart fell and she closed her eyes as her last bit of hope that he hadn't been involved faded.

"I have business there," he finally said.

"Your business is driving drugs from Tijuana to Oakland," she spat. "You're out of your territory."

"And what concern is it of yours?"

"Because you just firebombed my workplace, asshole."

He sighed, and she could imagine his look of impatience. It would be the same one he always got when she said something he didn't want to hear.

It was banked anger mixed with annoyance, hidden

behind a toothy smile meant to encourage her to shut her mouth and stop being a neurodivergent child.

Stay sweet and try to act like you're normal, muñeca pequeña. *Silence is your friend. Don't make me force your good behavior.*

"Mind your tongue, little one," he murmured, his warning tone sending a shiver down her spine. "Good girls don't say those nasty words."

"Berto, please. The Wolves—"

"Enough. You're exactly where you're supposed to be."

"What are you talking about?"

"The Horsemen are known for hiring nonviolent offenders when they're released. You're a beautiful woman. Do the math."

"You..." She closed her eyes and swallowed, unable to make the words come out. "Why?"

"All I need from you is information. Tell me what they do and who they talk to. I want their contacts, their schedules, and anything else you think I might like to know."

"I'll do anything, but—"

"Things happen, you know." Berto's voice went husky and soft, but she didn't mistake the threat. "Bad things sometimes happen to good little girls who don't listen. Wrong place, wrong time. It is always so, you understand, yes? I can't protect you if you misbehave."

The call dropped and she sank to the floor, then wrapped

her arms around her calves. Tears burned and she let them fall.

————

JAKE

His footsteps silent on the tile, he left the restroom. She'd been too busy with her phone call to hear him.

The evidence had been in front of his face, and he should have known better. Olivia was in bed with *Los Lobos de la Muerte.*

Pulling his shit together, he strode into the kitchen, then slammed his fist into the wall.

"God damn it! Fuck!"

By her words, she knew who had attacked Club Apocalypse. She called the fuckwit by name. She'd set them up, but he didn't know why. What did a gang want with an adult resort in another state? Judging by what he'd overheard, she knew Berto, but hadn't said anything about the nature of their relationship.

He hauled in a breath and exhaled, then checked his bruised knuckles. It was all good. They weren't going to get away with their bullshit.

Olivia was the weak link, and she was within his grasp. Although he could take the problem to the rest of the Horsemen and get her ass thrown back in jail where she belonged, he had a better idea. She'd brought trouble into his domain, and it was his responsibility to deal with it.

By the time he finished with her, she'd beg to be locked in a cell.

Calmly, he finished cleaning the kitchen and got rid of the waste bucket.

"Can I help?" she asked from the swinging doors. Her lips were parted, letting him know she was breathing with her mouth instead of her nose.

"Sure. I think I have the worst of it cleaned up. I'll rinse if you load the dishwasher."

"Yes, sir."

He tried to ignore the surge of pleasure from the address. She'd be calling him Master soon enough. He'd let her think she was safe—for now.

"And after that, you can make *pupusas*."

A faint smile blossomed, and she nodded without looking at him. "I have fresh mango salsa to go with them, and I could grill some shrimp. There's some in the cooler we should eat before it goes bad."

"Where did you get mango salsa?"

She grabbed dishes as fast as he could rinse them, obviously well familiar with the routine. "I like it with tortillas and eggs. Everyone told me it was okay to make small batches for my own use, and it isn't wasted."

"And the tortillas?"

"It's just flour, salt, oil, and water," she murmured. "I'm sorry. I didn't think anyone would mind."

"We don't." He studied her for a moment, then eased closer to her. "Will you tell me where you learned to cook? I'm trying to figure out how you can make such delicious food when you could barely open a can when you got here."

He didn't actually care who taught her. Information was ammunition.

"My Tia Jozefina." She smiled again and drummed her fingers against a plate before sliding it into the dishwasher. "She tried to teach Berto too, but he..."

Her smile faded and she scraped a piece of dried food from a bowl with a thumbnail. He gave her a moment, resisting the urge to shake her until she spilled her secrets.

"He, what?"

"He always wanted to be with his friends. Cooking was women's work."

"I beg to differ."

She giggled and stole a peek at him when he handed her the last of the flatware. "He gathered the wood for Tia's stove though. It was a blessing he recognized food didn't happen without fire."

That explained why she had trouble with modern kitchen appliances. If she'd grown up cooking on a wood-fired stove, she certainly wouldn't have seen an industrial mixer or a food processor. It probably made her a better chef though.

"Who's Berto?"

"My cousin." Her smile faded and her hand shook as she started the dishwasher. "He...we're not close."

Jake hid a grimace. He couldn't tell if she was lying when she wasn't looking at him, but close or not, she was culpable. Of course, her whole life was a lie. She hadn't learned to cook in prison at all. He pressed his lips together, deciding to let her dig her own grave.

"What do you need for *pupusas*?" he finally asked once they'd gotten the dishes stored and the floor sanitized. Olivia might be a lying gangbanger, but she had a good work ethic.

"Masa harina, salt, water, and..." Her voice trailed off and she strode to the coolers. "I think this white cheddar to give the queso fresca a bit of body. Water buffalo mozzarella would be better, but we don't have that."

"And what's your wine pairing?"

She grabbed the cloth bag of corn flour from an overhead shelf, then stilled. "Maybe a chardonnay? A white without too much oak, I think. I'm not very good with wine pairings."

"How do you pick them? You do a pretty fair job at it."

"I just know what smells good together. I don't drink, so it took me time to figure it out."

Without waiting for a reply, she returned to the kitchen and grabbed a large steel mixing bowl. Instead of weighing ingredients as he'd asked, she used her hands to mix corn flour, water, and salt into a soft dough.

Despite his anger, watching her work was fascinating, and the *pupusas* did indeed resemble hand pies.

"You could fill those with meat or vegetables too," he said.

"Yes. They're popular in many countries, and everyone has a different spin on them." Using her fingers, she transferred the treats to the grill.

Without thinking, he slapped her ass hard, making her cry out and spin around.

"Jake!"

He pinched her chin and forced her to look at him but ignored the fear in her huge brown eyes. "Is it too much to ask for you to use a fucking spatula?"

"I—"

"Do you see those?" He turned her around and made her look at the rack of kitchen implements hung over the grill. "Tools. Right in front of your face. You can't miss them."

She wriggled to get free. Although he didn't want to lose the feel of her curvy body against his chest, he let her go. He shouldn't have touched any part of her but watching her put her hands so close to the hot grill sent him over the edge.

Although she belonged in jail, he wasn't about to let her hurt herself under his watch.

Her fingers drummed madly against her thighs, and she looked at the floor as she backed away. "I... I'm sorry, sir."

"Where are you going?"

"You promised you wouldn't shout." Without another word, she raced from the kitchen.

"God fucking damn it!" His bruised knuckles met the wall once again before he turned off the grill and chased after her. He had broken his promise, and she had every right to run, but he wasn't about to let her wander around by herself.

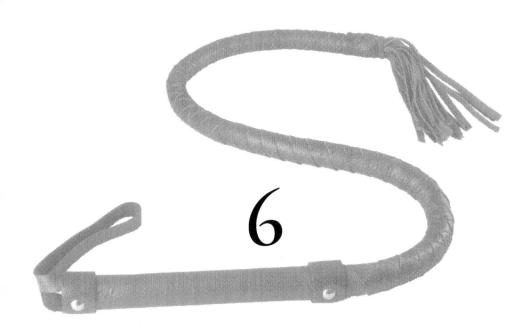

6

OLIVIA

"Olivia! Stop!"

Her head ached with unshed tears, but she didn't obey Jake's barked order. She should have known better. He'd been nice to her just long enough for her to let her guard down, and because she was an idiot, she'd let it happen.

As usual.

Worse, she still had to tell everyone about the Wolves, but she couldn't do it now. Jake was already furious with her, and she didn't have enough courage to face it yet.

His pounding footsteps grew louder behind her. She wouldn't make it to her room before he caught up. There was only one place where she might be safe, and praying for deliverance, she skidded to a stop and pounded on Kendra's office door.

"Come in," Kendra called.

Nearly crying in relief, she stumbled into the office and shut the door, praying he hadn't seen her.

"Hey, Olivia." Kendra finished writing something on her legal pad, then looked up and frowned. "Are you okay?"

"Yes, I mean...is there a housekeeping position I could have instead of the kitchen?"

Kendra studied her for a moment, then folded her hands on her desk. "Not really. We're going to be closed until we get the lobby finished. Then again, having you in the kitchen isn't gaining us anything either, so I guess it depends on why you're asking."

The door opened behind her, making her flinch and duck her head. Out of the corner of her eye, she saw Jake's white sneakers.

"Why, yes, Jake. Of course, you can come in. Thank you for knocking," Kendra said. "Olivia, I think it's safe to assume this asshole is why you want a different job."

"I—"

"She either stays in the kitchen, or she can go back to jail," Jake said, interrupting her.

"And why is that?" Kendra asked.

He grabbed Olivia's arm and pushed her into a chair, then stood over her, his fingers biting into her sore shoulder.

"Ask her about her cousin Berto and *Los Lobos de la Muerte*. I heard her talk to him."

Her stomach settled in her shoes, and she swallowed hard, trying not to throw up. She should have known the kitchen troll spoke Spanish. Even if they weren't fluent, most people in the southwestern states knew at least a little.

Why was she always so stupid?

"How about you back the fuck off and remove your hand," Kendra snapped. "You're scaring her."

To Olivia's surprise, Jake let her go, but didn't move from his position behind her chair. She resisted the urge to run, knowing he'd catch her before she reached the door. Aside from that, she had nowhere to go.

"She deserves it," he muttered. "Now, ask her."

"Okay." Kendra turned her focus to Olivia. "I promise nobody will hurt you. Will you tell me why Jake is losing his marbles and his good sense?"

Olivia resisted the urge to roll her eyes, wishing people would stop making promises they wouldn't keep. "My cousin Berto is the leader of *Los Lobos de la Muerte*. I don't know why he set fire to the lobby or what he hopes to gain."

"Hmm." Kendra made a few notes on her legal pad. "Do you think he's trying to harm you personally?"

Jake inhaled sharply and she felt his body heat against her back. She leaned forward in an attempt to escape, but it didn't help. Before she'd gone to jail, she wouldn't have believed Berto would purposely harm her, but everything had changed. The boy she used to idolize was gone.

As if they had a mind of their own, her fingers drummed against her thighs. "I don't know."

"How did he shut down the cameras and our computer system?"

"He must have hired someone, I think. He doesn't like computers."

"I see." Silently, Kendra gazed at her, making her want to squirm under the steady perusal.

"I'll call Walt so he can take her back to jail where she belongs," Jake said.

"Pick up that phone and I'll break your fingers," Kendra replied, her voice calm despite the violence in her words.

"Excuse me?"

"I said no." After rising from her chair, Kendra rounded her desk and sat on the edge. "I know you don't like Olivia but pull your head out of your ass for once."

"I should have Mark beat your butt," he muttered. "Is there any hope you'll be respectful to your employers at some point?"

"Not when you're being a jackass." She crossed her ankles, then gave Olivia a small smile. "Is it possible someone hired your cousin to attack us?"

Frowning, Olivia considered the idea, then nodded. "Yes, Berto likes money. If he was paid enough, he would do it."

"I'm assuming you called Berto and Jake overheard. Is that right?"

"Yes, ma'am."

"Okay, what did you talk about?"

"I heard her," Jake said before Olivia could answer.

"You heard her, but not Berto," Kendra replied. "Be quiet."

Thankful she couldn't see Jake's face, Olivia said, "He wants me to spy for him, and he..."

She fisted her hands to make her fingers be still and looked up. Although she could only manage a few seconds of eye contact, Kendra didn't look angry.

"Jake, fetch Olivia a glass of wine, please. She needs something to soothe her nerves."

"No, I...it's okay. I don't drink." She exhaled, then forced herself to look at Kendra's chin. "He said I'd get hurt if I didn't obey, but he didn't say how or why."

"Would you say you and Berto are close?"

"No, ma'am. We were as children, but..." Olivia shrugged and dropped her gaze to the floor. Even looking at Kendra's chin was discomfiting. "And then he asked me to deliver that stupid package, so I would get arrested and convicted, all so you would hire me so I could spy on you."

Saying it out loud made it real. Maybe she could have pushed it away as fantasy, but hearing the truth from her own lips... She blinked hard, desperate to keep her angry tears at bay.

"Interesting." Kendra reached out and touched her arm. "Do you want to go back to jail?"

The word yes was poised on her lips. She'd be away from Jake and wouldn't be forced into doing something she didn't want to. She'd finish out the rest of her sentence where she couldn't hurt anyone or give Berto the means to ruin Club Apocalypse. The idea sounded better with each passing minute.

Yet...she couldn't. There had to be something she could do to make amends, get rid of her worthless cousin, and show everyone she wasn't useless or stupid.

"No, ma'am. I don't."

"Great." Kendra scribbled something on her notepad. "You're not going back to jail, Olivia, but you might wish you were before this is all over."

JAKE

Olivia glanced between him and Kendra like she was watching a tennis match. "I don't understand."

"Neither do I," Jake snapped. "What the hell are you talking about?"

Ignoring him, Kendra picked up her phone and tapped out a text message. A few minutes later, a knock sounded on the door and Sean and Mark joined them.

Mark kissed her cheek and perched on the desk next to her. "What's up, troublemaker?"

"If Jake can cool his jets and think like a SEAL, we might be able to solve our stray wolf problem." She gave Olivia a brilliant smile, baring teeth. "We just found the right bait."

"Care to share with the class?" Mark asked.

"Olivia has an interesting story for us. You might want to sit down."

Despite his anger, Kendra was right to tear into him. Jake knew better than to fly off the handle without all the information. His temper and inability to listen had cost him his only serious girlfriend, and he didn't blame her a bit for leaving him. Even then, he'd known better. He'd thought going through BUD/S had knocked it out of him, but apparently not.

Maybe Olivia was lying and was setting them up for something worse than a fire in the lobby. That didn't mean he got to abuse her.

Her fingers drummed her thighs so rapidly they were almost a blur of motion, and a rapid pulse beat in her neck. Despite her obvious discomfort, she lifted her head.

"What do I need to do?"

"Nothing yet," Kendra said. "We need to make some plans, but first I want you to tell Mark and Sean what happened."

Her chin dropped and she relaxed her shoulders. "I over-heard who set the fire, so I called Berto and—"

"No, from the beginning. Start with Berto setting you up."

"Um...yes ma'am." She tightened her hands into fists in an obvious attempt to keep them still but didn't move her gaze from the floor. "Berto asked me to transport a package. I didn't know what was in it. He said it was a gift for someone, and I thought I was doing a favor for my cousin."

"You didn't look?" Sean asked.

"No. It was wrapped like a wedding present with white paper and ribbons. I didn't want to ruin it."

"And it was full of drugs," Jake said.

"Yes. I was supposed to take it to an address in Holbrook, but the police were waiting with a drug dog when I got there." She shivered and laughed softly, then added, "Yes, I am that big an idiot. I walked right to them, carrying the box."

"No," Mark said, "he's your cousin and you should have been able to trust him."

"I also know his gang makes most of its money running drugs. It was stupid."

Jake agreed, but kept his mouth shut. He couldn't help feeling a little sorry for her though. That didn't mean he was ready to forgive her. Stupidity had consequences.

"Hmm." Sean took Kendra's desk chair and folded his arms over his chest. "What I'm hearing is he abused your trust, then set you up for a conviction, all so you'd be in a position to spy on us, right?"

"Yes, sir. I think so."

"That's a lot of planning." Jake scrubbed a hand over his face and paced the office. "Just out of curiosity, did your parole officer give you other choices aside from Club Apocalypse?"

"Oooh, there's a good question," Kendra murmured.

"No. He said you were the only ones hiring."

"Which I know is bullshit," he replied. "I have to outbid the recycling center for bus people."

"Exactly." Kendra straightened, then recrossed her ankles.

He tuned out the conversation, trying to think his way through the problem. If Olivia was telling the truth, she was every bit as much a victim as they were.

Unfortunately, she was presenting all the signs of lying —except maybe she wasn't. He couldn't get a good read on her. It wasn't her fault, and he wasn't about to pin the blame on her, but it didn't make it any easier to trust her.

"—and it might go further than that," Mark said, pulling him from his thoughts.

"I'm sorry, what?"

"I was just wondering if Olivia's cousin paid her parole officer to send her here."

"It's also obvious someone called in the tip when she was arrested," Sean added.

"We don't know any of that for fact," Jake countered. "If

any of it is true, we have more problems than a burned-out lobby."

It was a whole lot of coincidence crammed into a short time span and would have started about the time the Shepherds of the Coming Peace had begun hassling them.

He could push it a little further too. If they sent Olivia back to jail, would she end up dead in her cell like the leaders of the Shepherds?

"If it's not true, then we're not out anything," Kendra replied. "We can feed Berto the information we want him to hear and let him reap the consequences. If there's no shenanigans in the judicial system, we'll have this done by the time the lobby is renovated."

"And if there is?" Mark asked.

"We'll burn that bridge when we come to it, but I want to keep this meeting quiet."

"We should tell Walt, at least," Jake said. "He'll want a heads up."

"No. In fact, we're not even telling Ryan."

"Harsh."

"Expedient. I want everyone to think it's business as usual here. That means Ryan and Carrie stay on their honeymoon, and we have no need for police presence."

"I agree," Mark said.

"I also want Gabby and Olivia moved into the apartment," Kendra said.

"Why?" Sean asked.

"I want everyone in one place. The apartment is also somewhat separate from the rest of the resort and has good fire suppression."

"It has too many windows, but we'll keep the drapes closed." Sean rose to his feet. "I'm assuming you and Mark will be taking his old room. Gabby and Olivia can share Ryan's room, and I'll pretend Olivia and I are dating. We don't want one of those assholes catching her by herself, and that will give me an excuse to keep her close."

"No. If anyone's going to watch Olivia, it's going to be me."

His shout echoed and everyone stared at him, but he wouldn't back down—not even when Olivia darted from her chair to hide behind Sean.

"Sean, please escort Olivia to her room so she can rest," Kendra said softly.

"Sure." He stood and offered a hand to Olivia. "I'll help you."

"Wait!" Jake got between her and Sean. He might not believe her or trust her motives, but he couldn't let her go without apologizing. "I'm sorry I shouted at you. I promised I wouldn't, and I did."

Instead of answering, she ducked around him and escaped the office. Sean gave him a dirty look, then followed.

"Olivia!" Before he could chase her down, Kendra grabbed his arm.

"Jake, leave her alone. It's more than obvious you scare

her. Give her a little time before you start bullying her again," she said. "Or better yet, don't bully her at all."

Ignoring her, he opened the door then scanned the corridor in both directions. Unfortunately, Olivia had already vanished. He let out a soft curse, then nodded. "Fine."

He might have to wait until Kendra stopped playing Mama Bear, but he and Olivia were going to have a chat. It was time for them to come to an understanding.

7

OLIVIA

Her lungs seized and she was lightheaded from lack of oxygen, but she managed to get her door open and collapse on her bed before she passed out.

Thankfully, Sean left her alone.

They knew...everything. All her stupidity and every bad decision that had led her to this point. Her secret place on the escarpment was no longer a refuge either.

It didn't help that she felt awful for breaking Berto's confidence. Maybe he was a bad person, but she had to live with her conscience. Sharing a secret when she'd promised not to was wrong, and it didn't matter whether Berto was worth it or not.

Someone knocked on the door, but she ignored it and huddled in bed with her pillow over her head. It was probably Jake, and she couldn't talk to him until she'd put her brain back together and her heart rate slowed.

It had all been too much. Her shoulder still hurt, her head ached from too many voices, and her blood sugar was dropping. All in all, she was more than ready to call it done and stay in her room until morning. In fact, she'd sleep in. It wasn't as if she'd be doing her normal five-mile run.

Unsurprisingly, the door opened, then shut. A few seconds later, someone sat on the edge of her bed and massaged her shoulder.

"Hey, are you okay?"

She stuck a thumb out from under the covers and turned it up but didn't answer Sean's question.

"I think you're fibbing, so I'll check on you later to make sure. I have a present for you, and I promise it doesn't have any drugs in it. I didn't even wrap it."

Slowly, he lifted the covers, then laid something against her chest before standing. Along with inoffensive unscented soap, she caught a faint whiff of chocolate and pastry before the covers fell.

"I'll leave you be, but if Berto calls, write down what he asks you, and tell him you'll find out, okay?"

She heard his footsteps as he crossed the room, then the sound of the door locking behind him.

Lifting the covers a scant inch, she scanned the room,

then let out a sigh of relief and sat up. On the bed next to her was a black and white stuffed cat with blue eyes and a fluffy tail, and there was a glass of milk and a massive chocolate croissant surrounded by fresh strawberries on the nightstand.

Tears trickled down her cheeks, but she smiled and cuddled the stuffed animal as she ate. When she finished, she tucked herself back under the covers and closed her eyes.

Although Sean was probably being nice to her because he wanted her to help them bring Berto to justice, it felt... good. As long as she remembered people weren't going to do anything out of the kindness of their hearts, she'd be fine.

It was dark by the time she woke from her nap, and her stomach growled. Sitting up, she stretched her sore shoulder and grimaced at the lingering ache. She probably should have iced it, but it was too late to mess with it.

"Is something wrong with your shoulder?"

She screamed and launched herself across the bed, then stumbled and fell to her knees as brilliant illumination blinded her. Blinking, she tried to focus on Jake's white sneakers.

"I'm sorry I scared you. Are you okay?" He held out a hand to help her up, but she stood by herself and put a good amount of distance between them.

No, asshole. Stupid kitchen troll.

"I'm fine." Her hands shook, but she forced herself to keep them still. "Berto hasn't called, so you can leave now."

"Interesting." He stalked her slowly, one silent step at a time.

"What is?"

His lips quirked into a smile, and she shivered when she risked a quick glance at his predatory blue eyes.

"I figured out your tells. Maybe I am a stupid kitchen troll, considering how long it took me."

"I don't know what you're talking about."

He was between her and the door, and she didn't hold any hope he'd let her escape—not that she had anywhere to go.

"When you tell the truth, you don't look at the person you're talking to. When you lie, you stare at their nose and pretend you're making eye contact."

She froze in place, then glanced at the door as her muscles clenched in preparation for escape. "That makes no sense."

"Yes, it does."

Jake was right. He'd pegged exactly how she reacted when talking to people, but she didn't have to admit it. His body heat touched her, and she bit back a whimper, then tried to dodge out of reach. As she reached for the doorknob, he caught her, caging her in a heated embrace as he let out a soft breath, tickling the skin under her ear.

It was chase and capture fantasy, wrapped in a dangerous package she wanted but couldn't have. Jake would demand too much. He'd take her secrets, her will, and her self-respect, and he'd never look back.

He'd be no better than Berto, and she'd be discarded like trash.

"Calm down," he murmured, his growly voice sending a shiver through her body. "I'm not going to hurt you, but I need you to listen."

She held herself very still, praying he'd let her go, but her eyes cut to the softball bat leaned in the corner. "I...okay," she finally said after calculating the distance.

"We're going to move you to the private apartment." His lips brushed against her ear as he spoke. "You're going to sleep in my room because I just don't trust you quite yet."

"No!"

It was too much, too fast, and she hadn't had enough time to settle. She rammed her elbow into his gut and broke free, then curled her fingers around the bat and came up swinging. He ducked, then threw himself to the side.

Something crashed and she felt the impact jangle in her injured shoulder, but she screamed a battle cry and swung again, aiming at his head.

He rolled out of reach and leaped to his feet. "Olivia, stop!"

"I said no!" she shouted, letting her anger free.

The word had never been in her vocabulary. She'd never been allowed to say it, but Club Apocalypse was the one place it was accepted.

People could say no here and expect to be heard.

"Put me back in prison if you want, but I'm not doing this anymore. I'm calling red."

Holding the bat in front of her, she scrabbled for the doorknob. Thankfully, it opened, and she took off. Her cliff wasn't a safe space, but she'd find another.

She just needed to run.

———

JAKE

His ears rang and his scalp still twitched from the brush of Olivia's bat too close to his head. Sitting up, he chuckled and rubbed his neck. He'd wanted her to stand up for herself, but he hadn't expected it to include a skull fracture.

He got to his feet and picked up the shards of a broken lamp, dropping them in the wastebasket. He left the remnants of the television she'd demolished for maintenance.

Two lies and a truth.

She wasn't okay, and she sure as fuck wasn't safe. Maybe he didn't know the whole story about her and *Los Lobos de la Muerte*, but he knew that much.

He also knew he had to catch her before she did something stupid, like standing too close to the edge of a cliff.

She'd looked so sweet while she slept. He'd watched her

for over an hour, watched her curl her body around a stuffed cat as daylight faded and sent shadows across her golden skin.

The plate containing a chocolate croissant and fruit was empty, as was the glass of milk. He sighed with relief, silently thanking Sean for delivering her something to eat. It had been a peace offering of sorts, but clearly hadn't worked.

He strode to the apartment he shared with Sean and Ryan, knowing she wouldn't go back to the escarpment. It would have been the first place he looked, and Olivia wasn't stupid. Thankfully, there weren't that many places to hide within running distance.

As he passed the workout center, he paused, his ears pricking at the sound of Spanish curses. Careful to quiet his movements, he peeked inside and let out a relieved sigh.

"Stupid fucking kitchen troll," Olivia muttered, her bare feet a blur of motion on the treadmill. Without warning, she leaped off, then paced the room, her arms flailing to communicate her anger. Thankfully, she didn't pick up the bat.

"*El troll de la cocina exige un peaje*," he murmured, revealing himself. Wisely, he kept his distance.

She glared at him, then jerked her head away. "You've gotten enough tolls from me already. Please go away."

"You broke a lamp and the television."

"Take it out of my prison wages." She turned and crossed the room, putting as much space between them as possible.

"You're not going back to jail, *querida*." Still keeping his distance, he moved to a chair near the free weights and sat. "How much of what you told us was the truth?"

"I'm not your *querida*," she snapped. "I answered your questions with no lies."

"Yeah, except when I asked if you were okay." He crossed an ankle over his knee. "You said you were, and that is complete bullshit, which makes me question everything else."

"Why do you care?" She folded her arms over her chest and hunched her shoulders. "What possible interest is my health to you?"

"Olivia…" He stood, then moved slowly as if he was approaching a dangerous animal, making sure he didn't block the door. It wasn't far from the truth. She'd already proven she'd strike out if threatened. "We do care."

"And you accuse me of lying." She let out a bitter laugh. "You'll care as long as I'm useful, right? Your interest ends the moment I give you what you want."

Halting, he studied her for a moment. She, like any other cornered animal, was inches from flight. "I'm not going to say we don't want you to help us, but you'd be helping your-self too. If you—"

"Can you give me back my job?" she asked, her tone thick with acidic derision. "My real job, which isn't as some-one's kitchen slave. Can you have my conviction over-turned? How about giving me back the time I spent in a cell? Oh, I know, you could erase the hours I spent being interrogated by ICE while they figured out if my citizenship was valid."

Wincing, he resisted the urge to give her a comforting hug, knowing she wouldn't welcome it. He might not trust her, but she'd had her life upended.

"I—"

She sighed and edged toward the door. "You can't. I'll help you because it's the right thing to do, but don't expect more from me."

Her phone rang before he could reply. She said a filthy word in Spanish and laid the device on the weight bench.

"Is that Berto?"

"Yes. Do I answer?"

He nodded and pulled out his phone, then opened his voice recorder app. "Put it on speaker. I want to hear."

As if she was touching something foul, she tapped the icon to accept the call. "What do you want now, Berto?"

"Do you have information for me?"

She rattled something in Spanish he couldn't quite catch.

"Slow down," Jake mouthed, pointing at the recording app on his phone.

"You're a pretty girl," Berto said, the insinuation making Jake want to tear out his throat. "How long do you need to seduce one of them?"

"That's disgusting. I'm not going to do that."

"Then I suggest you find another way to learn what I need."

"The resort is closed until the lobby is repaired. They serve two meals a day, plus box lunches on request. The dungeon is open until three in the morning, but it's closed on Monday. That's all I know."

Her fingers drummed wildly on her thighs, and she kept her eyes fixed on the treadmill. Even on the phone with someone she obviously didn't like, she couldn't lie well. The dungeon closed at two and didn't open on Sunday.

"What about the computers and security system?" Berto asked.

"I have no idea. I work in the kitchen."

"Find out. I'll call you tomorrow at this time."

"Wait." Her fingers tightened into fists, and she glanced at Jake's face for a split second. "How did you disable the cameras?"

Berto laughed softly, then said, "It's good to have friends, cousin. You should try it sometime—if you live that long."

The call dropped and she shivered, then handed him the phone. "There's his number if you want it."

It took everything he had to stop himself from hunting the bastard down. It wasn't enough her own cousin had set her up for a felony conviction; he had to threaten her life too.

There was no way he was letting her out of his sight. Her life was measured in how long she was useful to her cousin, and he knew without asking she'd end up dead in a cell if she had to go back to jail.

It didn't matter if he trusted her or not. Maybe she was

setting them up, but he didn't care anymore. He'd keep her alive until her cousin was neutralized, then send her on her way.

Jake stopped the voice recorder, then snapped a photo of the number. "Thanks. I'll help you pack."

After grabbing a towel from the shelf above the weight bench, she wiped her face, then dropped it in the laundry hamper. "I'll move, but not if I have to share a room with you. I'd rather sleep with a rattlesnake."

8

OLIVIA

Why couldn't people just leave her alone?

Her life used to be quiet. She kept to herself, minded her own business, and never missed a day of work or school. She'd had *plans*.

Plans that hadn't included a felony conviction.

"Cat got your tongue?" Jake asked, pulling her from her thoughts. "I thought for sure you'd have something to add after that shot across my bow."

"I'm sorry, sir."

"That's another tell." Before she could fumble for her keycard, he used his to unlock her suite. "If you say something you mean, you don't call me sir."

Instead of replying, she gathered her things into the

cheap nylon duffle she'd bought at a thrift store to replace the prison-issue trash bag. She didn't have enough to fill either one, and once again wondered why she'd bothered.

"Where did you learn to swing a bat like that?"

"What?"

"Did you play softball in school or something? You almost took my head off."

If only...

She knew she should look at him while he spoke but didn't have the emotional strength to spare. Aside from that, she didn't care what he thought of her anymore. "Something like that."

Carefully, she wrapped her running shoes in tissue and nestled them in their box. Costing almost two weeks of wages, they were her one luxury and felt like clouds under her feet.

They'd be lost if she had to go back to jail. No shoelaces allowed, and she knew better than to think they'd be returned.

Hiding a wince, she glanced at the broken television and the remains of a lamp in the wastebasket. Strangely enough, Jake didn't seem upset about the damage, and she wasn't sure what to think about that.

To her surprise, he grabbed her bat, then presented it to her with a bow. Fingers trembling, she took it.

"I'm ready," she finally said, tossing the strap of her duffle over her shoulder.

"Good." He held the door for her, then followed her out. "Let's lay down some ground rules."

She hunched and watched her feet but didn't reply. There were always rules.

"No going off by yourself. If you want to run, use the treadmill."

"Fine. What else?"

He stepped in front of her, forcing her to stop, then tipped her chin up with a gentle finger. "Until we get your cousin out of the way, I'm your shadow. You'll have privacy in the bathroom, but that's it. I suggest you get used to the idea right now."

"But—"

"And I'll be holding onto your phone while you're in there."

She jerked out of reach and strode away. "I'm not a child."

A strong arm banded around her waist, and he pulled her against his side. "No, you're not, but you are in danger whether you admit it or not."

Although she knew better, Olivia inhaled his heated masculine fragrance. It was salt and smoke mixed with something almost sweet, and her mouth watered. Without the camouflage of chemical perfume, his personal odor was the most delectable thing she'd ever smelled.

She almost surrendered to temptation and licked him,

then reminded herself it was the scent of radioactive waste and wriggled free before she did something truly stupid.

"Berto isn't going to hurt me."

Sighing, Jake rubbed his face. "Olivia, he set you up to take the fall for a drug conviction. He also threatened you where I could hear it."

"No. He's my cousin."

"I don't think that matters to him as much as it does to you." Firmly, he pulled her close, but didn't move for several seconds. "Come on. It's safe to move you."

"I don't understand." She refused to contemplate his words—mostly because he was probably right.

"That's because you don't look up." When she tried to put some distance between them, he tightened his hold. "Snipers usually draw a bead on a target from above, and until we get your cousin taken care of, we have to take precautions."

He muttered something about Kevlar, then hustled her through the lobby, almost breaking into a run when they reached the atrium.

"What are you doing?" She finally managed to break free when they reached the restaurant, but he didn't let her go far before he caught her arm.

"The resort is empty, and we have no security." He held her still for several seconds, then kept her tucked against his side as he hurried down the corridor and past the dungeon. "It's the perfect time for an assault."

She rolled her eyes and held her peace until they reached her new home. The minute the door closed behind them, she yanked her arm free and hefted her bat, ignoring the shard of pain radiating from her shoulder.

The apartment reminded her of a dormitory suite with bookshelves, comfortable recliners, and a massive television. A breakfast bar separated the living area from a small kitchen. Four doors were closed, and she presumed they led to the bedrooms.

"Fine. We're here. You can stop playing GI Joe and leave me alone. Which room is mine?"

"That one." He scowled darkly, then pointed at the door closest to the kitchen. "You can go as soon as you promise you'll try paying attention to your surroundings. That means looking at something other than your fucking feet."

Horrible kitchen troll!

"I do look up, but not if it means looking at you!"

A door opened behind her, but she kept her gaze fixed on Jake's face. It almost hurt to meet his stormy blue eyes, but she was too angry to let it go.

It was like looking into a glacier—deep and fathomless, beautiful, but deadly, and all the more enticing for it.

"Bloody hell, will you two be quiet?" Gabby shouted. "Go hate-fuck each other but keep it down. Some of us are working."

The door slammed, the sudden shock of sound making Olivia jump.

To her surprise, Jake dropped his eyes, then chuckled. "Um...that was your room."

"I think I'll take my chances with my cousin."

He barked out a laugh, then went into the kitchen and poured himself a glass of scotch. "I'd offer you some, but—"

"I don't drink."

"I know." He turned on the faucet and let a few scant drops of water trickle into his glass, then took a sip before perching on a stool. "There's bottled fruit juice and milk if you want."

Her feet moved before she was ready, taking her to the breakfast bar. She sat across from him, then tugged the highball free from his hand and took a sip. The scotch burned a path into her belly, redolent with peat and cherries. She took a deep breath, letting the odors linger on her palate.

"I thought you didn't drink."

She took another sip and closed her eyes, relishing the scent. The mingled tastes and odors were almost more than she could tolerate, yet...

It was like a lover's embrace—intoxicating and warm, perfumed with sex and flowers.

She tipped the glass at him but couldn't meet his gaze any longer. At least she'd made some attempt at socially acceptable behavior. It might ease some of the outward manifestations of her sensory issues, but she didn't want to use crutches that might impair her judgment. Her brain had a hard enough time as it was.

"You made me decide to start."

———

JAKE

"Ouch." He rubbed his chest and tried to look affronted, but a smile crept out. "I'm going to be feeling that for a while."

Instead of taking another sip, she slid the highball across the table. "Sorry."

He'd never been accused of driving a woman to drink, but he deserved the shot. It hadn't even taken him a day to break all the promises he'd made to her.

"It's okay. Do you want more?"

"No, thank you." Without looking at him, she stood, then waved a hand at the couch. "I... I'll just sleep on the couch if it's okay."

"It's not okay. You can have my bed. I'll sleep in one of the recliners."

Her brow wrinkled and she shook her head. "No, I'm fine on the couch."

He crossed the room, then grabbed her bag before she could reach it. "Look, I know you don't like me, and I respect that, but I'm not letting you sleep in a room with a picture window that faces the road."

"Berto won't—"

Resisting the urge to shake her, he let out a breath. The

woman was determined to believe the best of a relative who didn't give a damn about her. "Olivia, he threatened you in my presence, and he's already proven he can disable our security. As far as I know, it's still out, meaning he can walk in with no one the wiser. Do you understand my position here?"

"He won't hurt me until I give him the information he wants," she retorted.

"That might be true," he said, trying to keep his voice soft and nonthreatening, "but are you sure?"

She looked down, and to his surprise, her hands stayed still. When she didn't immediately reply, he added, "And what happens when you give him what he wants? He already sent you to jail. How far do you think he'll go if he decides he needs to be assured of your silence?"

The more he thought about it, the less he liked it. A man willing to set his own cousin up for a drug charge would have no trouble murdering her. The space between his shoulder blades itched, and he glanced at the drapes to make sure they were closed.

They wouldn't stop a bullet, but a shooter couldn't see in.

"I don't know." She paced the room, her hands fluttering as if she was trying to brush away an insect. "My life is over, and it's his fault, but he's my cousin, and..."

Slumping, she collapsed to the couch and put her hands over her face. When she let out a soft whimper, he sat next to her and pulled her into his lap. Although she stiffened at first, she soon relaxed and laid her head on his shoulder.

His heart broke as her body quaked with silent sobs.

"It's going to be okay," he murmured, stroking her back, "but you have to let us in so we can keep you safe."

Sniffing, she sat up and wriggled free to sit next to him. "That's a lie. With a felony conviction, I'm going to be stuck working in a kitchen for the rest of my life. I was so close too."

"So close to what?"

She curled her legs under her and rested her head on the arm of the couch. "I was a semester away from graduating with an accounting degree. I'd even scheduled my CPA test and had a couple of really good job offers."

Jake couldn't decide whether to yell or laugh. "I was right. You're not a chef."

"I never said I was." She sat up and scrubbed a hand over her eyes but didn't look at him. "Sierra asked if I could cook, and I told her the truth."

He barked out a laugh and shook his head. "I have no idea what to say to that."

It made too much sense though. She cooked from her heart, and her ideas for recipes always changed depending on what was close to a sell-by date in the pantry. Even her use of fresh herbs varied based on some kind of eldritch testing. She was an amazing cook, but he doubted she'd ever be happy in a commercial kitchen—especially when she hadn't wanted to be there in the first place.

Her story explained why she cooked like a housewife instead of a trained professional chef, yet something twitched in his belly. All the pieces fit, but it was almost too easy.

"You don't have to say anything. I'm not your responsibility." She stood, then fetched her duffle bag. "I'm very tired. Where am I sleeping?"

He crossed the room and pushed open the door leading into his bedroom, then sidled past her to close the drapes. At least it was clean—more or less. Quickly, he picked up some dirty clothes and tossed them in the hamper. "Give me a sec. I'll get fresh sheets."

"Um...thanks." She moved across the room but didn't turn to face him.

Wishing he could see her face, he hesitated for a moment, then fetched clean sheets from the communal linen closet in the kitchen next to the washer and dryer.

Olivia was in the bathroom by the time he returned, and the shower was running. Instead of bugging her, he made the bed, then hauled a recliner in from the living room, along with a spare pillow and blanket, belatedly noticing she'd left her phone on the dresser. It was locked but didn't appear to have any missed calls or messages.

He used Ryan's bathroom to shower and changed into

sweats and a T-shirt, then made himself comfortable while he waited for Olivia to finish.

Eventually, she trudged from the bathroom wearing a baggy wifebeater and shorts. She carried a wide-toothed comb and a spray bottle in one hand. Humming to herself, she sat on the edge of the bed facing away from him and spritzed her hair with whatever was in the bottle, then worked the comb through the tangled curls.

Jake loved watching women while they performed intimate acts of self-care. He liked it even better when they let him help. He almost groaned when she lifted her arms, revealing the curve of her breast, but forced himself to focus.

She didn't once look up, and that was a big fucking problem. Did she care so little for her safety? Or was there some other reason she was sure her cousin wouldn't come after her?

Maybe she was meeting Berto during her morning runs.

There was only one way to deal with her. Olivia was going to accept a bodyguard until they could get rid of her asshole cousin. Between her reticence and perplexing disregard for her personal safety, his Spidey senses were tingling like crazy. He wouldn't rest until she was locked down.

She was going to hate it, but it would be with him.

Without a sound, Jake got to his feet and crept to the bed, using every bit of his training to keep his approach quiet. Considering how sensitive her hearing was, he'd have never managed it if he hadn't taken off his shoes. Instead of announcing his presence, he took the comb from her hand.

Shrieking, she leapt from the bed and raced across the room, then snatched up her bat. Breathing hard, she glared at him and tightened her grip on the handle. "You bastard! What the hell is wrong with you?"

"I thought I'd help you comb your hair while we discuss why you never noticed I was here." He stalked her, then gently eased the bat away. "You need a fucking keeper."

OLIVIA

Her heart pounded in her chest, and she couldn't quite catch her breath. As she tried to calm herself, she glanced around the room, noting the freshly made bed.

Maybe he had a point about paying attention to her surroundings. If he'd wanted to hurt her, she wouldn't have seen it coming.

"You're still not looking at me, so I'm going to help you to the bed before you pass out."

"I'm fine." Despite her words, her head swam when she tried to move.

"Uh huh. That's why you're almost hyperventilating." He wrapped an arm around her waist, then helped her sit. "I know it's hard for you to look at people and I'm sorry I scared you, but I need you to start paying attention to your surroundings."

His tone was too gentle...too caring, and she shivered when he touched her shoulder. It was a lie though. All he wanted was to use her as bait.

Just like Berto had.

At least Jake might not send her back to jail, and she might not end up dead. He was right about that too. If Berto was willing to set her up for an arrest just to put her in Club Apocalypse as a spy, it wasn't that big a stretch to imagine him having her executed.

After grabbing her comb from the floor, Jake knelt behind her and slowly eased the tangles free. It reminded her of all the times Tia Jozefina had done it when she was little, but it wasn't the same.

His body heat and gentle touch made her think things she had no business considering. She wanted to know how his large, callused hands would feel on her skin.

Physical contact had thankfully never been one of her issues. She liked to be petted and touched—especially when the person touching her was quiet and smelled good.

Jake could be very quiet—when he wanted to be—and she liked his scent when it wasn't covered by that awful rosemary soap. Thankfully, he'd removed it from his bathroom entirely.

"Feel good?" he asked, startling her from her thoughts.

He pulled the comb through her hair, then set it aside to untangle a stubborn knot with his fingers.

"I...yes, but you don't have to." She tried to ease away, knowing it wasn't a good idea to enjoy his attention, but he wouldn't let go of her hair.

"I know." His weight shifted behind her, and he leaned over the edge of the bed to retrieve the bottle of detangler. "Does this make it easier to comb?"

"Yes."

He sprayed a bit on the back of her head and worked it through with his fingers. Closing her eyes, she bit back a moan of pleasure. He'd obviously taken care of a woman's hair before, and the thought made her unaccountably jealous.

Being jealous of his past partners was about as stupid as trusting her cousin.

"Good girl," he murmured, smoothing his hand over her hair. "Do you braid it or wear a scarf to sleep?"

"Um... I can braid it."

"Shh." He gathered her hair at the base of her neck, then carefully wove it into a braid and secured it with the elastic she'd put on the comb handle. "Now, turn around and face me. We need to talk."

She shivered at his implacable tone but swallowed hard and forced herself to do as he'd asked. "Talk about what?"

To her shock, he cupped her cheeks and kissed her brow. "I know you probably think I'm overreacting, but I'm not willing to let you wander around by yourself if you're unable to register your surroundings."

"You're putting me under house arrest for being neurodivergent?"

"No. It's not so much your neurodiversity as it is my gut telling me your cousin will try to hurt you. Does that make sense?"

She studied the laugh lines under his blue eyes. It was the closest she could get to actual eye contact. In a way, it did make her feel better, yet not. He was forcing her to accept Berto didn't have her best interests in mind, and probably never had.

"Maybe it shouldn't, but it does, I guess," she finally said.

"I'll take it." He moved behind her, then pulled her against his chest. "I know it's hard for you to be face to face with someone, so we'll talk this way."

He was so damned warm. It was a mistake, but she let herself enjoy the cuddles.

"I...thanks."

"No problem." He brushed his lips against her hair, sending tingles down her spine. "Anyway... I'm sorry to do this, but you're not going to be running outside by yourself anymore. It just isn't safe."

"But—"

"Shh. I didn't say you couldn't run. I said you're not doing it alone. You'll also be wearing a vest, and I will personally beat your ass if you even think about trying to outrun us."

"Who is us?"

"Me and either Mark or Sean. Preferably both."

"There's no reason to go to so much trouble for me. I don't want to wear a vest."

She wriggled free, but he caught her before she could escape and tightened his arms around her. "Then you won't be running outside. You should feel lucky I'm considering the idea at all."

"Fine." She huffed out a breath, trying to control her irritation. At the same time, it was nice to have someone care what happened to her.

She tried not to feel sad about it too often, but the few friends she'd had in San Diego had ceased contact almost the minute she was arrested, and jail wasn't a place to develop lasting relationships.

Olivia didn't have friends here either though, and letting Jake pretend he cared what happened to her was about as close as she was going to get until she could leave and put her life back together.

"Just...fine?" He loosened his arms, but not enough to give her a chance to escape. "You're agreeing that easily?"

"It's not like you're giving me a choice."

His breath feathered over her ear, making her shiver. "No, I'm not."

―――――――

JAKE

Olivia was curvy and warm, and smelled like honey mixed with floral-scented hair product. Although he liked where she was in his lap, he let her go.

Maybe she had a point about the rosemary soap. It had been pretty strong, and now that it was gone, his sense of smell seemed more acute. Sadly, it would never be what Olivia's was.

"Please leave. I want to go to bed."

"I'm not stopping you." He stood, then went to his recliner and made himself comfortable.

"I thought you were sleeping in the living room."

"I said I'd sleep in the recliner. I just didn't say where the recliner would be." He tugged the handle to extend the footrest, then spread the blanket over his legs.

"Oh, for fuck's sake." She rolled her eyes and huffed, then got into bed. "Do whatever you want but do it quietly."

Without another word, she turned off the light. Smirking, he imagined steam pouring from her ears and considered crawling into bed with her. After all, she *had* said he could do whatever he wanted.

He pushed the idea out of his head. That would be taking things way too far—especially when she didn't like him, and he didn't trust her.

That wasn't entirely true. Jake trusted her, but he didn't trust her motivations regarding her cousin. It had to be hard to know a family member would do what Berto had done to her—especially when obedience seemed to be hard-wired into her psyche.

Maybe that was what he found so difficult. Olivia had blindly obeyed him in the kitchen when he'd purposely pushed her limits until she lashed out.

What would she be like if she obeyed because she wanted to? He closed his eyes, imagining her on her knees, with happiness filling her brown eyes instead of fear and hate.

Could he give her that? If he could show her she could obey and keep her sense of self at the same time... She'd be glorious, and with luck, he could teach her to protect herself from people like her cousin.

Grimacing, he included himself in that list, but he hadn't understood what she needed to thrive. Now that he did, he could fix it, and make sure she didn't do anything that might hurt herself or Club Apocalypse.

Knowing he needed to sleep, he settled back and tried to empty his mind. Tomorrow would be soon enough to tell Olivia about her new house rules.

Unfortunately, she didn't sleep restfully. Despite keeping him awake all night with her tossing and turning, she was up before four, and didn't seem to care she made enough noise to wake the dead.

Sighing, he rubbed his face and glared at her, then turned on the light when she exited the bathroom wearing shorts and a sports bra. "What the hell are you doing?"

"Going to the fitness center to use the treadmill." She returned his glare with interest, daring him to protest.

Interesting. She had no trouble meeting his eyes when she was mad.

"Fine." He found his shoes and put them on. "Ready?"

"I don't need a babysitter. Go back to bed."

"That's where you're wrong." He held the door open, then gestured for her to go first. "You don't go anywhere without an escort until we figure out what to do with your cousin."

She said a dirty word under her breath, then pushed past him. "Whatever."

"Hmm. Someone got up on the wrong side of the bed."

Instead of answering, she grabbed a water bottle from the fridge and strode from the apartment. He caught up to her and wrapped an arm around her waist.

"Stay close," he ordered.

"Yes, sir."

"So much snark in your tone."

"You deserve it."

To his surprise, she slowed when they reached the restaurant. Lifting her chin, she scanned the area before she continued to the atrium.

"Good girl. Nice job looking up."

She didn't answer, but she did blush and quicken her pace until they reached the fitness center. She took the treadmill furthest from the door, then set her program.

"I'll be about an hour," she finally said, putting earbuds into her ears. "Maybe a little more."

Before she could start the program, he took the earbuds from her. "Paying attention to your surroundings also means listening."

She stepped on the rails, twisting her body to look at him. "I thought you were supposed to be my watch dog, but fine. Just be quiet so I don't have to listen to you."

"Your mouth is going to get you into trouble, little girl."

"Sure, why not? Everything else seems to."

Fuck knew he'd tried to be patient, but enough was enough. He snatched her around the waist and hauled her from the treadmill. Screeching, she lashed out, nearly catching him in the face with a flailing fist.

"That's enough, Olivia. I've had it with your attitude." After capturing her arms, he carried her to the weight bench, then sat and yanked her over his lap.

"Let me go!" She kicked, nearly getting free, until he managed to trap her legs with his calf.

He slapped her ass hard, then followed up with several more spanks, all targeted on the tender spot where her ass met her thighs. Crying out, she dug her nails into his leg and tried to struggle free, making him clench his teeth.

"You know polite words," he finally said after giving her

ass several more hard slaps. "I get that you're upset, but you can't take it out on other people."

Although he'd given her a punishment, he rubbed her butt to ease the sting, then helped her up. She jerked out of reach, then spun around, but not quickly enough for him to miss the tears welling in her eyes.

"Damn it." He stood and slowly approached her, then hugged her from behind. "It's okay. I'm not mad anymore."

"Then why did you spank me?"

"You know why." Leaning down, he kissed her temple. "You can disagree with me, and I'll listen, but I need you to be respectful."

"I... I'm sorry."

"I know. It's all done now, and we can start over." Gently, he turned her to face him and leaned down to kiss her forehead. Instead of letting him, she lifted her head and touched her lips to his.

His cock thickened and he bit back a groan as she traced his lower lip with her tongue for a scant few seconds, then backed away, her hands fluttering at her sides.

"Olivia, I—"

"That never happened." Without waiting for an answer, she mounted the treadmill and started running.

"Oh, honey. You have no idea how wrong you are."

10

OLIVIA

Wishing she had her earbuds, she focused on the treadmill's readout, desperate to finish her run before she fell apart.

It felt as if Jake's eyes were boring into the back of her head like he was some demented shipworm. She tapped the touchscreen to increase her pace. Maybe he could see inside the squirrel-infested mess she called a brain and figure out why she was such an idiot.

She'd be forever grateful if someone could tell her why she'd decided to kiss him after having her butt thoroughly roasted. She'd been spanked before, but never by someone who meant it as a punishment. Although he hadn't truly hurt her, she'd be feeling it for hours.

It might also have been helpful to know why she'd decided to wake up and choose violence, and why she hadn't expected him to call her on her bad behavior. It was one thing to call him names in Spanish when he picked on her. It was quite another to be purposely rude to his face when he'd been trying to be polite.

Oh, and maybe do a memory wipe on both of them so their kiss was never mentioned again. She laughed inwardly, wishing it was a thing. There were plenty of memories she'd be happy to see gone.

The treadmill chimed, surprising her so much she almost fell off before she could slow to a walk for her cooldown.

"You okay?" he asked.

"I'm fine."

"Good."

She stepped off the treadmill and blinked when he handed her a towel. "Thanks."

"No problem." He offered her the water bottle, waiting while she drank greedily. "I figured we'd do breakfast around eight since we don't have to set up a buffet. We can do a big breakfast casserole."

"Sure." She wanted to tell him she didn't care about breakfast, but he was going out of his way to be nice.

"Or you could show me how to make *pupusas* as long as you use a spatula this time."

"Either is fine." There was another memory she wanted

to forget. She tossed the towel into the hamper, then walked to the door, unsurprised when he followed close.

Before she could open it, he touched her arm. "Olivia?"

"What?" She turned to face him, her gaze almost but not quite reaching his chin.

Without warning, he caged her in his arms, pressing her against the closed door as he kissed her violently, claiming her lips like he wanted to devour her. The ridge of his cock brushed against her belly, hard and...

Dios... He was massive. How did he manage to fit that thing into a woman? Thankfully, she'd never find out.

The touch of his callused hands on her bare skin sent pinpricks of electricity down her spine. She moaned and fisted his shirt, needing to touch him back.

His chuckle vibrated against her lips, making them tingle as he softened the kiss and drew away. Tracing a finger across her jaw, he kissed the tip of her nose.

"If you're going to be awkward over a kiss, it's going to be a real goddamned kiss." He smirked and tapped her chin, then opened the door. "Coming?"

"Fucking kitchen troll," she muttered, her face so hot she thought it might spontaneously combust.

"El troll de la cocina pasó factura."

He put his arm around her waist, making her curse under her breath. "When were you planning to tell me you spoke Spanish?"

"Sometime around when I hung my new wooden sign over the kitchen door. Want to know what it's going to say?"

"Probably not, but you're going to tell me anyway."

His laughter almost encouraged her to join in. "*El troll de la cocina exige un peaje.*"

"I was right," she muttered, "I didn't want to know. Are you still mad?"

"No." He stopped her before they reached the burned-out lobby, then turned her to face him. "I wanted you to be brave enough to say all those things in English."

Her lips parted and she risked a quick glance into his eyes. "Why?"

"Because you need to stand up for yourself." He pushed a piece of hair out of her eyes, letting it curl around his finger. "You need to tell people no, sweetheart. I hoped if I gave you a good reason, you'd say what I wanted to hear."

Tears welled and she jerked her gaze to his sneakers— the same ones he wore after she'd complained about his nonskid shoes. "I...that doesn't make sense."

"Sure it does." He wiped a tear from under her eye. "If you can tell me off, you can do the same thing to your asshole cousin."

She nodded, but fell silent, still trying to wrap her thoughts around what Jake said as he hustled her across the lobby. Illuminated with red security lights, it looked... haunted. Wind blew in through the gaps in the plywood

covering the broken windows, making her quicken her pace
as she remembered there was no security.

Nothing to stop Berto from coming for her.

She didn't dare breathe until they reached the apartment
and could barely hold herself still while he unlocked the
door.

Without warning, a sharp slap echoed an instant before
the burn in her ass woke up.

"Olivia, look at me." Jake cupped her cheeks forcing her
to meet his gaze. "I called your name three times. Are you
okay?"

"I..." She hauled in a breath, then shook her head.

"Shit." He swept her into his arms and kicked the door
open.

"Hey, what happened?" Sean asked from the kitchen as
he poured coffee into two mugs.

"Later," Jake snapped. The bedroom door slammed
behind him, and he carried her straight into the bathroom.
Without a word, he set her on the toilet seat, then knelt to
take off her shoes and socks.

"Jesus, you're like ice."

She tried to protest as he stripped her sports bra and
shorts away, but the words wouldn't come, and her vision
hazed as he helped her into the shower.

Stinging hot water coursed over her head. Teeth chat-
tering, she tried to avoid the pounding spray, belatedly
realizing Jake had managed to undress without her notic-

ing. Instead of letting her go, he held her as he crooned softly.

"I have you, baby. It's okay. I won't let you fall."

Maybe it was a mistake, but Olivia believed him.

———————

JAKE

After wrapping her in all the towels he could find, he carried Olivia from the bathroom and laid her on the bed, then retrieved his sweats. She'd somehow managed to fall asleep in the shower, so he'd only waited long enough for the color to come back to her cheeks. It was less falling asleep and more fainting though.

He gave her one last worried glance, then strode from the room, finding Sean and Gabby at the breakfast bar. As usual, they were glaring at each other, but he didn't have time for their bullshit.

"Get the crash cart from the dungeon," he ordered.

Sean nodded and left without replying but returned quickly with the medical supplies. "What's up?"

"I think Olivia had a panic attack and fainted. I want to check her blood pressure and sugar."

"I have electrolyte solution here."

Ryan was the real nurse, but both he and Sean had battlefield first aid training. Frowning, he tried to remember if he'd seen Olivia eat. She hadn't had breakfast before her run, and the last thing he could swear she'd eaten had been the croissant and strawberries he'd asked Sean to take to her room.

"She's asleep. I...yeah, let's wake her up. A bottle of that won't hurt her."

"I'll get her blood pressure before you wake her," Sean said.

"Can I help with anything?" Gabby asked.

"No, you're good." Jake gave her a small smile to show his appreciation for the offer.

"But eat something before you start working again," Sean added. "One woman passing out is more than I want to deal with."

"Yes, sir, Mr. Wanker, sir." Gabby sketched out a salute and took a banana from the bowl on the counter, then went into Mark's room and shut the door.

"Smart ass."

To his surprise, Olivia's eyes snapped open, and she grabbed at a towel, clutching it to her chest when Sean pushed the cart into the room. "What's this?"

"You had a panic attack and fainted. Hold out your arm," Jake said.

"Why?"

Sean secured the blood pressure cuff around her upper arm without replying, then put the stethoscope under it. After a few minutes, he nodded in satisfaction and removed the cuff. "Low, but not dangerous. Yell if you need me. I'll be keeping an eye on Gabby."

He nodded at Sean and thrust a bottle of electrolyte solution at her. "Drink."

"I'm fine." She tucked the towels around herself, then swung her legs over the edge of the bed.

"It's like you want me to beat your ass again," he said, pushing on her shoulder until she scowled and settled back against the pillows.

"Hey!"

He held the electrolyte solution out, tapping his foot until she took it. "Drink that entire bottle and keep your ass in bed."

She crossed her arms over her chest and frowned. To his surprise, she met his eyes, meaning he was making her mad.

Good.

"Fine, but you're wasting my time when I should be making breakfast."

He sighed and pinched the skin between his brows, then grabbed jeans and a T-shirt. There wasn't much point in whites when there weren't any guests. "You're not going anywhere."

"Don't be ridiculous." She finished the bottle of electrolyte solution and grimaced. "This is awful."

"Maybe so, but it'll get your blood sugar back up." Figuring she'd already seen him naked; he changed in front of her. Knowing Olivia, she'd escape the minute his back was turned.

That gave him an idea. He jogged into the main room and grabbed a pair of cuffs from the toy chest. To no one's surprise, she was already out of bed and reaching for her duffle by the time he returned.

The woman was stubborn as fuck, but he was learning to pick his battles. Instead of cuffing her to the bed as he'd planned, he shrugged, then said, "Are you really that determined to disobey me?"

"You hired me to cook. I can't do that if I'm lying in bed like a lazy slug." She pulled a shirt and leggings from the bag, then went into the bathroom and slammed the door.

"Be careful what you wish for," he murmured, knowing he'd been the one to encourage her to speak up for herself.

A few minutes later, she came out fully dressed, holding her running shoes in one hand. "I just need to do something with my hair."

"It's fine the way it is."

Rolling her eyes, she put on her work shoes, then grabbed a scarf from her duffle and quickly restrained her curls in the colorful purple silk. "It's fine until it falls into someone's food. Then it's disgusting. Besides, it's still wet."

He didn't bother glancing away from the curve of her lush breasts. He might be a lecherous pig, but Olivia Rivera without a bra was a wonder of the universe.

Although he wanted to unpack her stuff into the dresser,

it smacked of intimacy he wasn't sure he wanted. Still, the thought of rummaging through her panties for a T-shirt was inexplicably hot.

It's one step away from sharing a fucking toothbrush.

"Fair enough. Do you really insist on cooking?"

"I do." She glanced at his face, then quickly looked away. "I'm fine."

"All right," he nodded agreeably, keeping the cuffs out of her sight. "Ready?"

"Yes. How many are we cooking for?"

"Six. We sent non-critical staff home, so it's just us."

"I'm non-critical," she countered.

"Yes, but you live here." Keeping her nestled against his side, he escorted her to the restaurant, noting how her gaze darted everywhere.

Maybe she was learning.

The interrupted meal from the day before still rested on the grill, cold and coagulated. In an effort to put her attention on something else, he said, "Grab all the mushrooms from the pantry, a package of bulk sausage, plus a couple of pounds of bacon, please."

"Mushrooms? What for?"

"We'll sauté them with an onion and sausage for the casserole."

"Not Gabby's Welsh dragons," she countered. "She'll murder us in our sleep."

"True. Make that three pounds of bacon."

"For six people?"

"Have you seen Kendra eat bacon before?"

Laughing, Olivia went to the pantry and came back with a bus pan full of stuff he hadn't remembered was in there. He normally had a better idea of the contents of his pantry, but she seemed to make every last thought leave his head.

"What's all that for?"

She pointed at several plum tomatoes, a couple of peppers, and green onions. "I'll make *pico de gallo* to go with the casserole for everyone who isn't a heathen, and the mangos are for a tart. They'll be overripe by tomorrow."

"Sounds wonderful." It would also work perfectly for his plans. "The worktable is all yours."

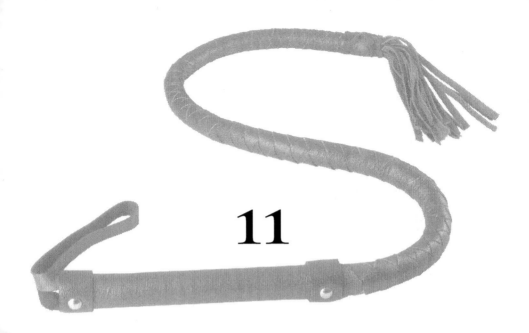

11

OLIVIA

Thankfully, Jake let her panic attack go and gave her space to do what she was being paid for. Although it was nice to trust someone to take care of her when she faltered, she couldn't let it happen again.

That way lay madness.

Or, more specifically, getting attached to a man who saw her as a fixer upper.

Of course, she'd been an idiot and decided to run for almost an hour without eating anything first. Maybe she did need a keeper as he'd mentioned.

"How's it going?"

"I'm good. The mushrooms and onions are almost ready, and the *pico de gallo* is resting."

"Thanks." He set an empty bowl on the worktable, then used the edge of a chef's knife to scrape the vegetables into it. A few mushrooms fell to the floor, and he cursed, then knelt at her feet.

"Give me a sec and I'll clean these up."

"No, it's okay. I'll get them." Something wrapped around her ankle, then tightened, making her look down. "What the...what are you doing?"

"Making sure you stay still," he replied, affixing a bright red cuff to her free ankle before she could consider escape. He'd looped the chain connecting them through the stool legs, meaning she couldn't get up unless he let her go. If she tried to unbuckle them herself, she'd probably overbalance and dump her dumb ass to the floor.

Slowly, enticingly, he ran his hands up her thighs as he stood, then cupped the back of her head and kissed her hard. He tasted sweet and smoky—just as intoxicating as the scotch she'd sipped from his glass.

"Jake, I—"

"I'm sure you're not just about to argue with me, are you?"

"This is... I don't know what it is but get those cuffs off me so I can help."

"I have something better for you," he murmured, moving behind her. Without warning, he tugged her T-shirt, then stripped it off over her head.

"Jake!" Terrified someone would come in, she crossed her arms over her breasts. "What the hell!"

He took a step back, then studied her. "You'll be my odalisque. My little cooking muse. But I think something is missing."

Without warning, he lunged at her, then grabbed her hands. Holding them in one large fist, he unwound the scarf from her hair and secured her wrists behind her back.

"That's better," he murmured, arranging her hair over her shoulders. "You look good enough to eat."

"Jake, no. This is so unsanitary!"

"Shh." He stroked her arms, then kissed the sweet spot under her ear, sending a shiver down her spine.

"¡*Dios*! What if someone comes in?"

Her protests rang false, even to her own ears. She could have said red. Although she hadn't spent any time in the dungeon aside from serving for parties, she knew with everything she had that Jake would stop.

But the word wouldn't come, and she didn't want it to.

Sleeping with Jake was a bad idea and she'd probably regret it. He was her boss and had been bullying her for weeks, but it was impossible to deny herself. She wanted his touch—his hands on her.

Why should she refuse him? Things might get awkward for a while, but it wasn't as if she'd be staying at Club Apocalypse forever.

He wrapped an arm around her waist, then lifted her just

enough to pull down her leggings until they bunched around her ankles. "They'll see a beautiful woman inspiring me to culinary brilliance."

"*Ay—*"

He slid a hand under her thigh, then lifted it and kissed a path from her knee to her core. "You smell so fucking delicious."

Beautiful. Delicious. Good girl.

The words arrowed into her, and she gasped. It had been so long since she'd had anything but her own fingers, and no one had ever told her such things.

"*¿Verde, amarilla o roja, querida?*"

This was her chance to end it. Stop it now before it was too late. The word was on the tip of her tongue, and all she had to do was spit it out. He'd even let her know he'd listen if she said it in Spanish.

"Green."

"There's my good girl." Still petting her, he knelt between her knees and spread them wide. "All good chefs need to taste though."

Without warning, he pulled her clit into his mouth and sucked, swirling his tongue around the tender bud. She cried out and arched her back, desperate for more contact. More...something.

More of everything.

He scooted her toward him, nearly unbalancing her. He didn't let her fall though, keeping her safe in his arms as he ate her like she was his last meal, driving her to the edge of the abyss when he stabbed a finger into her core and curled it to press against her g-spot.

"Jake!" Her scream echoed in the empty kitchen, and she pressed her lips together, desperate to keep silent so no one came to see what was going on.

His shadow beard scratched against her inner thigh, and he turned his head to nip her. She tried to wriggle her hips closer, but he held her too tightly.

"Oh, fuck!"

"Yeah, scream for me, baby." He pushed a second finger inside her and bit her clit, nearly sending her over the edge. "Come all over my face. Drench me with that sweet honey and let me see how fucking hot you are when you let go."

He rubbed her g-spot until she saw stars and screamed her pleasure just like he'd ordered. Her belly tightened with need, and when he sucked her clit into his mouth and lashed it with his tongue, she came so hard her vision went dark.

Slowly, and almost too gently, he softened his touch and eased her down. Air tore through her lungs as she tried to reach the surface of the tide of passion dragging her under.

Still holding her steady, he stood and moved behind her, then wrapped his arms around her. Cuddling her against his chest, he brushed soft kisses over her cheeks. "There's my good girl."

"Why?" She swallowed hard and tried to organize her scattered thoughts into coherence. "I...okay, you need to let me go so I can get dressed, then we'll sanitize everything and never speak of this again."

"You forgot one very important thing." He pressed a kiss to her temple, making her close her eyes.

"What's that?"

"I don't want to."

————

JAKE

Olivia lifted her chin and tried to turn on her stool. "Excuse me?"

Her cheeks were still pink, and she glowed with a faint sheen of perspiration. Even her eyes were softer, somehow warmer. She smelled fucking divine, and he wanted another few days of burying his face in her succulent pussy, but she had a point. There was a breakfast to be made for everyone who didn't get to eat Olivia.

"You have only yourself to blame," he murmured, scooting her stool away from the workbench.

"Jake, let me go. I need to clean up. You can't leave me sitting naked in a kitchen without breaking all the health codes."

"Yes, I can." He arranged her hair over her shoulders but made sure not to hide her beautiful tits. "In fact, I might have you sit just like this every time I cook."

She sputtered and her flush deepened. "Jake!"

He moved in front of her. Careful to let her keep her eyes off his face, he kissed her forehead. "You could have stayed in bed and rested, but you decided not to. What else was I supposed to do?"

"Not commit a health code violation making breakfast?"

"Ah, but you're not touching any food, and I moved you away from the worktable. I'll wash up and everything will be fine."

After giving her one last kiss, he whistled as he walked to the sink and washed his hands and face. Although he missed her scent, she had a point about sanitary kitchen practices.

"Are you serious?" she shouted. "Jake!"

"Yes? I haven't heard the magic words you can use to tell me what you want."

Wondering if she'd use a safe word, he got the sausage started, then laid several slices of bacon on the grill. He wanted Olivia to have a protein snack before he did anything else. Soon, the savory fragrance and sizzle filled the air, almost but not quite drowning out her irritable mutters as he threw the casserole together.

As he was putting it into the oven, he heard a throat clear behind him and turned.

"Am I interrupting something?" Mark asked, jerking his chin toward Olivia.

Her face flamed scarlet, but she lifted her chin and glared at him. "Yes, Mr. Luciano. You are interrupting, and I thank you. Will you please let me go? I'd be especially grateful if you punch the kitchen troll in the face."

"She refused to stay in bed and rest after having a panic attack and fainting," Jake said, resisting the urge to remind her of how fucking perfect she looked when she came.

"I see." Mark studied her for a moment, making Jake clench his fists. "Kitchen troll?"

Maybe tying her to a stool naked had been a tactical error. He didn't like the idea of other people looking at her, but it was too late. Still...it was one of his best friends who wouldn't touch her even if he hadn't been in a committed relationship.

"Yes. He's a fucking kitchen troll," she snapped.

"Hmm." Mark moved to stand in front of her. "I need you to look at me, Olivia."

"No." Jake pushed him out of the way, setting himself between Mark and Olivia. "She doesn't like making eye contact."

He met his friend's confused gaze and shook his head. After so many years together, they could communicate without a single word, and he made sure Mark understood how far he'd go to keep Olivia safe.

"Okay. Olivia, you can look wherever makes you comfortable, but I need to hear your answer to this question. Did Jake tell you that you could say red to stop everything?"

She blinked, then lowered her head and nodded. "Yes, sir."

Although he was insulted by the question, it was better for her to have outside corroboration.

"I'm not surprised, but good. Jake wouldn't play without a safe word. Now, do you want to stay here as you are, or do you want me to escort you back to bed?"

"I..." She glanced at Jake for a split second, then swallowed.

"You can say red," Mark said, moving to the side so she didn't have to look at him.

"I...can you keep everyone out?"

Her answer surprised him, yet at the same time it didn't. Obedience might be her first reaction, but she was learning to put down limits.

It was his job to make sure they were heeded.

"Absolutely," Mark promised, "but we need your verbal consent to stay where you are."

"Yes, sir. I'm...green."

"Good girl." He gave Jake an abrupt nod, then winked and sauntered from the kitchen.

"Well, that was fun." He plated the crisp bacon, then carried it to her.

"I can't believe I didn't say red," she muttered. "I—"

He stopped her words with a slice of bacon, holding it for her while she took a bite. "You can say red at any time," he reminded her.

She chewed and swallowed, then nodded. "I know."

"Good girl," he murmured. "Now, you can tell me how to make this mango tart."

"That doesn't seem right. I thought I was supposed to help."

"You are." He leaned against the worktable and smiled. "You're my own piece of living art, sitting there to inspire my culinary brilliance, remember?"

She flushed, but her lips twisted into an unwilling smile. "Cheesy."

"Oh, that's what we forgot. How does grilled brie on toast sound?"

"Like a supper appetizer. Use cream cheese mixed with..." She glanced at the spice cupboard. "A bit of fresh dill, a touch of dried onion flakes, and white pepper. We'll taste it to see if it needs salt."

It would be an interesting flavor profile, but the more he thought about it, the better it sounded. He especially liked the idea of having her teach him her mystical measuring ways. Aside from that, he enjoyed talking food with her.

"And for the bread?"

"The leftovers from supper service. Slice it lengthwise and toast it. Oh, and get the smoked salmon from the back of the walk-in."

"I assume you already know when it expires."

"Don't you? I was going to add it to the omelet station today, but..." She shrugged and looked away, then sighed. "Guess that isn't happening."

"Hey." He put down the handful of spice jars, then cupped her chin and kissed her cheek. "None of this is your fault and nobody is blaming you, okay?"

She nodded and sniffed, then gave him a watery smile. "Yes, sir."

Unfortunately, he still wasn't sure if the words were true. There was too much potential for violence hanging over their heads, and she was the catalyst. The biggest question in his mind still remained unanswered.

Where did her loyalties lie?

12

OLIVIA

Although she'd never once thought she'd be naked and tied to a stool in a commercial kitchen, it was strangely comfortable. She trusted Mark to keep people out, and once that worry was gone, she could relax and enjoy the way Jake looked at her.

It was like he truly believed she was beautiful—even with her hair a mess of frizzy curls and the dew of her climax still slicking her inner thighs.

She wasn't good with facial expressions. It was hard for her to know what people were feeling because she didn't often look above their shoulders. She could tell the difference between a smile and a frown, but people lied with their faces sometimes. She didn't know how to distinguish a mean smile from a happy one.

It was so much easier to listen to them when she wasn't confused by conflicting body language.

Jake was different. He didn't think less of her when she didn't look at him, and he'd even protected her when Mark asked for eye contact.

That had never happened before, and she wasn't sure what to think. And what was she supposed to do with the physical attraction zinging between them?

It didn't take a mind-blowing round of oral sex to make her aware of their chemistry, but he didn't trust her. He didn't have to say it either. His actions told her all she needed to know, and it left her unaccountably sad.

He smiled, but everything he did was carefully planned to ensure her compliance. He didn't want her out of his sight, so he made his version of confinement so pleasurable she forgot who he was.

It was cruel to show her the heights of passion, then use her desire to control her.

"Olivia? How much salt?"

She jerked and nearly toppled the stool. "Sorry, what?"

He held a spoon filled with whipped cream cheese. "Taste this. I think it needs a few pinches of salt."

"I...okay."

Frowning, he slid the spoon between her lips. She closed her eyes and let the cream slide over her tongue. "One generous pinch. No more than that and give it another tiny bit of onion flakes."

"You got it." He turned back to the worktable and incorporated the additions, then held out another spoonful. "How's that?"

Forcibly, she focused her attention on him and what they were doing, then tasted the mixture. "Better."

"Thanks." He studied her for a moment, then knelt to release her ankles. After untying her wrists, he helped her with her clothes and waited while she tied the scarf around her hair. "I guess playtime is over."

"I guess."

Playtime never started. Their interlude was simply a moment out of time meant to make the chick on the spectrum think somebody liked her.

He was truly no better than Berto.

"I'll let everyone know breakfast is ready while you wash up."

"Okay."

As she walked to the sink, he said, "Oh, and Olivia? Don't wander off."

She flinched but nodded and turned on the water. It wasn't as if she had anywhere else to go, nor did she need the reminder of how he truly felt about her.

He returned quickly and helped her set up a small buffet in the dining room. Kendra and Mark came in first, followed by Sean and Dr. Knox.

"This looks delicious," Kendra said, filling a plate with bacon and the cut mango that had never made it into a tart.

As long as it didn't go to waste, she supposed it was good enough.

"And this dilled cream cheese is lovely," Gabby said, spreading a generous amount on a piece of toast. "It's perfect with the salmon."

"The *pico de gallo* is inspired on the casserole," Jake said. "Olivia made it."

Everyone looked at her and she dug her nails into her thighs in an effort to keep still. "Um...yeah. It's good."

"Why aren't you eating?" Sean asked, after taking a huge bite of casserole. He swallowed, then added, "This is delicious."

"I'm...um... I ate some bacon earlier."

"You need to eat more," Jake said. He made her a plate, then set it in front of her.

She stared at the food, feeling everyone's eyes on her as her stomach roiled until she thought she'd be sick. "I... Sorry, I have to go."

Her chair fell with a crash, and she pushed past Jake in her haste to escape to the kitchen, but that wasn't a safe place either. The only safe place she'd had was gone.

"Olivia!"

"Red!" She evaded his grasping hands and raced toward the storage areas, then hid in a corner behind a sack of flour. Wrapping her arms around her calves, she tried to control her breathing and push down her inexplicable, unwarranted panic.

It was so stupid. Nobody had done a single damned thing to her. She was perfectly fine and in no danger. Tears pricked her eyes, and she lowered her head to her knees, wishing she could be normal just one fucking time.

"Olivia?"

"I'm fine. Go away." She didn't look up, unwilling to see the judgment on Jake's face.

"I'm not going to leave you alone, but I won't come any closer."

She heard the skid of chair legs on tile but didn't say anything.

"I'll sit here in case you need anything, but you don't have to talk."

"I feel stupid."

"Why?"

"I want to go back to my room. I want to be by myself, and I don't want to talk to anyone." She hauled in a breath, trying to ease the ache in her chest. "I know you don't want me running around, so just lock me in, I guess."

"You're not stupid. We want you to be guarded because of your cousin."

"That's a lie." Tears burned hot tracks down her cheeks, but she refused to let him hear her cry. "You're afraid I'll call Berto and tell him something that will hurt your business.

You think I went to jail on purpose just so I could spy on you."

"Olivia—"

"You think I'll do whatever my cousin tells me, and considering what happened, I understand it. Maybe you're right, and I'll cave when he pressures me. That doesn't mean I have to smile at you and your friends and pretend I'm happy about being locked up again."

Gathering her courage, she stood. Her body ached—a soul deep pain she couldn't shake. "You're in luck though."

"How so?" Thankfully, he was still seated in a dining chair.

"You don't need to worry about making me feel good, so I behave myself. Can I go back to my room now, or is that too far out of my jailor's reach?"

———

JAKE

He had no idea what was going on in Olivia's head and didn't want to ask. That didn't mean he wasn't desperate to find out, but the middle of a meltdown wasn't the time. And he really fucking hated seeing her hide behind that bag of flour like she thought someone would attack her.

Like she thought he would attack her.

Jake knew his inner desires. He wanted a slave. He

wanted her obedience, wanted her focus to be on him alone, and he wanted to be the person she relied on for everything down to the air she drew into her lungs.

He didn't want her fear and seeing her cower from him shattered something in his chest. He wanted to hold her and tell her everything would be okay, but there was too much at stake.

It was too much to ask of her, and it was a promise he couldn't make—no matter how much he wanted to.

Slowly, giving her time to adjust to his movements, he stood and laid his keycard on the chair. He could give her a taste of the freedom she so desperately needed.

"There's a keycard for the apartment on the chair. You can use the access hallway to bypass the dining room."

Making sure she heard his footsteps, he walked away, but doubled back and squeezed himself into a crevice between the wall and one of the coolers. He quieted his breathing, his heart slowing to match. It was an unconscious response, developed after years of being positioned behind a sniper rifle. He could hold it for months if needed.

Thoughts of those years often made him wonder. Society told him he should feel something for all the lives he'd snuffed out from distant shadows, yet he didn't. It was hard to feel guilt when one carefully placed bullet could save thousands of innocent lives.

Society told Olivia she was broken. Flawed. Not normal.

Fuck, he hated that word. Who the hell was normal these days?

People like her cousin took advantage of her.

People like him too. Jake was worse though. He was purposely using her neurodiversity against her, and he felt no guilt. The only thing saving him from being a complete asshole was that he wanted to make things better for her.

One bullet to buy the safety of thousands.

He didn't delude himself. It would get worse before it got better. He wanted her safe and able to protect herself from the rest of the fuckwits seeking to drag her down. She just had to live through the sucking chest wound.

So did he.

As much as he wished it could be different, at the end of everything, he'd let her go. She didn't belong with him, or in Club Apocalypse, and he couldn't force her to stay when she'd made so many plans. Unfortunately, she'd take a piece of his soul with her. And for once, he'd miss it.

Her head lowered, Olivia darted past him, then escaped through the service exit leading into the main corridor. Taking advantage of her inattention, he followed until she unlocked the door and let herself inside.

When he returned to the dining room, he sat across from Gabby, then rested his elbows on the table. She arched a pierced brow and took a bite of her toast.

"Is it done?" he asked.

She finished eating, then leaned back in her chair. "All

you Horsemen are right bastards, you know? Instead of telling us Olivia is all right, the first thing you ask is whether I've put spyware on a woman's phone without her knowledge."

Kendra coughed and held a napkin to her mouth. After clearing her throat, she asked, "Is Olivia okay? She seemed upset."

"I think she got overwhelmed by too many people. She went back to her room to rest." It might not have been the truth, but it seemed to satisfy Kendra.

For a moment, he wondered if Olivia was experiencing sub drop, yet there hadn't been a real scene between them. Then again...

It wouldn't hurt to check, but he'd give her a few more minutes. He'd cause more harm than good if he was wrong.

Still giving him a beady stare, Gabby held out her hand. "Olivia's phone is successfully bugged. I put it on the dresser where she left it. Give me yours and I'll install the monitor."

It took surprisingly little time to give him the ability to track Olivia's location and listen to her calls. When Gabby slid it back, he inclined his head. "Thanks."

"You're not welcome." After touching a napkin to her lips, she stood. "If you'll excuse me, I have work to do, but I'm expecting a visitor soon."

"What kind of visitor?" Sean asked.

"The kind you don't need to know about. Mind your own business."

"Gabby." Kendra held up a hand, stopping her. "We are minding our business when you tell us something like that."

She rolled her eyes and huffed, then crossed her arms over her chest. "If you must know, I've asked a business associate to deliver some...supplies."

"What kind of supplies?" Mark asked.

"New cameras, an off-grid and masked hotspot, a dedicated power supply, and perhaps a small bit of other miscellaneous technology you probably wouldn't understand."

"How much is it going to cost, and how do you know it won't get hacked?" Sean asked.

Gabby scowled at the question. "The cost is definitely none of your business. If you read my contract, you must know I'm personally liable for any intrusions after my work is installed. I have no intention of letting it happen again."

"I'd like to say I'd let the insurance cover the fire damage, but jail time for fraud doesn't sound appealing," Kendra said. "I'm sorry, but I remembered that clause in your contract and didn't want to file a claim until I talked to you and an attorney."

"You don't need to be sorry, and there's no reason to file an insurance claim as I'll be paying for the renovation." She shrugged and smiled at Kendra, then added, "It certainly didn't occur to me there was someone good enough to hack me of all people, so I suppose the old cliché about pride making me fall on my face is quite true."

Jake didn't remember that part of Gabby's contract, but

he hadn't spent a lot of time reading it. It explained why she'd been so furious though.

"Just out of curiosity, how do you know the new system won't be hacked?" Kendra asked.

"You can't hack what doesn't exist. Ta!" Giving them a wave, she skipped away and down the hall.

"That woman is a menace," Sean muttered.

"Maybe." Kendra ate the last of the bacon, then let Mark spoon some casserole to her plate. "But you can't say she doesn't live up to her agreements."

13

OLIVIA

The room smelled like Jake. He haunted her even when he wasn't there.

For the thousandth time she asked herself why she hadn't said a safe word. She should have called red before he touched her, but as usual, she was too busy trying to make people happy.

Don't be weird and look at me when I talk to you. Stop waving your hands. Stay sweet and shut up.

She'd found a place where saying no was accepted, and she still couldn't do it. And *dios*, Jake had done more than please her. His tongue should have been registered as a lethal weapon.

Her phone chirped with an incoming text, but she

couldn't bring herself to climb out of bed to answer it. Knowing her luck, it was Berto. Again, she'd been an idiot and hadn't set up a ringtone for him.

"Fuck off, asshole," she muttered, putting a pillow over her head.

A soft knock sounded at the door, but she ignored it. She'd used up her emotional pennies for the day and couldn't deal with talking to anyone else.

The knock came again, and she gritted her teeth when the door opened, then shut again.

"Oy, *mo cridhe*." Gabby sat next to her, then squeezed her knee. Strangely, the scent of mangoes and bacon followed her into the room. "Are you okay?"

"No. Go away."

"Sorry, that was a dumb question." Without warning, Gabby stretched out next to her and played the big spoon. "It's good not to have to look at people, yeah?"

"People lie with their smiles."

"Sometimes. Anyway, I have a pressie for you."

"I'm sorry, what?"

"A present." Gabby pressed something large and covered with plush fur into her hand. "This is Uther Penunicorn. He's very good for catching tears. He says you need him."

Olivia clutched the toy to her chest and let out a breath, then sat up. "Thanks."

"My pleasure." Gabby moved to sit behind her,

dislodging the pillows from the bed. "Is it hard for you to look at people?"

"Yes, sometimes."

"Me too. I prefer my computers."

She leaned against Gabby's chest and inhaled her ginger perfume, allowing herself the scant moment of comfort. "Sorry there weren't beans this morning."

"No worries." Gabby hugged her, then let out a sigh. "Anyway, I need to tell you something."

Olivia sighed and extricated herself from Gabby's embrace, wondering when her fresh hells would stop. "What now?"

"Jake asked me to install a tracker on your phone. He can read your texts and listen to your calls too."

"Unsurprising." She glanced at the device, laying so innocently on the dresser exactly where she'd left it. "I'm assuming he asked you not to tell me."

"Got it in one. I agreed only because I believe it will help keep you safe, but not telling you isn't in your best interest." Gabby squeezed her tightly, then reached for a plate piled with bacon and cut mango, plus a piece of toast spread with cream cheese. "I reckon you could use a snack since the bastards put you off your food."

"I—"

"Eat. The sugar and protein will make you feel better."

"Or I'll throw it up," Olivia muttered. "I was an idiot this morning."

"How so?"

Olivia ate a piece of bacon, more to give herself time to think than from hunger. She had no idea why she was telling Gabby her sad story to begin with, but she needed an understanding ear. "I let Jake tie me to a stool, and...anyway. You get the idea."

"They are bastards, but easy on the eyes, yes? The sex appeal oozing from them should be illegal."

"You could say that." Olivia set the plate aside, then squirmed to the other side of the bed and curled around the stuffed unicorn. "You're very kind, and I'm sorry, but I'd like to enjoy my pity party by myself."

"No worries." After giving her shoulder a squeeze, Gabby hopped out of bed. "I put my number in your phone. Call or text if you need anything."

"Thanks."

"Oh, one more thing." Gabby took her hand and closed her fingers around something wrapped in cellophane. "You deserve one of my special cock lollies."

"A...excuse me?" Olivia opened her eyes and stared at the phallus sucker, then giggled. "Where did you get this?"

"Kendra hooked me up. They come from a wonderful lady in Oklahoma named Rhonda. I call her my penis princess, and she's a right gem. She makes other flavors too, but I save those to throw at people when I tell them to suck my lady dick."

Olivia laughed until tears poured from her eyes and her

stomach hurt. When she managed to calm herself, she said, "This is why you always smell like ginger."

"Aye. I'm an addict." Leaning down, Gabby kissed her cheek. "I'll trot off and let you rest."

The door closed behind her, and Olivia unwrapped the candy. The ginger was powerful, almost sharp, but sweet too. Although she'd eaten candied ginger many times, the sucker sent warmth deep into her belly, and she felt better almost immediately.

Gabby was so kind, and Olivia didn't think she'd ever met a more generous person. Although she appreciated the cat Sean had given her, Uther Penunicorn was a priceless gift. He was cherished by someone who thought enough of her to share.

The idea sent a surge of contented joy deep into her heart.

With her stomach settled, the mango and bacon looked much more appealing, and she soon cleaned the plate. Unfortunately, the food did nothing to soothe the Jake-shaped turmoil in her head.

His nickname was apropos. She supposed most people thought it was funny to call the chef Famine, but to her, he was the starvation of the soul. He gave her just enough to ensure her cooperation, but it would never fill the empty spaces.

That wasn't his job though. They weren't dating, and she

couldn't even call him a lover. His task was to keep her compliant long enough to get rid of Berto.

Her eyes popped open, and she sat up. If she could prove Berto orchestrated her arrest, maybe she could have her conviction overturned. She'd need a better lawyer, of course. The public defender she'd been assigned hadn't done her any favors.

Unfortunately, she didn't have the money for an attorney like that, but she could save up. Gabby would likely be happy to loan it to her, yet she didn't want to borrow from a friend.

She laid back down and cuddled the stuffed unicorn, knowing she was getting ahead of herself. Until Berto was caught and brought to justice, she couldn't even start the process.

It was enough to have a plan. Best of all, she had hope.

———

JAKE

After cleaning up from breakfast, Jake stood in front of the apartment door, wondering if he should check on Olivia. The spare master key he'd gotten from Sean's office was warm in his hand, but he couldn't decide if it was encouraging him to go inside or warning him away.

He decided to leave her alone but checked his phone to make sure she was where he expected her to be. Frowning, he watched the red dot representing her phone move away from him, then stop.

"Fuck. I told her to stay put." Turning on his heel, he strode down the corridor. Before he reached the lobby, where the app pinned Olivia's location, he heard a shrill scream.

He broke into a run, then skidded to a stop at the sight of Gabby leaping at some strange dude. He laughed and caught her easily, and she enveloped him in a full-body hug with her legs wrapped around his waist.

Looking to be in his late thirties, the man had salt and pepper hair, and topped six feet easily. He was darkly attractive with full lips and a large Roman nose. Graying stubble covered his jaw, and he wore an obviously hand-tailored suit that Ryan would have drooled over. Judging by how easily he'd caught Gabby, he didn't skimp on time in the gym either.

Olivia stood behind Sean, who looked like he wanted to insert bullets manually into the man's skull. Jake almost laughed, wondering when his friend would get the stones to act on the sparks flying between him and Gabby.

Mark and Kendra stood near where the front desk had been, matching expressions of bemusement on their faces.

"Nicky! I'm so glad to see you!" Gabby kissed both his cheeks, then hugged him tightly. "Did you have a nice flight?"

"*Sì, cara.* It was very comfortable. Thank you for the use

of your jet." He winked at Sean, then carefully eased Gabby to the floor. "You're as beautiful as ever."

Frowning, Jake noted the telltale bulge under the man's left arm. He said nothing, but Gabby would have some questions to answer once they got rid of her friend.

As long as he didn't pull a weapon, he'd get to keep breathing.

"It was the least I could do for such a good friend."

"Ah, my sweet highland rose, be honest. You demanded expedited shipping, remember?"

Jake rolled his eyes at the Italian's smarm but didn't say anything. Sean looked about ready to beat the man down just for existing anyway.

"And I spent a fortune for it," she retorted, still grinning. "So, where are my new toys?"

He tapped her nose, then shook his finger at her. "Where are your manners, young lady? Introduce me to your friends first."

"I'd rather not."

"*Cara...*" The endearment held warning, but the man's eyes twinkled.

"Fine." She huffed out a breath and stomped a foot covered in a fuchsia Doc Marten. "Left to right, Jake McBride, Sean Franklin, Mark Luciano, and Kendra Hall."

"Ah, at last, I meet the famed Horsemen and their lovely vice president of operations," he murmured. "I am Nicolo Bianchi, and it is my very great pleasure to make your acquaintance. I'm despondent to miss Ryan Wood, but perhaps I'll catch him and his blushing bride in Scotland."

Jake shared a glance with Sean. It wasn't as if Ryan and Carrie's location was any great secret, yet...

Maybe Gabby was right, and they were better off not knowing, but she'd definitely have some explaining to do.

Nicolo's eyes brightened and he stepped past Sean, then bowed to Olivia and offered his hand. "And who is this charming goddess?"

She blushed scarlet but laid her hand in his. To Jake's annoyance, she actually looked at the bastard's face. "I—"

He brought her hand to his lips and brushed a kiss over her knuckles. "*Tesoro*, you stop my heart with your beauty."

"That's Olivia Rivera, and I will personally kick your ass and tell Ella on you if you bother her," Gabby said, leading him away.

Nicolo laid a hand on his chest in mock injury. "You wound me. It's like you don't trust me."

Jake certainly didn't and had a little more sympathy for Sean. Despite Nicolo's playboy mannerisms, he sensed there were more dangerous layers under the surface and wondered if he was one of Gabby's contacts from the Italian mafia. Between the concealed shoulder holster and the suit, Nicolo had the look down pat.

"Your fiduciary honor is unimpeachable. I trust you with my toys, my plane, my houses and cars, and my banking passwords," she retorted. "I would even trust you with my stuffed animals, but not with my female friends, and probably not with the male ones either."

"But you have so many, and they're all so beautiful." He smiled, baring teeth, making it hard to tell if he was teasing. "Surely, you wouldn't miss just one or two?"

"Toys, Nicky." She smirked and gave Sean a sideways glance, then added, "But Sean's yours if you can coax him out of the bushes. Oh, I almost forgot. Mark, would you hold the door, please?"

Surprisingly, Sean's head didn't burst into flames, but Jake suspected Gabby's ass would be feeling his displeasure sooner or later.

Nicolo laughed and tickled her under her chin. "You spoil my fun, *cara.*"

"I'm sure you'll live."

"As you say."

Jake followed Mark to the service entrance, then whispered, "I think Sean is going to lose his mind if we don't get rid of the Italian."

"Maybe, but I'm happy to let him stay if he helps keep my woman safe," Mark replied.

He had a point.

Nicolo snapped his fingers, and two men carried in a large wooden crate, then set it in front of Gabby. Without acknowledging anyone, they went back out and returned with a second, smaller container. After leaving Nicolo with a crowbar, they retreated, then got into a small panel van and drove away.

"Squee!" Gabby clapped her hands and jumped up and down. "Toys!"

"Patience, little one." Nicolo's expression went flat as he gazed at everyone. "Do you wish me to open the crates in front of your friends?"

"Well, it's all being installed here, and they're the property owners." Gabby shrugged, then added, "It's okay, but not in the lobby."

"And you wish to do the install yourself?"

"Yes." She studied him for a moment, her expression pensive. "I'd ask you to help, but I have to provide fair disclosure. A gang set fire to the lobby, and I believe they were hired by someone who managed to break my system."

"I see. That's quite an accomplishment." He winked, then tousled her rainbow hair. "It's very sweet of you to try to protect me, but I will be fine."

"Aye, I suppose you would be, at that," she murmured. "All right, then! Play Father Christmas and let me see my toys!"

14

OLIVIA

Nicolo reminded her of Berto. They were both far too charming, but where Berto was ingratiating and only nice when he wanted something from someone he couldn't bully, Nicolo's charm was elegant and seemed as much a part of his personality as the bespoke suit. If she didn't know better, she'd have thought he actually meant the things he said.

He was also one of the very few people she'd ever met who could match his facial expressions and vocal inflections to his words, and make it look like he was telling the truth.

And that made him dangerous—especially when she didn't trust her judgment regarding people's motivations or honesty.

She still didn't know why Gabby had dragged her out here. It hadn't been to meet Nicolo—not after she'd explicitly warned him away from her. Gabby's excitement was contagious though. Maybe it was better than hiding in Jake's bedroom by herself.

"Little one," Nicolo said gently, "shall we find a more private location to open your toys?"

Gabby hummed her agreement and ran a loving hand over the smaller of the two crates. "Kendra, may we stage these in the large conference room next to the restaurant?"

"Um...sure. What's in them?"

"Bits and bobs and all manner of fun things. You'll see."

"Your idea of fun is slightly scary," Kendra countered. "I'll get you a master key so we can keep it locked."

"You're a love. Thank you."

Olivia had to admit to some curiosity too. The crates looked heavy yet were marked with prominent fragility warnings. She also didn't think they were toys as Gabby claimed. It was as if she resisted saying what the crates contained where people could hear her.

The men paired up and soon had the crates moved, positioning them on the floor at the front of the room. After closing the door, Nicolo hefted a crowbar. "Are you ready, Gabrielle?"

"Eeee! Yes!"

"So excitable." Without another word, Nicolo wedged the crowbar under the lid of the larger crate and pried it free, then repeated the process with the second. Both containers were filled with mounds of shredded paper concealing what was inside.

"I'll find a garbage can," Olivia said.

"I'll show you where they are," Jake replied. "We might need two."

Biting her lip, she nodded. Being alone with him was about the last place she wanted to be, but she couldn't refuse after offering to get the bins.

When the door shut behind them, he said, "Olivia, look. I—"

"Stop. I don't want to talk about it, and I would rather just forget this morning ever happened."

"Not sure how we're going to do that when we're sharing a room."

"Try harder, because that's all we'll ever share," she snapped, angry enough to look at his face. "I agreed to help you trap my cousin. I agreed to you attaching yourself to me like a fucking tick. I didn't even complain when Gabby told me about the tracker on my phone."

He had the grace to look uncomfortable, but Olivia wasn't done. "The next time you lay a hand on me, I will be calling red, so keep whatever you wanted to say to yourself, and leave me alone!"

His lips quirked into a half smile. "I think I need to make you angry more often. It's the only time I get to see your beautiful eyes."

"Ahhh! That's what you're thinking about right now? I suppose I should be glad you're not looking at my chest!"

"Oh, I'm looking at that too."

"You utter—"

From her pocket, her phone shrilled the discordant ringtone she'd chosen for Berto. Her anger at Jake faded as the sick feeling she always got when she had to talk to her cousin took up residence in her belly.

"Back inside the conference room," he ordered, spinning her to face the door before unlocking it. "Set your phone on the table and put it on speaker when you answer."

"I...okay." She did as he asked, unable to meet anyone's eyes. "It's Berto."

"Don't answer yet. Let it roll over to voicemail," Sean said. "I want to see if he leaves a message. If he says something incriminating, it can be used as evidence."

"And keep him on the line for at least five minutes when you call him back, if you can," Gabby said. "We'll pinpoint his location."

Olivia nodded and choked back a whine. Berto hated when she didn't answer her phone. He'd yell and...

She took a deep breath and reminded herself she wasn't alone. Although she still had to deal with Jake, there were other people who were kind and wanted to help.

When the message notification chimed, Jake tapped the icon to play Berto's message.

"Stupid *puta*. Answer your fucking phone when I call,

you little cunt. I want to know if they've hired guards to protect that dump, and where they are."

The message ended and Olivia looked at her hands, then shrugged. "My loving cousin, Berto."

Nicolo sniffed and tipped his nose in the air. "The gentleman who bombed this fine establishment, I presume?"

"Yes, according to Olivia," Kendra replied. "Quite a peach, isn't he?"

"Indeed." He pulled a slim phone from his pocket and placed a call, speaking rapid Italian she had no hope of following. When he finished, he pocketed his phone and inclined his head toward Olivia.

"*Tesoro*, do be so kind as to tell your cousin there are only two unarmed guards who leave at approximately ten o'clock every evening, please."

Gabby groaned and rubbed her forehead. "Shite. How much is this going to cost me?"

"That half case of Gordon and MacPhail in your Paris loft."

"Are you trying to make me cry?" she demanded. "Do you know how hard it was to find?"

"I do know. You outbid me, remember?"

"Bloody wanker." She folded her arms over her chest and pouted. "You have the security code already."

He bowed, then pulled her hand free and kissed her

knuckles. "As always, it's a pleasure doing business with you, my good doctor."

"Shut it before I hurt you."

After giving her hand a fond pat, he turned his attention back to the group. "As I was saying, two unarmed guards who leave at ten. We'll see what that tasty bit of bait flushes out, and renegotiate after say, seven days."

"Can I just pay in cash next time?" Gabby asked.

"Oh, I suppose," he replied.

"Asshole."

Olivia blinked and her hand trembled over the touch-screen, trying to work up the courage to return Berto's call.

"How many will there be?" Jake asked, taking her hand away from the phone. "And what kind of weapons will they be carrying?"

"A good number more than two, I expect, but rest assured, they are every bit as well trained as you and your comrades. You shall have no problems, and they will endeavor to capture rather than kill."

"You didn't answer the question," Olivia murmured.

"Quite right, my dear. Nor shall I. You and your companions will be tucked safe inside and away from the windows, so truly, there is no reason for you to know."

He might not be giving them the answers they wanted, yet his refusal was kind. Nodding, she decided she liked Nicolo Bianchi, but it would be unwise to trust him.

———

JAKE

"Are you ready?" he asked, still holding Olivia's hand.

It was that or pound the Italian's face into hamburger. Who the fuck did he think he was, telling three retired SEALs to stay inside?

And that supercilious Eurotrash attitude was starting to fucking grate.

Then again, maybe it wasn't such a bad idea. Professional mercenaries would be less likely to become emotional. Although they wouldn't hesitate to kill, they'd stay on task, do the job they'd been paid for, and give the Horsemen all the plausible deniability they'd need.

Damn that fucking Italian.

At somewhere around thirty grand a bottle for the whiskey Nicolo had extorted from Gabby, they'd be paid very well indeed. No wonder she'd been about halfway to tears.

"Remember, *tesoro*, a gentleman does not call a lady those filthy names. You deserve better. He is not worth your tears, nor do you owe him a single instant of your consideration," Nicolo said as he stroked Olivia's hand.

"He's right," Jake said, hating to agree with the smarmy bastard. "If we're very lucky, Berto will show up tonight and this will all be over before morning."

She nodded and swiped her phone awake, then brought up her contact list. "I...okay, I'm ready."

Everyone went silent as they waited for the call to connect. Before she could speak, Berto's voice boomed out in snarled Spanish.

"Where the fuck have you been?"

Her hands fluttered madly, and to his surprise, Nicolo took one and laid her palm against his chest. She stilled and let out a breath, visibly calming herself. Swallowing his pride, Jake took her free hand and did the same thing.

"I... I had to work."

"I... I... I... You're so stupid you can't even speak. Tell me how many guards there are."

She straightened and pulled her hands free, then rested them on the table in front of her. "I have some questions first."

"Fine. Whatever."

"When did you start plotting to send me to jail?"

"That's your question?" Berto asked. He let out a braying laugh. "It's not like the information will help you because you know better than to tell, but it was about six months before your arrest. I called in the tip, paid off your lawyer and parole officer, and you're exactly where you need to be."

"I was supposed to be going to my college graduation, remember?"

"Watch your tongue or it might get cut out."

Wishing he could reach through the phone and rip out Berto's heart, Jake leaned toward her and stroked her back.

She tightened her hands into fists but didn't respond to the threat. "The resort has two unarmed guards who leave at ten every night. Is that what you wanted to know?"

"Unarmed? And what about the old men running the place. They do anything useful? Any guns or weapons?"

"No. There are no guns. Like you said, they're old."

Jake didn't take offense at Olivia's comment, but his fury grew every time Berto opened his fucking mouth. It wasn't enough to send her to prison, he verbally abused her too. Part of his anger was directed at Olivia herself. Why did she take it?

"And the English computer chick? She still there?"

"Um... Why do you want to know?"

"She's worth an extra half million if we can bring her in alive." He barked out another ugly laugh. "The bounty just says alive. She's cute, so I might take a little extra before we turn her over."

"No." Olivia lifted her head, her expression fixed with hate. "She's gone home."

Nicolo blew her a silent kiss, the asshole. When she returned his grin with a weak smile, Jake decided not to rearrange his face...yet.

"Fuck. Anyway, that's enough for now, but I'll call later. I want to know if she left anything behind."

"Like what?"

"Computer equipment, cameras, anything electronic. Hell, just save whatever you find, and I'll pick it up."

The call dropped before she could reply, and she managed a small, tremulous smile. "Um...so that's Berto."

"Hmm." Nicolo drummed a finger on the table, then typed a message on his phone. "His disposal will be... I believe the American phrase is...on the house?"

"Who, aside from Jake, Olivia, and Nicolo understood the conversation?" Sean asked.

"I did." Gabby said, seemingly unconcerned with what she'd heard. "Olivia told Berto what we agreed she'd say about the guards. Then he asked if I was still here. She told him I went home because she's a delightfully clever provider of magnificent breakfasts."

To Nicolo, she added, "You really must try her full English, Nicky. It's the best I've ever eaten."

"Can we stay on topic, please?" Sean asked. "Why would he ask about you?"

"It seems there's an insultingly small bounty on my head, and he wanted Olivia to find anything I'd left behind. I'm considering letting him have my unwashed socks and perhaps a few used tissues."

"Indeed," Nicolo said, giving her a warm smile. "A half million dollars won't get them far, and certainly not out of my reach. I'm sorry for the insult, darling."

"I'm sure you'd have paid at least seven figures, right?"

"Of course, a bargain at twice the price."

"Excuse me," Sean said, his jaw clenched tight as he spat the words. "I don't think you appreciate how dangerous these people are. Why are you making jokes?"

"It's fine, Sean," Gabby replied. "They won't get in here, and even if they did, they'll find I'm not so easy to capture."

"I would normally agree," Nicolo murmured, "but you are not in your own environment here, and without proper security, you are at some risk."

"Shush you. I'm well able to—"

"Mr. Franklin, I suggest preemptive spankings. Thoroughly and often, to remind the good doctor of her manners."

"Hey!"

"Gladly." Without warning, Sean picked her up from her chair, then sat her on his lap. When she tried to wriggle free, he said, "I could start right now."

Nicolo threw back his head and laughed. "I quite like you, Mr. Franklin. I believe this will work very well indeed. Now, back to the matter at hand. Gabrielle, were you able to track our friend's phone?"

"Yes. He's in Tucson."

"We can't kill him," Olivia murmured.

"Why not?"

The question was echoed by more than a few people, and Jake nearly roared his anger. Even after being threatened with disfigurement, she still wanted to protect her worthless cousin?

It took everything he had to stop himself from shaking some sense into her—or strapping her to a spanking bench next to the other incredibly stubborn woman in the room so he and Sean could explain the concept of personal safety to them.

"Because I want my life back, and I want my conviction overturned. Berto needs to testify and tell people he arranged my arrest, and I want the people who helped him to face prosecution. I can't do any of that if he's dead."

Nicolo sighed and sent another text, then pocketed his phone. "Well, shit."

Damn. Jake really hated agreeing with the man.

15

OLIVIA

"Nicky and I will handle the install, but it will probably take the rest of the day," Gabby said.

"I'll help," Sean offered. "Just show me what you need."

"All right. Thank you." She held up a tiny white object on the tip of one finger. "This is what we're installing."

"What are they?"

"Cameras." She held up a small pistol-grip tool, then added, "They're mounted with specialized pop rivets, and take a minute or two per camera to install. We'll put one every five meters about eye level on the exterior walls."

Sean frowned and squinted at the object. "That's not a camera. It's a breath mint."

"Ye of little faith." She retrieved her phone and tapped the screen, then gave the camera to Sean. "Use the tip of a small darning needle to turn on the camera, like so. Now, watch my phone."

She carried the camera from the room, leaving Sean and Jake frowning at the screen.

"Holy shit! Look at this!" Sean turned the phone to reveal a wide-angle view of the entire lobby where several people were setting up tools and equipment for the renovation. The screen went blank, and Gabby returned a few moments later.

"Gorgeous little buggers, aren't they? They're nearly invisible when they're installed and give color video even after dark. Anyway, we have about four hours in which we can be assured Berto isn't here, so we'll do the outside walls first, then move inside. We can't do the lobby yet as my darlings would get painted over, but our movements will be hidden by the contractors if anyone is already watching."

"Are they weatherproof?" Sean asked.

"Of course. They'll last about five years."

"What's the catch with them?"

"As I mentioned, you can't paint where they've been installed. They're also hideously expensive, but I'll set up the system to work with different cameras when the time comes."

"Do I want to know how much they cost?"

"No. You really do not. Shall we?"

Carrying Styrofoam boxes of cameras, she, Nicolo, and Sean left the conference room, followed quickly by Mark and Kendra.

"Come on," Jake said, breaking the uncomfortable silence. "We should talk."

"There's nothing to say." She tried to squeeze past him, but he blocked the door before she could escape.

He took her hand and tucked it into the crook of his elbow, then led her to the apartment. "We're going to talk about what happened this morning."

"That's the last thing I want to discuss with you or anyone else."

"I know." He unlocked the door and ushered her inside before she could think up an escape plan. "But we need to. Have a seat."

"Fine." She stomped to the breakfast bar and took a stool. "Let's get this over with."

He sat across from her and reached for her hands, but she put them in her lap before the tremors started. "Olivia, I'm sorry for this morning. I don't know what I said or did that set you off, but I want to fix it for you."

"Can you get rid of my cousin or put my life back together?"

"No, not yet."

"Can you stop treating me like a criminal?"

"I don't—"

"You performed a sex act on me this morning. I consented, so that's on me, but the minute it was over, you told me not to wander off. Tell me, Jake, where do you think I'll go?"

He was silent for several seconds, then got up to grab two bottles of water from the fridge. "I am...was worried you'd return to your cousin."

"The one who threatened to cut out my tongue? Can you give me just a little credit for not being as stupid as he thinks?"

"You said you didn't want us to kill him."

"I also told you why, but once he tells the truth about what he did in front of witnesses, I'll probably throw a party if he gets shanked."

"There's also the issue of your inability to watch your surroundings," he murmured, pushing the water toward her. "I don't believe you'd willingly return to him, but if he wants to take you, I'm worried you won't see it coming."

His words stopped her budding diatribe, and she bit her lower lip. He wasn't wrong. "And your answer to that was to tie me naked in the kitchen and go down on me?"

"Seemed like a good idea at the time."

"It wasn't." She uncapped the bottle and took a long drink. "I'm not going to lie. It was a bad idea, but it was good."

"Just good?"

Her lips curled into an unwilling smile, matching his. "It

was more than good, but I'm not going to let you use sex to distract me from being little more than your slave."

Reaching over, he cupped her chin gently. It was a movement meant to hold her still, yet he didn't force her to meet his gaze. "No, you're not a slave, sweetheart. A slave would trust their master enough to let them be their eyes when they can't see, their air when they can't breathe, and their safety when they can't protect themself. For the price of their obedience, their master would still their hands and take those burdens."

That didn't sound like slavery. It sounded like...freedom. She couldn't imagine what it would be like to allow someone to take over the responsibility of all the shit constantly bouncing in her head—to make the squirrels be quiet in their cages. His words were a dream though.

The years of sporadic therapy when she could afford it had never given her the peace he described, nor had self-help books, meditation, or any of the dozens of things she'd tried.

It would never give her back the time she'd spent believing herself broken because she didn't perceive the world like everyone else.

Maybe it was a fantasy, but what did she have to lose by trying?

"Can you...if I let you do that, will it make it easier to think?"

"I have no idea."

She barked out a surprised laugh. "At least you're honest."

He stood, then moved behind her and rubbed her shoulders. "I said I didn't know if it would help. I didn't say I wasn't willing to try. Are you?"

She tried to turn to face him, but he stopped her. "First order is that we talk like this, with me behind you."

"Um...okay?"

"Good girl." He kept up the massage, easing the tension from her shoulders. "As much as I loved making you come this morning, I realized something just now."

She closed her eyes, relishing the touch. "What's that?"

His body heat sent prickles down her spine and his breath washed over her ear. "I gave that rosemary soap to Mark. Even I could smell it on him, and you didn't say a word."

———

JAKE

Olivia's hands were quiet in her lap and the muscles in her shoulders and upper back relaxed under his touch. Despite her physical stillness, he could almost hear the gears in her head grind as she tried to change her perspective.

He was getting in too deep with her, but he couldn't help

it. Every time he thought about the expression on her face when Berto threatened her...

Most likely, he'd fuck it all to hell, but it was impossible to let her go without trying to help her.

"I didn't notice," she finally said. "I hate that soap, and I didn't...that's so odd."

"Want to hear a theory?"

"I guess so?"

"You were focused on me. Maybe not your sight, but your hearing and sense of smell weren't getting distracted." He unwound the scarf from her head and massaged her scalp, making her let out a tiny moan. "I think you shut down your nose for a bit."

"Hmm."

Maybe there was something to her way of experiencing the world. Without the benefit of looking at her face, he had to rely on the tone of her voice, respiration, and her body. He wouldn't say it was easy, but it was enlightening.

"I'm probably bullshitting you. I don't know. I'm not a therapist and I have no idea how your senses work, but I think maybe you really liked it when I made you come. It made you feel good, right?"

He caught the edges of a smile before she spoke. "You know it did."

"And you felt good until I opened my stupid mouth and made you remember you don't want to be here. I'm sorry for that. I did want you to stay put, but I didn't mean it the way it came out."

"That's part of my problem." She slumped and rested her head on the breakfast bar. "I don't get nuances of speech. Sarcasm is a mystery because I can't read expressions very well."

"Oh, I'm pretty sure you understand more than you think." He moved down her back to massage the tight muscles at the base of her spine. "What was your initial impression of Nicolo Bianchi?"

"He confuses me."

"Why?"

"I don't know. I think I like him, but he's too kind, maybe too perfect. I've never met anyone like him before."

"Would you trust him?"

"Do you?"

"I asked first."

Olivia laughed softly, then straightened and took a sip of water. "I think trusting him would be dangerous, but I'm not the best judge of character. Why did you ask about him?"

"Would it surprise you to know I had the same thoughts?" He moved to the side and held out a hand where she could see it. "Come with me. I want to show you something."

She nodded and let him lead her into Mark's room. Gabby had taken over the space until even the bed was covered with computers. He took some care to lead her through the maze of cables so neither of them touched anything.

With his luck, he'd trip over something and launch a missile from one of the silos in Colorado.

"What is it?"

"A surprise. Close your eyes."

"Um...okay?"

When her eyes slid shut, he opened the hidden latch set into a piece of paneling, making a door swing wide. Although he'd show her the secret later, he wanted to see her reaction.

"I'm going to kneel and take off your shoes. Keep your eyes shut for just a few minutes longer."

"Must be some surprise." She chuckled softly but lifted her feet to let him remove her socks and sneakers.

"I hope you like it." He took her elbow, then added, "Three steps down. I'll help you."

"You have roses. They smell nice. I think I hear water too."

"Focus on the roses." He helped her down the steps, then walked her forward a few feet.

"Can I open my eyes?"

"Yes."

She blinked a few times to adjust her vision, then gasped. "*Dios*. What is this place?"

He gave her a moment to take everything in. Surrounded on all sides by wooden privacy fence and a rose-covered overhead trellis to block the sun, the outdoor lounge was the Horsemen's oasis. The ground was even covered with artificial turf meant to be easy on bare feet. Comfortable couches surrounded a free-standing firepit, and a hot tub with an outdoor shower was positioned in one corner. Against the far wall, there was a small fountain. It didn't do much of anything except provide background noise. He'd turn it off if it bothered her.

He couldn't remember how many evenings he'd sat out there with his friends, drinking and shooting the shit after a long day.

"Shh." He moved behind her, making sure her attention was on her surroundings. "One sense at a time. You don't need to experience everything at once."

Closing her eyes, she smiled and lifted her face to one of the blossoms and inhaled. "The roses smell like apples and cloves, but soft and sweet. It changes when the breeze mixes it with sagebrush."

"Good girl. When you're done with the roses, listen to the water."

"Who made all this?" She ran a hand across the back of a weatherproof suede couch. "It's...everything is so beautiful."

"We built the enclosure years ago. Jolene Stratton gave us the roses, and Kendra put all the furniture in. Used to be just some lawn chairs and a couple of cheap plastic tables. We had the hot tub and the shower, but not much else."

She lowered herself to sit on the couch and kept petting the fabric. "I could live out here. Everything...works."

"Can you tell me what that means?"

He sat next to her but tried not to interrupt her sensual exploration. He'd never seen her look so at peace with herself and her surroundings and wondered if she'd found the same contentment on her cliff.

To his surprise, she reached over and brushed her hand over his. "It's like everything makes sense together. The roses make the fountain quieter, but the fountain makes the roses smell sweeter. This couch is soft, but kind of thick and rough. I like to touch it because it makes the breeze tickle my skin."

She spared him a quick glance, then blushed. "I'm sorry, that sounded really dumb."

"No, it doesn't. Want to try an experiment?"

"What kind?"

"You'll see. Stand up for a second." When she got to her feet, he lowered the sofa back until it was flat, extending it into a double bed.

"Oh, man. I need this couch."

"It's yours. You can undress and find out how it feels against your body. Best of all, no one will see you out here, except me."

16

OLIVIA

J ake's suggestion was too seductive...too tempting. She wanted that plush fabric against her skin almost more than she wanted to breathe, and the desire drowned out her other senses.

When she didn't immediately reply, he said, "C'mon. You know you wanna."

She shook her head and took a step back. "No. You'll restrain me again."

"How about if I promise I won't until you beg for it?"

"That won't happen." She had a feeling they both knew she was lying.

"Never say never." He lifted the top of an end table and

drew out a plush throw, then spread it over the cushions. "I even have something else for you to touch. It feels like real fur."

"I—"

"Imagine fur against your body," he whispered, suddenly behind her. "Tickly and warm, and so, so soft, but not as silky as your pretty skin."

She closed her eyes and whimpered softly. The kitchen troll was easy to resist, but this version of Jake was impossible to deny.

He traced a finger down her arm, leaving a trail of fire in its wake. "The sunlight makes you look like someone's wrapped you in edible gold leaf."

Laughing, she tried to pull back from the sensual haze he cast upon her. "It's always food with you."

"I am a chef." He grabbed the throw and rubbed it against her cheek. "Take a chance, Olivia. Let yourself feel in a safe place. Let me be your eyes so you can enjoy the rest of what you're feeling. Please."

Her knees almost buckled, but she managed to stay on her feet. The temptation of his voice was bad enough, but hearing him say please...

She pulled her T-shirt over her head with shaking hands, then kicked off her leggings, leaving her panties. The soft evening breeze caressed her like a lover, enclosing her in a rose-scented cocoon as the fountain draped her in sound.

For once in her life, her brain went...quiet. Not even her cliff had given her such peace.

"There you go," Jake murmured, almost too softly to hear. "Try the couch when you're ready."

"Why are you doing this for me?"

"I want you to see possibilities and tools you can use when things get overwhelming." He kissed a path across the back of her shoulder. "Hell, I don't know. Maybe none of this will work and I'm pissing up a rope."

One step at a time, she walked to the couch, then laid on her stomach. The suede upholstery was almost abrasive compared to the opulent synthetic fur and she giggled at the contrasting sensations.

Before prison, she'd had a tiny apartment filled with things to touch. There were plants, soft bedding in a multitude of textures, and different essential oils. She'd even had a weighted blanket covered in similar faux fur.

"There's my good girl." He knelt next to her, then straddled her hips. The rough denim of his jeans sent a counterpoint of sensation into her core, and she shivered with delight.

His callused hands worked very bit of tension from her body until she felt like she'd melt into a puddle. He kept his voice soft too, and his personal fragrance blended perfectly with the roses.

"Do you like that?"

"Yes. It feels nice."

"Good. How's your brain doing?"

She laughed softly as he feathered his fingers along her ribs and brushed the curves of her breasts, almost but not quite tickling her. "I think that's the strangest question anyone has ever asked me."

"Yeah, it didn't come out the way I meant."

"What did you mean?"

"I want us to move forward, Olivia." He lowered himself until she felt his weight against her back, then kissed her shoulders. "I want to keep being the person who takes the bad things away so you can experience what makes you happy."

"Sounds too good to be true. What do I have to do?"

"It's the easiest thing in the world. All you have to do is obey."

"Blind obedience got me into this mess in the first place."

"You obeyed the wrong person." His breath wafted across the side of her face, smelling of peppermint. "I might punish you for disobedience, but I will never harm you emotionally or physically."

After Berto's betrayal, giving someone her trust as Jake was asking should have sent her running a two-minute mile to escape. Yet...the small things he'd asked of her had helped. He'd changed so much for her; his soap, his shoes, and even his voice to accommodate her needs.

"What kinds of orders would you give me?"

"I think my first order will be for you to never look me in the eye."

She snorted out a laugh and shifted her hips, liking the feel of his weight pressing her into the fur blanket. "That one is easy."

"Except you look at me when you're mad. Could you do it then?" he asked, his voice a sultry purr. "Or would I have to punish you?"

Whuh.

The scent of roses faded as his voice trapped her in a sensual web. "How would you punish me?"

"I believe in making the punishment fit the crime. If you look at me, I might blindfold you while I jerk off. You'd be able to hear me, but I wouldn't let you watch or touch me. If you climax without permission, I'd make you come again and again until you're sobbing."

"*Dios.*" Her dry throat clicked as she tried to swallow. "You make it sound like I'd be your sex slave."

His weight suddenly left her and he slapped her bottom hard. "You are not a sex slave." His voice was flat with an angry edge she hadn't expected, yet he didn't shout. "You'll be my sensual slave. I will control what senses you use and when. I will drag you through sensation after sensation until you can't focus on anything but me, and sometimes I'll take them away."

"Jake, I—"

He moved to kneel in front of her, then grabbed her hair to lift her head. She caught a fleeting glimpse of his blue eyes before she dropped her gaze to his shirt collar. The sting from his grip on her hair traveled like electricity into her pussy and his laugh sounded like razor-edged temptation.

"And sometimes, beautiful Olivia...sometimes you'll beg me to."

———

JAKE

She exhaled slowly, then breathed in through her nose. Aside from her heartbeat and respiration, she was utterly still and didn't make a single fucking sound.

He let go of her hair and allowed her to sit on her heels. For a moment, he wondered if he'd pushed too hard, too fast. Although she'd worked in his kitchen for weeks, they didn't *know* each other. He hadn't asked her limits or any of the dozens of questions he should have known the answers to before proposing a master/slave dynamic—especially since the relationship had an expiration date.

Olivia hadn't belonged in jail, nor did she belong in his kitchen, or even at Club Apocalypse. The only thing he could offer was a little bit of calm before she went back to her regularly scheduled life.

When she remained silent, he touched her shoulder. "What do you think?"

She laughed softly and folded her hands in her lap. "It sounds like I'm making a deal with the devil. What's in this for you?"

"Will you be offended if I say I get off on the control?"

"Judging by how you are in the kitchen, I'm not surprised." Her smile faded and she chewed on her lower lip. "What kinds of things will you ask me to do?"

"The first thing is that the kitchen is yours until we get this shit with your cousin straightened out."

"Excuse me?"

"You heard me." He got to his feet, then tugged the blanket out from under her and wrapped it around her shoulders. "We have six people to feed and a ton of food that will go bad before we can open again. Take care of it, starting with supper tonight."

"One condition."

"What's that?"

"You can watch, but the minute you shout or throw away my food, I will brain you with a cast iron skillet."

He choked out a surprised laugh, then nodded. "Fair enough. What's for supper tonight?"

It was good to see Olivia communicating her needs. He'd been desperate for her to stand up for herself for so long, it hardly seemed real, but he'd take it.

"We're having the snapper. I refuse to let such expensive fish go to waste and feeding six will let us use it all."

"Good girl. Are you going to make that crema fresca sauce again?"

She shot him a look and scowled. "You said it was incompetent and threw it out."

"I lied." When she didn't look away, he tapped her nose. "Eyes down, sweetheart."

"You are such a fucking kitchen troll."

"Very nice! You said it in English right to my face. What's for breakfast tomorrow?"

"I would have said blinis and caviar service, but I gave the last of it to Ryan and Carrie."

"That was you? I thought Ryan stole it."

Blushing, Olivia dropped her head. "It was their wedding breakfast. He said it was Carrie's favorite, and it wasn't going to be used soon enough."

"It's okay, I'm not mad." He studied her for a moment, then added, "You really hate wasting food, don't you?"

"I grew up poor. We had enough, but not so much we could afford to throw food away." She lifted her head for a split second, then smiled. "And there wasn't money for your fancy gadgets either."

"All right." He sat next to her and pulled her against his chest. "We'll call food waste the first of your hard limits. What else can you think of that you hate?"

"Didn't I give you a list yesterday morning when you thought I was trying to kill myself?"

"True, and you don't like to be shouted at. I'll make every effort to remember all the things that bother you, but if one comes up, I want you to tell me instead of holding it all inside until you have a meltdown."

"I...okay. I can do that."

"I also want you to talk to me when I say something you don't like. I don't want you to have any more panic attacks."

She squirmed out of his arms and went to sit near the fountain but didn't look at him. "Jake, panic attacks happen. You can't exactly stop them."

"Maybe not, but I can fix what's causing them." He rolled his eyes and considered smacking himself in the forehead. He wasn't a fucking counselor and had no business trying to advise her on her mental health. "Okay, you're right. I can't stop them or fix it so they don't happen. Will you at least let me get you to a safe place so you're not alone?"

She drew her knees to her chest, obviously needing time to think. Finally, she nodded, then said, "Okay, I'll try."

Although he wanted to be close to her, he forced himself to stay still. "Good girl."

"I like when you say that." She laughed softly, then pushed her hair out of her face. "It's stupid, but you said the crema fresca sauce was adequate, and I thought that was the biggest praise ever."

Fuck, he was an asshole. He'd gone way too far trying to get her to stop letting him abuse her.

"By adequate, I mean it was the most delicious sauce I've ever put in my mouth. It was a close second to your delectable pussy."

"Jake!" She tossed the blanket over her head and groaned. "I can't believe you said that."

"What?"

"You...my..." She peered at him from under the blanket, then sighed. "You're utterly filthy."

"You have no idea." He moved to sit close to her, then tugged the blanket away from her face. "So, here's the deal. I promise not to shout or do any of the other shit I know you hate. In exchange, you'll let me control your senses."

"What does that mean?"

"If sound is setting you off, I'll make you wear earplugs. If it's smell...well, there's not much I can do about smell, but maybe a surgical mask if I can't remove you from it. Those are the two that seem to trigger you the worst."

"Um...okay?"

"You seem fine with touch and sight, but I want you to tell me if that changes. Oh, and try to watch your surroundings more, maybe pretend you're driving or something."

"I'll try."

She shivered, then leaned against him, making him realize the evening chill had descended. He stood and walked to the door leading inside. "Wait here for a minute. I have something for you to wear while you're cooking."

"I'm hoping that means I won't be cooking naked."

He laughed, then went up the stairs to the door. "No, but maybe we'll do that if it's just the two of us. I like the idea of you cooking in nothing but an apron."

There was one thing he was absolutely certain would shut down all the unwanted shit her senses were telling her, and he wanted to rub his hands together like a supervillain.

Supper was going to be very interesting.

17

OLIVIA

She'd had no idea this secret patio existed. Maybe it was for the best though. Jake was going to have a hard time getting her to leave as it was, and it wasn't her space.

That didn't mean she couldn't daydream. One day, after her conviction was overturned and she finished her degree, she'd have a house of her own with an outdoor lounge surrounded by flowers.

Instead of getting dressed, she decided to wait for Jake to return. If he was bringing her something to wear, there was no point if she was going to have to change again. Besides, the fur blanket was just too wonderful against her skin, and she wanted to nest in it forever.

It seemed odd to willingly obey a man who had bullied her for so long, yet she couldn't deny how tempting he was. His words, spoken softly in that deep baritone voice, tempted her. His touch...the way he made her come...

How had Jake gone from being so abrasive she wanted to push him off her cliff to wanting to help her?

Maybe he was just being nice until she slept with him, but that didn't make sense either. He was gorgeous enough to have any woman he wanted and was impossible to resist when he wasn't being an asshole.

He returned quickly, holding something wrapped in what looked like a pair of her running shorts. "I have a treat for you," he murmured as he crossed the patio.

"What is it?"

"Something I hope you like." He knelt at her feet, then slowly eased her thighs apart.

"What are you doing?" She giggled and tried to close her legs, but he wedged his shoulders between them. "Um... I don't think we have time for this."

"We have plenty of time. Lie back and close your eyes."

Hiding a smile, she did as he'd asked. "I think that's the first order you've ever given me that I want to obey."

"Smart ass."

Something cool touched her mons, then a drip of wetness slid down her folds. "What are you doing?"

"Giving you a treat."

Without warning, he slid something inside her. It went

in too easily, making her realize he'd coated it with lubricant. It wasn't large enough to be uncomfortable, yet she almost sat up when he seated it, and pressed something over her clit. Her core clenched around the object, and she gasped when it bumped against her g-spot.

"What is that?"

"Just a little toy to help you focus. It's brand-new, and I already washed it with hypoallergenic cleanser."

"Um...thanks?" She'd been too muddled in the head to even consider whether the toy was clean or not.

He patted her knee, then stood. "You can sit up and get dressed. I brought a pair of your running shorts to make sure it stays where it belongs."

"How will a dildo help me focus?" Despite her words, she sat up and reached for the shorts. Her movement made the toy sink even deeper inside her, nearly making her eyes cross. It seemed to hit every sweet spot she had.

Maybe he had a point about it helping. The only thing she could think about was the way the toy stimulated all her nerve endings.

"It looks like you're enjoying it."

He grabbed her shirt from the ground, then passed it to her and let her finish dressing. Thankfully, the dildo wasn't too obvious, and it was easy enough to tug her T-shirt down to cover the faint outline in the front of her shorts.

"Please don't tell me you're going to make me go out in public like this."

"Define public."

She planted her feet and crossed her arms over her chest. "Yellow."

He moved to stand in front of her, then stroked her arms until she relaxed. "Yellow on wearing the toy, or yellow on leaving the resort while wearing the toy?"

When she didn't immediately reply, he added, "You're allowed to look at me during safe word times if you want to."

Olivia risked a peek at his face. He didn't look angry or like he was about to yell at her, and his voice was soft and gentle instead of shouty.

"I..." Her words trailed off as she realized her only objection was moot. She wasn't going to be allowed to leave the resort until Berto was caught. In fact, Jake probably wouldn't let her use the pool either because it was outside. The thought was both comforting and irritating.

She hated having her freedom curtailed, yet this was different. Jake was trying to keep her safe.

"Do you need to sit down?"

"No. I'm sorry." She tried for a smile, surprised when it actually appeared. "I was about to say I didn't want to leave the resort, then remembered I can't because of my stupid cousin."

He sighed and squeezed her shoulders, then kissed her forehead. "It won't be forever, sweetheart, and don't ever be sorry about using a safe word."

"Yes, sir."

Laughing, he put the blanket away, then took her hand to lead her up the stairs to Mark's bedroom. "That's the first time you've called me sir and meant it."

"It's a term of respect. I'm supposed to say it to my boss."

"Maybe, but I could always tell you wanted to call me something less polite instead."

He leaned close and brushed his lips over her ear, sending a shiver of anticipation into her belly. "I like kitchen troll, but if any of the others happen to pop out of your pretty mouth, we'll be discussing it while you're over my knee for a spanking."

The thought of another spanking made her entire body clench with a mixture of trepidation and need, but she tried to brush it off. Unfortunately, the toy lodged in her pussy wasn't helping. "I speak a little bit of Italian and Portuguese. Maybe I'll have to get more creative."

He crouched to grab their shoes, then led her through the maze of Gabby's computer equipment. "Those are fun, but if you really want to curse at someone, try Russian or Greek."

"Oh, really?"

"Yeah." He laid her shoes in front of her before putting on his own. "Just remember learning a new language won't save you from a bare-assed spanking, and I won't stop until your cute butt is hot and red, and you're ready to do anything to show me how sorry you are."

———

JAKE

He'd thought Olivia was hard to read, but he'd been wrong. All it took was learning her cues—a task made easier now that he wasn't picking at her until she exploded.

Even better, he'd get to see her explode again, but in a much more entertaining way.

Her face didn't reveal her emotions very well. She smiled and frowned, yet he wasn't sure if those expressions were a good barometer for what she was feeling. She'd probably gotten therapy to help her interact with other people, but it wouldn't help him understand her. Hell, he needed a translation guide for that, but he could ask the on-call counselor for a better way of communicating with her.

Maybe he was going about things the wrong way. He might not be able to trust her facial expressions, yet her body didn't lie. The blush of her arousal was pink, but darker red when she was angry. Her hands stilled, and she cocked her head slightly to the right when she was happy. Even her walk changed.

He'd always hated how she hunched when she moved but understood it had been because of nerves and discomfort. Now, her hips relaxed and swayed, and her arms pumped naturally instead of being held tight to the sides of her body.

Damn... Her ass had the cutest little wiggle. Probably had

something to do with the vibe in her pussy, just waiting to make her come.

He almost reached for his phone to get her little surprise party on the road but forced himself to leave it alone. He needed to get her into the kitchen before he started tormenting her.

"So, the snapper you wanted the other day?" he finally asked as they approached the staff entrance to the kitchen.

"Yes, it won't be fresh for much longer. I'm glad to have a chance to use it before it goes bad."

"Sounds delicious." He held the door for her and followed her in. "You're making that crema fresca sauce, right?"

"I don't know." She flashed him a quick smile, then retrieved her knives from the shelf above her workstation. "If you hadn't discarded what I already made, it would have been perfectly rested by now. I'm not sure you deserve it."

"Ouch! That's just mean."

"Maybe it will teach you not to throw away my food."

As if. He'd commit murder for the woman's leftovers as it was.

Without waiting for an answer, she unwrapped her knives, then went to the walk-ins. "You're in luck. There's one duck egg left."

He followed, watching with interest as she picked through the produce and loaded her choices into a clean bus pan. "Just out of curiosity, what made you think of using a duck egg?"

"Mostly for the additional fat, but the flavor worked with the sauce too. They kind of remind me of umami, and..." Her fingers fluttered at her sides, then she appeared to shake herself.

"You okay?"

"Yes, thanks."

"How does the toy feel? Still in there good and tight?"

"It's distracting, but fine. I'm fine." Her hands twitched again, and she pressed them against her thighs in an obvious attempt at self-comfort. "Actually, I'm going to replace it with a chicken egg, add a touch of sugar, and use it as dressing for the slaw. Do you have a tortilla press?"

She was getting lost in her senses again, meaning the distraction he planned wouldn't come a moment too soon.

"I thought you didn't use gadgets."

"That's not a gadget. It doesn't get plugged in or make loud noise." She retrieved the fish from the meat cooler, then added, "I can roll them out if you don't have one."

"Can you explain what you're planning?"

"Fish tacos with slaw of Napa cabbage dressed with the crema fresca sauce and served on homemade tortillas with some of these tomatoes and avocados. It's easy, and there's plenty for six, well, seven if Mr. Bianchi stays for supper. I'll make *arroz con leche* for dessert."

Jake crossed his fingers behind his back, praying the

damned Italian took his smarmy ass back to Italy. "That requires a rice cooker. I thought you didn't use gadgets."

She blushed and her lips bowed into a smile. "You can cook rice in a pot on the stove, you know."

"True, but you don't have to pay attention to a cooker."

"You caught me. A rice cooker was the only appliance I owned before jail." Her smile faded, and she tapped her fingers against her muscular thighs. "Anyway, the tortilla press?"

"I'll see if we have one. Be right back."

"Thanks." Carrying her prizes, she returned to the kitchen.

He knew exactly where the press was. Instead of fetching it, he took his phone from his pocket and waited just long enough for her to set the bus pan next to the sink before opening the app controlling her vibrator.

"It's showtime, Ms. Rivera." He tapped the screen, then slid his finger in a circle to activate the clitoral stimulator.

She screeched and doubled over, her hands flying to her crotch. "Jake!"

"Can't hear you!" he called. "I'm looking for that tortilla press."

Resisting the urge to cackle, he started the vibe inside her, making it rock and roll against her g-spot. She screamed again, then followed it up with a litany of Spanish curses, almost too fast for him to follow.

Still snickering, he grabbed the press from the storage

cupboard, then hurried to the kitchen. He wouldn't put it past her to strip down to get rid of the toy. Or come without permission—not that he planned to deny her for long. Maybe a good climax would keep her brain squirrels at bay long enough for her to eat a decent meal.

He needed to find a better way to say that. Brain squirrels sounded rude—even to him—and he made a note not to mention it out loud.

Her hand still pressed to her pussy, Olivia shot him a glare. "Jake! Please!"

"What?"

"Turn it—" She whined, then hauled in a breath. "Turn. It. Off."

"No." He increased the vibrations on her clit and set the inner vibe pulsing, then sauntered toward her.

"I... I'm supposed to be cooking, and—" She groaned and bucked her hips, then shuddered. "Please."

He moved into her space. Caging her in his arms, he nibbled her throat, noting her rapid heart rate. "Not until you come for me. Close your eyes."

"Why?"

"Because I'll be kissing the fuck out of you when you come. I want you to relax and let it happen, and you can't do that if you have to look at me."

18

OLIVIA

Her heart thundered in her chest, keeping time with the constant pulsing of the vibrator against her clit. It was maddening, overwhelming, and...the most wonderful thing she'd ever experienced.

Jake made it okay to let go. For once in her life, she felt safe. It wouldn't last, but she'd take what he offered for this moment out of time, then keep it as a fond memory when it ended.

Despite his words, he didn't immediately attack her mouth. Instead, he started his kisses on her shoulders, then worked his way up her throat to the sweet spot under her ear. Everything he did was for her pleasure.

Her delight, her...

"*¡Esperar! ¡Deténgase!*"

He stepped back and fumbled with his phone, making the vibrator still inside her. "*¿Qué ocurre? ¿Estás bien?*"

"*Shit.*" She pressed her fists against her eyes. "No...yes. I'm fine."

"Total bullshit." Gently, he turned her to face the sink, then massaged her shoulders. "You can tell me in Spanish if that's what works for you, but I need to hear what's wrong."

She hauled in a breath and exhaled, wishing she could pick out the right words in one fucking language for a change. Gathering her courage, she turned to face him, but didn't have the strength to meet his concerned gaze.

"I just...why are you doing this?"

"Why am I doing what?"

"I don't understand. You've given me so much. It's like..." She leaned against the sink and tried to think her way through what she wanted to say. "You haven't even tried to make love to me, and I feel like... I don't know."

"And that confuses you," he murmured.

"Yes." She straightened, then lifted her chin. "Do you want me at all? Or is this just a game?"

"The answer to those questions is yes." He turned her around once more, then dug his thumbs into the tense muscles at the base of her neck. "I want to fuck you. I want to sink my cock into your pussy and wreck it. I could list all the bad things I want to do to you, but I'm afraid you'll run."

"I—"

"It's a game too. I like to see how far I can push...how much you can endure. How long will it take before you beg for my cock in your sweet cunt?" He nipped her ear, then wrapped a hand around her throat. "How long will it take before you beg me to fuck that beautiful ass?"

She swallowed hard. Although he wasn't cutting off her air, the threat was there, and her eyes nearly crossed with need as she imagined doing exactly what he was telling her. No one had ever said such dirty things to her before or made them sound so enticing.

Although his language was raw and coarse, he even made the c-word sound sexy. She usually despised that term. Of course, he hadn't used it to refer to her personally like Berto always did when he talked about women. Thankfully, Jake spoke before her brain squirrels took her thoughts in the wrong direction again.

"Maybe I should save fucking your ass for when you're being punished." He brushed kisses across the back of her neck, making her shiver. "I'll tease you...fill you with my cum until it leaks out and makes a filthy mess all over you, but I won't let you get off."

His thick cock prodded against her backside, and she whimpered. "You're too big."

"For now." He moved his free hand down to caress her bottom but didn't let go of her neck. "I'll use butt plugs to train your ass to take all of me. Maybe I'll have you wear a chastity belt to keep it inside. I'll just have to fuck your mouth until you're ready."

"*Dios.*"

He pumped his hips against her, then licked the sweet spot under her ear. "You'll be a good girl and swallow my cock, right? You'll let me fuck your throat until tears run down your face because you'll wish I was fucking your pussy instead."

She coughed and nearly choked on her own spit. "I... wow. You have this all planned out."

"I haven't thought of anything else in weeks."

Without warning, the vibrator surged to life inside her, making her cry out. He didn't give her a single moment to think about his words. No time to parse them out or twist them into something else, and no chance to prepare herself.

"Jake!"

He tightened his arm around her waist to hold her still, then slid his free hand up her shirt to pinch her nipples. "I just realized I've been neglecting these fantastic tits. It's a crying shame they aren't decorated with clamps. I'll even give you a special treat and put weights on them."

"Fuck..." Olivia wasn't much for swearing, but he drove her to it. There was no middle ground with Jake McBride—he either made her mad enough to swear or aroused her until she lost her vocabulary.

"You like that idea? Good. We'll do it tomorrow. Right now..." The vibrator jerked inside her, then throbbed against her g-spot as he twisted her nipple almost painfully. "You're going to come for me when I tell you to."

He left her no choice. Disobedience wasn't an option—not that she wanted to refuse. Instead of fighting, she leaned back, allowing him to support her weight as she cleared her mind of all but the feel of his muscular chest against her...his body heat and the clean scent of plain soap and male.

He scratched his nails down her bare stomach and she gasped, then let her head fall back to his shoulder. Everything he did...every touch, every movement—even the sound of his breath rasping against her ear—drove her need higher.

He laid his palm against the vibe positioned over her clit and pressed down, forcing the buzzing toy more firmly against her.

"Jake! Please!" Her knees buckled, but he held her up, bearing her weight with unconscious ease.

"Good girl," he crooned. "I love hearing you beg, but you'll have to do better than that before I let you come."

———

JAKE

There was nothing more beautiful than a woman in the throes of sexual arousal. The only thing that would have made it better would be kissing her, but he worried he'd already pushed her too far as it was.

It was a dick move to compare a person's skin tone to food, but Olivia really did remind him of the edible gold leaf his pastry chef sometimes used on truffles—and fuck, she was just as sweet.

Maybe it was more because he was beginning to think of her as hidden treasure. It took patience and diligence to unearth the gem secreted under the fragile shell.

"Ask me again to let you come," he murmured, getting his mind back on business.

"Yes." The word left her lips with a hissed breath of air. "I need to come."

"Say please."

She trembled and moaned softly, then ground her pussy against his hand. "Please, *por favor*, let me come!"

"So beautiful," he crooned, pressing against her lower abdomen. "You're such a good girl for me, and I'm proud of you."

"God, please!"

Her praise kink matched his begging kink. He gritted his teeth, wanting nothing more than to replace the vibrator with his cock. "Come for me. I want you to let go."

"Ahhh!"

He cupped his hand around her pussy, wishing he could taste the wetness drenching the front of her shorts as she spasmed against him. She stiffened and let out another shriek, then sagged in his arms, panting like she'd run a marathon.

Holding her up with one arm, he fumbled for his phone and turned off the vibe. Only one thing stopped him from making love to her as she deserved.

Their first time wasn't going to be in his fucking kitchen. In fact, he wouldn't touch her again until they were in bed— or at least in his bedroom. Maybe if the lights were dimmed, she'd feel more comfortable when he kissed the fuck out of her as he'd promised.

"Shh." He kissed her neck, feeling her pulse thunder against his lips. "Such a good girl."

She laughed softly, then got her feet under herself and straightened. Although she didn't face him, he caught a glimpse of red on her cheek and her fingers twitched before she locked them into fists. "I...um... I should go change."

"Sure." He forced himself to let her go. It was a wrench, and it felt like he was cutting off his own arm, but she needed space. "I'll get started on the vegetable prep."

When she moved out of the way, he went to the sink and turned on the water, meaning to wash the produce she'd chosen.

"Jake?"

"Hmm?"

Her fingers tightened on his upper arm, and she pushed gently to turn him around. She met his eyes for a split second, then stretched up on her toes and pressed her lips to his in a slow, painfully sweet kiss that sent his need soaring.

Although he knew better, he couldn't resist the urge to

pull her against his body. When she didn't protest, he deepened their kiss, trying to decide if beds and bedrooms were overrated.

Even the dungeon didn't sound appealing. Olivia would look fucking amazing strapped to a bondage bench, but that could be a game for another time when she was more comfortable. Then again, she hadn't seemed distressed when Mark caught them.

She pulled away and touched a trembling finger to her bottom lip. "I... I better go."

Before she reached the door, he pulled his shit together and said, "Hey, Olivia?"

She put her hand on the lever but turned to face him. "Yes?"

"This did happen."

Her eyes flickered to his face, and she smiled. "I know."

She vanished before he could reply, and he got started on the produce. Maybe the dungeon would be better. It would allow her to have the bedroom for rest, and the dungeon for nasty, dirty sex games.

Maybe he should just ask her what she wanted instead of assuming. She'd agreed to the haphazardly sketched-out Master/slave dynamic, but that didn't mean he could give orders without considering her comfort level.

He didn't fucking know her comfort level.

She returned as he was transferring the cleaned produce to the prep table. Instead of running shorts, she wore jeans under a clean chef's jacket. Her hair was secured in a red and gold scarf.

"I thought we weren't wearing whites," he said. "It's just family."

"Ugh. Don't mention family. Call them... I don't know, but not family."

"Bros by other hoes?"

"I don't know how you managed to come up with something worse." Shaking her head, she fetched flour from the pantry and dumped several cups into a mixing bowl, followed by salt, oil, and water, none of which she measured.

"I can totally do worse."

"This is going to rate up there with my top ten stupid ideas but give it your best shot."

He hadn't intended to tell her what he privately called her sensory issues, but maybe it was better to learn what she wanted to hear.

"You have brain squirrels. That's what I call what happens in your head when you have a hard time processing things."

Her spoon fell to the prep table with a clatter, and she spun to face him. "Are you kidding?"

Shit. He mentally backpedaled and tried to come up with something he could say to make it better, but as usual, he opened his dumbass mouth and shoved his foot into it.

"Um...yeah. I'm sorry. I know it's insulting and—"

"How did you know?"

"What?"

She crossed the kitchen and got into his space, then looked at his chin. "How. Did. You. Know?"

"You lost me."

"I call them that. They live in little gilt cages with crap locks, and they always get out and..." She stepped back and rubbed her face, leaving a streak of flour on her nose. "*Dios*. You're in my head now."

Slowly, being careful not to startle her, he wiped the flour from her face. "No, but if it helps you, I want to be."

19

OLIVIA

Still in shock from Jake's revelation, she mixed the tortilla dough on autopilot. After covering it with a tea towel, she started the rice for *arroz con leche*.

It was almost uncanny how he'd guessed her childhood name for the overwhelming things going on in her head.

Granted, lots of people mentioned squirrels when their minds went off on a tangent. Maybe it wasn't so surprising.

That killer orgasm had knocked those furry little assholes into a coma. For the first time in ages, her mind was clear, and she could focus. It seemed he was right about making her come hard enough to shut them up.

She resisted the urge to giggle but wondered how many orgasms she'd need in a day to function in a commercial kitchen. Somehow, she had a feeling Jake would oblige.

Instead of running five miles a day, which would eventually kill her knees, she'd have a pre-breakfast orgasm. Or maybe Jake could run with her, then fuck her silly on top of her cliff.

There would be a sign posted in front of the restaurant:

Breakfast service is delayed while the sous chef comes hard enough to speak in tongues. Thank you for your patience.

Those were orders she wouldn't mind obeying.

"You're not mad?" he asked, pulling her from her thoughts.

The giggles broke free. She snorted, then cleared her throat and held a jalapeno over a gas flame to roast it for the slaw dressing. "No."

Unfortunately, the giggles wouldn't stop, and soon she was bent over and almost crying with laughter.

He moved behind her and rubbed her shoulders. "I've never heard you laugh before, but I don't understand what's so funny."

She'd never know how he guessed exactly where to massage. It seemed like a different muscle group relaxed every time he touched her.

"You. Me. Us." She waved a hand in front of her face in a vain attempt to dry her tears, then peeled the pepper. "Brain squirrels."

"What about them?"

"Nothing. I'm sorry, I thought it was funny."

"It was." He pulled up a stool and rested his chin in his palms as she mashed the pepper with spices. "Do you want me to do the fish?"

"Yes, please. I want whole fillets. Also, save the heads and bones for stock."

"Sure." He grabbed the fish from the cooler and got to work. "I'm assuming the stock is for later?"

She pulled off her gloves and washed her hands. "Risotto, or maybe bouillabaisse so we can get rid of the fennel and any fish we have left. Can you rinse the scraps and dump them in the medium stock pot?"

"Sure." He did as she asked, then used the pot filler above the cooktop to cover them with water. "What else?"

"Onion, a whole garlic clove, carrots, and celery. Sauté everything but the garlic in unsalted butter until the onions are translucent."

"You do the seasonings." He chopped the vegetables she wanted, then dumped them into a pan. "I'll never know why I thought you couldn't cook."

Her amusement faded. To give herself time to answer, she whisked the dressing ingredients harder than they needed, then realized she'd forgotten the egg. "I can't really. I just make things that smell good together. I never had so many different ingredients before."

Chuckling, he shook his sauté pan to toss the stock

vegetables, releasing a cloud of fragrant steam. "I was right. You have been trolling the internet for recipes."

Her cheeks heated, and she tried to make her hands behave as she tempered the egg yolk, whisking it over a double boiler until it was creamy yellow. "Kind of, yes. Mostly, I just see what's about to go to waste, then search for that ingredient."

"Have you ever made anything to the recipe?" He washed his hands, then stood next to her to watch.

"I didn't know it was a requirement." She put the egg into the cooler along with the dressing, then moved to the prep table to start the tortillas.

Before she could uncover the dough, he grabbed her hands, then brought them to his lips and kissed her fingers. "It isn't, and it doesn't matter if you search the internet for ideas. You're still one of the best cooks I know."

"Not a chef?"

"No." He laughed softly, then added, "But that's okay because you don't want to be a chef."

"I do like to cook."

He let her go, then studied her for a moment. "You know, I think maybe that's why your food is better than mine."

"It is not!" Except sometimes...it was.

"Hear me out." He returned to his stool and helped her form balls of dough for the tortilla press. "I used to be that way. I tasted my own food so much I had to buy bigger whites."

"Tasting is important," she murmured.

"Yeah, but then I got to the point where I had signature recipes that had to be the same every time." He sighed and rolled a wad of dough into a ball. "I stopped experimenting. Stopped trying to make them better, or even get out of my comfort zone for something different."

"I'm sorry."

"Don't be." He plopped a dough ball on the press, then laid the finished tortilla aside. "You waltz into my own fucking kitchen, pretending you couldn't cook, and then you made my recipes better. I was furious, and absolutely convinced you were lying about everything."

Tears pricked her eyes, and she hunched her shoulders. She should have known he'd only been kind to give himself a better chance at tearing her down. "Please, I—"

"And then I wondered if you were purposely trying to make me angry because the things you didn't know how to do didn't make sense with the food you created."

Her hands trembled and she forced them to be still before she made a mess. "I didn't mean to do that. I was just...you know."

He leaned across the prep table and cupped the back of her head, then pulled her toward him. "Shh."

Without giving her time to reply, he touched his lips to hers in a sweet, slow kiss that fanned the flames of her arousal once more. He nipped at her lower lip, encouraging her to open to accept him.

She moaned, then tangled her hands in his hair, praying he'd never stop as he swept his tongue into her mouth and teased the edges of her teeth. He tasted like peppermint and warm, spicy man, and she couldn't get enough.

With a muttered curse, he drew away, then kissed the tip of her nose. "You don't get to apologize, Olivia. I'm the one who owes you an apology, and also my thanks."

She glanced up but couldn't hold his steady blue gaze. "For what?"

He kissed her again, almost brutally as his fingers dug into the back of her neck. It didn't seem possible, but it was even better than when he was gentle. She whimpered and leaned closer, desperate to make him keep kissing her.

Sadly, and way too quickly, he ended their kiss and rested his forehead against hers. "Thank you for reminding me of what I used to love about cooking."

———

JAKE

Instead of answering, Olivia focused on the dough that would soon be fresh tortillas. Her face didn't show any emotion, but he was beginning to recognize her tells.

She was relaxed. Her shoulders weren't hunched around her ears, her spine was straight, and she had her head cocked slightly to the right.

He'd unloaded every bit of his past frustration with her, and she didn't seem upset. He still felt like the world's biggest asshole though.

It was one thing to demand excellence in a commercial kitchen. Abusing her because he didn't understand how her senses worked... That was different, and he owed her more than an apology.

"I used to sit with Tia Jozefina like this. We would make tortillas and she'd sing while she cooked them."

"I bet they were wonderful."

She laughed and lifted her head for a scant second. "It's hard to mess up a tortilla."

"True."

As she covered the finished tortillas with a cloth, the rice steamer chimed. "*Arroz con leche* now. Once it's chilling, I'll cook these, and you can do the fish last."

"What? You're putting me to work?"

She glanced at him, then hunched her shoulders as she dumped the rice into a large saucepan. "I'm sorry, you don't have to."

Shit. She'd flat told him she had a hard time with sarcasm. Careful not to startle her, he moved behind her and rubbed her arms. "It's okay. I was teasing, and I forgot."

She let out a sigh, then slumped. "No, don't be sorry. I'm just weird."

"Call yourself a name again, and I'll paddle your cute butt, Ms. Rivera," he warned. "I have all kinds of spatulas, spoons, and other implements in this kitchen that will teach you better."

"Oh?"

"Yes." He dropped a kiss to the enticing spot just below her ear and inhaled her faintly floral perfume. "We don't say weird or normal when referring to ourselves or other people."

"Can I say I'm unusual?"

He stepped to the side so she could see him if she wanted, then stroked his chin as he considered the word. "Unusual is good. It means you're unique and special."

"Short bus special," she muttered.

He didn't give her time to say anything else and let his hand crash against her ass.

"Ouch!" She rubbed her butt, then glared at him. "What was that for?"

"I just said you weren't allowed to say nasty things about yourself." He forced himself to calm down but was seriously tempted to do a more thorough job of spanking her. "I wasn't kidding."

She pressed the heels of her hands against her eyes, then leaned forward to rest her elbows on the prep table. The position almost invited another spank, but he resisted the urge.

"I... I'm sorry. You were teasing first, then you weren't, and now I'm confused."

Jake cursed himself again. It wasn't her fault he was

fucking everything up. "Let's try something else. You said you don't always understand when people are teasing, right?"

"Yes, sir."

He moved behind her and rubbed her shoulders, knowing it soothed her. "Cool. So, let's try this. If I say something and... I don't know, maybe snap my fingers, that will mean I'm teasing. Do you think that would work?"

"Maybe." She cocked her head toward him, then looked at his chin. "And maybe clap your hands if you're serious about something?"

"I can do both if it will help." He stepped back, then clapped his hands. "Do not call yourself names again. If you do, you're going to get a spanking, and I'm fucking deadass serious about it."

She swallowed hard and looked at the floor. "Just telling me you're serious will probably work."

"I'll clap too. It'll remind you of the spanking you'll get if you disobey that order." He touched her jaw but didn't force her to look at him. "Actually, if I say anything that is in the best interest of your health and well-being, I won't be kidding, okay?"

She licked her lips, then lowered her eyelashes. "I...yes, sir. I understand."

Thank fuck.

"There's my good girl." He brushed a kiss over her forehead, then swatted her butt gently. "Now, let's get the *arroz con leche* done so we can put supper on the table."

"Um...okay?"

Deciding to take a quick inventory of the pantry, he left her alone while she threw together the rice pudding. It was finished by the time he came back, so he helped her ladle it into custard cups.

"Fuck, this smells amazing," he said, inhaling the perfume of cinnamon and rum.

Blushing, she handed him a spoonful. "I boiled golden raisins in rum with a cinnamon stick, then added seeds from a vanilla bean after I took it off the heat."

He sucked the spoon clean, then moaned. The shit almost had him in tears. "You used Arborio rice."

"Yes. I...it tastes more robust, I think."

"Good choice. I love it."

"Thanks." Her hands fluttered at her sides, and she rushed to the grill to check the fish. "These have another minute or so to go. Is the table set?"

"Yeah. I already put out the slaw and tortillas, and all the toppings too."

"Great. I mean, good. Thank you."

"No problem." He checked the temp on the fillets, then transferred them to a serving platter. "You know, I'm actually starving. I can't remember the last time I anticipated a meal so much."

"It's mostly just leftovers."

For a moment, he wondered if she was hunting for praise, but that wasn't her way. Although she loved being told when she did well, she didn't necessarily seek it out. She just did her best and hoped it was good enough.

"No, well, maybe it is, but you made something wonderful." He set the tray down and clapped to let her know he was serious. "Take the compliments when they come, okay?"

She let out a breath and chewed on her lower lip. "They're already waiting for us. I can hear them."

He moved to stand in front of her, then cupped her pretty face in his hands. "No, honey. They're waiting for you."

20

OLIVIA

"Nicolo Bianchi, I swear by the Pictish gods of my ancestors I will stick this fork in your left eyeball if you steal another bite from my plate!"

She couldn't decide if Gabby was serious or teasing. Judging by the way Gabby hunched over her meal, fork at the ready, she'd been serious, but nobody stabbed people in their eyes with forks over fish tacos.

At least, she didn't think so.

"She's kidding," Jake murmured softly, petting her shoulder.

"No, I am not," Gabby retorted. Still glaring at Nicolo, she took a huge bite of her food.

"I thought you loved me, *cara*." Nicolo winked at Olivia, then made himself another taco.

"Not that much."

He laid a hand over his heart and threw his head back. "I'm mortally wounded." Sobering, he inclined his head toward Olivia. "*Tesoro*, this is utterly divine. I would be most pleased if you'd entertain an offer to come cook for me in Italy."

She blinked and her belly swooped and soared. Unfortunately, she couldn't tell if the praise made her feel good or scared her. "I...um... I'm on parole. I'm not allowed to leave the state."

"Ah, yes. Those pesky legal details are such a bother. However, you need only say the word, and you'll live a life of luxury in the shadow of Vesuvius as my personal chef." His green eyes seemed to pierce her, and she shivered. "I can make everything...go away."

Jake touched her thigh, making her jump. She looked down at his hand, and he brought the other over to silently clap them together. "Olivia was studying to be an accountant," he said. "She's a fantastic cook though, and we're blessed to have her with us."

The clap was confusing. Whose comment was it for? His, or Nicolo's? Maybe it was both. Then again, she got the feeling Nicolo didn't say things he didn't mean. He scared her and she didn't trust him, yet despite his florid language, Nicolo was the easiest for her to understand.

Even when he was using words like *disposal* and *go away*, she knew what he'd meant. He was a predator in an expensive suit.

"She'll be missed when she leaves to finish her education," Sean added, meeting Nicolo's steady gaze.

"Give it up, Nicky." Gabby spooned more slaw into a tortilla, then added a few slices of avocado. "The Horsemen aren't going to let you have her."

Underneath the table, Jake clapped his hands, then gave her an encouraging smile and snapped his fingers. "It's self-preservation. Kendra will hunt us for sport if we do anything to stop the flow of Olivia's full English breakfasts."

Even if they were confusing sometimes, she'd had no idea how helpful Jake's cues would be. It was so much easier to follow the conversation and react appropriately when she knew what people were saying behind their words.

His cues would work even better when there weren't so many people in the conversation, but for once, talking to a group didn't make her anxiety spike.

"Yes... I mean, thank you for the offer, Nicolo, but I can't accept. If...when my conviction is overturned, I want to finish my degree and find a job." She tried for a smile, then added, "I like cooking, but not as a career."

"Although I love Olivia's food, I think I might have a better idea," Kendra said. "Olivia, how close were you to graduation when you were arrested?"

"Um...I was in my last semester." She stole a peek at

Kendra's face, then lowered her head. "It took forever because I was working full time and taking classes at night."

"Nice! How would you feel about coming to work here when you finish?"

Jake clapped his hands, then whispered, "Kendra is always serious."

She'd already suspected that about Kendra, so it wasn't entirely surprising. "Why would you offer me a job?"

"Frankly, I need the help. I can do the work, but I hate it with a passion and it's taking too much time from my schedule. I've been meaning to hire someone anyway, but I'd prefer to have you."

"But... I'm a convicted felon."

"For a crime you didn't commit—at least not intentionally." Kendra reached across the table and touched her hand. "It's a legitimate offer. All I ask is that you think about it. As a side bonus, you can have free run of the kitchen when you get the urge to cook."

Jake snapped his fingers under the table. "Hey! That's my kitchen. Don't I get a say?"

"No." The word was echoed by Kendra, Mark, and Sean, making everyone laugh. It was a happy sound and pleasant to her ear, even with so many people.

"And because you're brilliant and studying in a math related field, I'll set you up with a scholarship. If you don't want to work here, I'll make sure you have an offer more to your liking," Gabby added.

"That's very generous, but you don't have to."

"No worries." Gabby finished her taco, then swiped a finger across her plate for the last of the dressing. "I have a scholarship fund set up for deserving women, and it's only one semester."

"Yes, she's helped many women." To her surprise, Nicolo's gaze softened, and he smiled. "Ms. Rivera, even if you don't wish to cook for me, it is within my power to repair your reputation."

"Nicky—"

He held up a hand, cutting Gabby off. "Let her answer, *cara*."

Jake squeezed her knee, then traced something on her thigh. It took only a second for her to realize he was drawing the word *no*.

She blew out a breath through pursed lips, then met Nicolo's gaze easily. "In exchange for what?"

"Certain...accommodations to be named at a later date."

For once, the brain squirrels were quiet and let her focus. Maybe they'd decided not to be furry little idiots in the presence of someone who might eat them.

It was very odd to understand someone whose words were so obtuse, yet she did. Nicolo Bianchi wasn't her friend, and she doubted his "accommodations" would be any better or safer than what she was already dealing with.

She almost wanted to thank him though. He'd taught her what a predator looked like, and she didn't have the cloud of a familial relationship obscuring her vision. It was an education she wouldn't squander.

"No. I won't bargain like that." She stood and stepped away from the table. "I... I'll be right back. I need to check the dessert course."

She hurried into the kitchen, praying she didn't look like she was running away, then leaned against the prep table and tried to settle herself.

Except she didn't need it.

She'd gone toe to toe with someone more dangerous than Berto, and...won.

———

JAKE

Olivia scampered into the kitchen, leaving him wondering whether he should follow or break every bone in the Italian's body.

Instead of doing either of those things, he put his rage in time-out, then folded his hands on the table. She needed a chance to decompress, and he needed to not commit assault on his own property.

"Mr. Bianchi, Olivia isn't—"

"You have my apologies," he interrupted. "I meant no harm to her or the Horsemen, but I saw the signals you gave her to help her cope."

What. The. Fuck?

"Then what did you mean?"

"She..." Nicolo sighed and looked over Jake's head, his attention seemingly far away. "There is something about people like her which invites either abuse or the urge to wrap them in silk blankets and hide them away from that which might harm them."

"People like her..." Sean gave Nicolo a dark scowl. "Do you understand how insulting that is?"

"My apologies. It's been some time, and perhaps my language is no longer considered appropriate." Nicolo took a sip of wine, then set the glass aside and rested his elbows on the table, an impassive poker face firmly in place. "I wish for Olivia to be protected, gentlemen. If you are unable to do so, then I will."

Who the fuck did he think he was? Jake tensed and tightened his fists. Nobody was going to touch Olivia—least of all some asshole who thought he could waltz in and start giving orders regarding a grown woman he didn't even know.

Before he could leap across the table and break Nicolo's face, Kendra gave him a pointed look and held up her hand. "What's in it for you?"

"Nothing, Ms. Hall." He rose to his feet and bowed. "It grows late. I'll take my leave of you and prepare for tonight's amusements."

He walked away before anyone could reply, leaving Jake with more questions than answers—and a lot of unspent anger he needed to get rid of before he even considered going near Olivia.

"His brother was autistic," Gabby murmured.

"Was?" Sean asked.

She smiled, but Jake didn't miss the sheen of tears in her eyes. "Will someone fetch me a nip of scotch? This story requires a wee dram."

"Sure." Jake went to the bar and returned with a highball glass and a bottle of his best. Gabby was picky about her whiskey.

"Thanks." She drained the double shot he'd poured, then held out the glass for another. He obliged, but she cradled her drink in her hands and didn't look at them. "Mattia was murdered about a year ago. One of Nicky's enemies lured him away with the promise of a puppy."

"Shit." Sean wrapped an arm around her shoulders, but she shrugged him off.

"Indeed. He'd just had his thirtieth birthday. He'd always begged for a dog, and Nicky and I wanted to surprise him, but we…" She sniffed, then wiped her eyes with the back of her hand. "Anyway, say what you will about Nicky, but he won't allow Olivia to come to harm. Knowing him, her cousin will stay alive just long enough to give a statement exonerating her. Her parole officer and attorney won't live much longer, I reckon."

"Although I'm very sorry for your loss, please don't tell

us the details. I'd like to keep at least a little plausible denia-bility," Kendra muttered.

"Of course." Gabby finished her drink, then stood. "I'm off to watch the camera feed."

"I'll help," Sean replied.

"Suit yourself."

Jake had no idea what to do with the information he'd been given. Sympathy welled, for both Gabby and Nicolo, yet he couldn't allow Olivia to be dragged into the dangerous world they inhabited. Maybe she wasn't as trusting as Mattia had been, but he couldn't stomach the thought of her living as a prisoner.

Again.

Before Gabby and Sean could leave, Jake stood and said, "Wait."

"What's up?" Sean asked.

"Stay long enough for dessert. Olivia made *arroz con leche.*"

"Of course. I'd nearly forgotten." Gabby's smile didn't reach her eyes, but she sat. "You had me at Olivia made dessert."

"Great. I'll help her bring it out."

He went into the kitchen and paused, simply watching her. Humming softly, Olivia grated fresh nutmeg over the custard cups, then arranged them on a tray. She looked up and smiled when he cleared his throat to catch her attention.

"Did the clapping and snapping cues help?"

"Yes." She chewed on her lip, then nodded. "A few were confusing, but I figured it out, I think. Thank you."

"My pleasure. Need some help?"

"No, I...yes. Is Nicolo still out there?"

"No. He went to...actually, I don't know what he's up to."

"Okay...yes. I mean, no." She frowned and set her grater aside. "What's a polite way of saying I'm glad he's gone, but I feel bad because he's missing dessert?"

"Don't let the door hit him in the ass on the way out?"

"That's mean." She arranged fresh berries around the custard cups. "I mean, I think it's mean. Brain squirrels."

"Maybe the furry bastards understand more than you think."

"Maybe." She collected dessert spoons and fresh napkins. "It's weird, but—"

He clapped his hands. "What did we say about that word?"

"I didn't mean me, but something else." She turned to look at him, managing to hold her focus on his collarbones. "It's just weird that I think I understand Nicolo."

"How so?"

"He's dangerous, but... I don't know. He makes sense for some reason. It's like I know what he's saying even when he's using all those formal words." She lifted her lashes for a split second. "That's what's weird to me. I can't explain it any better."

Maybe Olivia believed she had problems reading people,

yet her assessment of Nicolo was incredibly astute. It was probably dishonest, but he decided not to share what he'd learned about the man's brother. The news would upset her, and he didn't want to disturb the delicate peace he'd managed to help her find.

"It's okay." He took her hands and squeezed gently, then brushed a kiss over her lips. "You're okay. Okay?"

She giggled softly, then nodded. "Okay."

"Hey." He kissed her again because he couldn't not kiss her. "I might or might not have a surprise for you in the dungeon after we clean the kitchen."

Her hands fluttered, but she stilled them and grabbed the dessert tray. "What kind of surprise?"

"The kind where you come a million times and forget your cousin exists." He leaned closer and traced her lower lip with the tip of his tongue. "The kind where I fuck you like you deserve."

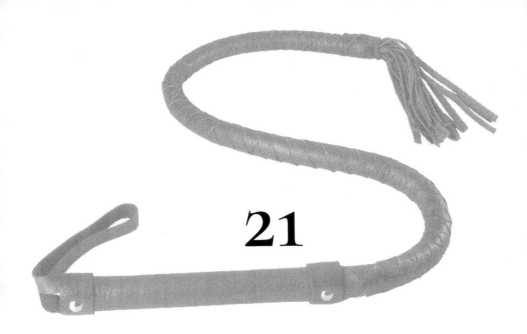

21

OLIVIA

D*ios.*

Jake had found the one sure way of quieting the random stimuli throwing her brain off its tracks. He just needed to talk dirty to her, and...

China rattled and she nearly dropped the tray when she walked headfirst into the door.

"Whoa, careful!" He put his hands on her shoulders to steady her but didn't let go. "Do you need me to carry that?"

"Um...yes, please." She let him take the tray and her arms fell to her sides, but she didn't feel the need to stim as she normally did when her hands weren't busy.

"Are you okay? What happened?"

"You... I..." She swallowed and risked a peek at his face. "I can't think when you say things like that."

"Things like what?"

Her heart raced as she tried to come up with a reply that wouldn't make her look so needy and awkward. "Like when you told me what we'd be doing in the dungeon."

"Good to know. Are you ready to serve this magnificent rice pudding?"

"I...yes." She reached for the door to hold it open for him, but a brain squirrel nipped at her synapses to jog her memory. "Wait! What about tonight? Do you think Berto will come?"

"He might."

"We have to watch for him. What if—"

Dessert dishes clattered as he set the tray on the prep table. Cupping her cheeks, he pressed a gentle kiss to her forehead. "Shh. It's going to be okay."

"He might get inside though." She jerked out of reach and shivered, then crossed her arms to keep her hands still. "What do we do if he... I'll never forgive myself if he hurts someone!"

"Olivia—"

"No! I have to... I don't know. Maybe if I try to catch him... I'll lie and tell him you threw me out. Or something. I—"

Without warning, Jake grabbed her by the shoulder and spun her to face the prep table. He pushed hard, forcing her chest to hit the wood surface, then delivered several stinging swats to her bottom.

"Ow! That hurts!" She tried to cover her backside with her hands, but he caught them and held them out of the way while he blistered her unprotected ass. Even through the thick fabric of her jeans, the spanking set her skin on fire.

"It's supposed to hurt." His voice was calm and measured as he spanked her. "Do I have your attention yet?"

"Ouch!" No matter how hard she struggled, he wouldn't let her go, but at least he stopped and rubbed her abused flesh. "Yes! I'm sorry."

"Good girl." He helped her straighten, then lifted her up to sit on the prep table, sending prickles of pain and heat into her core.

"What are you doing?"

His sudden kiss bruised her lips, leaving them swollen and tingling. "You're not leaving. You're not going to look for that little asshole, and you're not getting out of my sight. Understood?"

"I...yes, sir."

"Good girl." Gently, he brushed a few tears from her cheeks, then kissed her forehead again. "I promised I'd help you with the squirrels. I also promised I'd keep you safe from your cousin, but you have to listen and let me in, okay?"

"I'll try, but... I don't know."

"Are the brain squirrels out of their cages?"

She heard the smile in his voice. Although it was hard to

judge someone's expression, she could sometimes tell what they were feeling by the sound of their words. It was easier if she knew them well.

"A little?"

"Well, I can't spank the squirrels." He brushed another soft kiss over her lips, sparking the tingles once more. "But I can spank you."

She shivered but wasn't sure if her trepidation was from worry or desire. "Are we still going to the dungeon?"

"Yes. There are no windows, and the door is kept locked." He helped her down from the prep table, then picked up the dessert tray. "Aside from Sean's office, it's the most secure space in the building."

"Okay."

He stopped before he reached the door and studied her, his gaze seeming to penetrate deep under her skin. "You can say no if you're not feeling it, but I promise you will be completely safe no matter what you decide."

She didn't need him to clap to know he'd been serious, meaning she was beginning to understand his vocal inflections and mannerisms. Jake hid deep emotion behind coarse language and sometimes outright bullying. It made her wonder if someone had hurt him in the past, and if he used abrasive behavior to protect himself.

It seemed to her he'd lived a charmed life, yet maybe he hadn't. Maybe—underneath the bluster—he was just as messed up as she was. She hid amusement at the idea, knowing he'd spank her again if she referred to herself as messed up, but she liked having someone care if she said mean things about herself.

Olivia wondered if something had happened to him during his military service. Once, during her sporadic attempts at therapy, she'd met a woman with crippling anxiety from her time serving. She'd had a service dog which kept her grounded. The memory made her wonder if an emotional support animal would help, but she wouldn't know where to start looking for one, or how she'd keep it if she had it.

There was another problem. She couldn't decide if her suspicions were correct. It was so hard for her to understand other people, and she still wasn't sure she trusted him.

What would happen if she messed up again? If he heard something out of context, would he go back to hating her?

Would his attention and care cease the minute Berto was in custody?

She chewed on her lip and tried to keep her hands still as she followed him from the kitchen. It was too much to think about, and worse, the indecision woke up the squirrels in her head.

You can't do anything right. You're stupid. Worthless. Nobody wants you.

Even with so few people, the conversation was loud and overwhelming. They were laughing at her, pointing out her deficiencies, making jokes at her expense...

She hauled in a breath and tried to swallow a sob as she pushed down the urge to run and hide. The squirrels were wrong.

They had to be.

JAKE

Something was wrong.

Although he had no idea what was going on in Olivia's head, it was more than clear she wasn't okay. Her hands were in tight fists, and she had her elbows pressed to her side as if she was trying to hold herself together by sheer force of will.

In an effort to make everything appear as if nothing was amiss, he smiled as he served dessert. "Here you go. Enjoy!"

"Thanks! This looks delicious." Gabby took a bite, then closed her eyes and moaned. "Bloody hell, woman. I could live off this and die happy."

Olivia sat but gave every indication she was about to run. She also didn't touch her dessert. "Um...I'm glad?"

Jake took the chair next to her and tried to think of something—anything he could say to get her mind off whatever was upsetting her.

Wait. Hadn't she said she couldn't think when he told

her all the things he planned to do to her delectable body over the next several hours?

Leaning close, he brushed his lips over her ear and made sure to keep his voice down. They were seated across the table from everyone else and nobody was paying them any attention, but it wouldn't do to let anyone hear him. "Hey, Olivia?"

She flinched at the touch and didn't look at him. "What?"

"It's nothing important. I just wanted to say your pussy tastes better than this rice pudding."

"Jake!"

Her face bloomed with an embarrassed flush, and he smirked. "What?"

"I can't believe you said that!"

"Why? It's true." He kept his voice to a soft whisper and added, "I have personal experience, and I'm going to get even more tonight. I can't wait until you come all over my—"

A sharp pinch on his thigh made him cut off what he was about to say, and he caught her angry glare. She actually met his eyes, meaning she was furious.

Mission accomplished. If she was mad, she wasn't letting the brain squirrels have a chance to send her into another anxiety attack. Giving her another dirty smile, he saluted her with his spoon and finished his dessert.

Gabby arched a brow at him but kept her thoughts to

herself. To Olivia, she said, "That was delicious. I'd love to give this recipe to my cook, plus the one for the sauce we had with our tacos."

"I...yes, ma'am." Olivia shook her head and looked at her barely touched pudding. "Sorry. Gabby...not ma'am. I'll write them down for you."

"Thanks." Gabby touched her napkin to her lips, then stood. "I'm off to monitor the cameras."

Sean followed her from the restaurant, along with Mark and Kendra, thankfully leaving him alone with Olivia.

She waited just long enough for them to disappear, then spun on him, her face red with anger. "I have no idea if I should slap you or never speak to you again! How dare you say all those dirty things where people might hear?"

"Are you protesting me saying them, or that I said them in company?"

Her lips parted and she huffed out a breath. "Could you at least try not to embarrass me in public?"

"You weren't complaining when Mark caught you tied to the stool in the kitchen."

"Ahhhhh!" She flung her arms in the air and let loose with a litany of Spanish curses that singed his ears. "You are such a fucking troll!"

The best part was... She never once took her eyes off his face.

"Kitchen troll, if you please."

She screeched again, then sent a custard cup flying at his

head. Thankfully, he managed to catch it before it smashed into his face.

Still glaring at him, she said, "Why, Jake? Why must you torment me?"

He approached her slowly, keeping an eye on her hands in case she reached for something else to throw at him. Before she could escape, he got into her space and turned her to face away from him, then pulled her against his chest.

"I didn't do it to embarrass you." He kept his voice soft and soothing but made sure she was listening. "You went pale, and your hands were in fists like you were trying not to stim. I was afraid you were gearing up for another anxiety attack and remembered you said I could make you stop thinking if I told you how delicious your pussy is."

She shivered in his arms and didn't speak for several seconds, but he wasn't sure if it was from the praise or because she was still upset.

"I never said that," she finally muttered.

"Yeah, you did. You said you couldn't think when I told you how much I want to stick my tongue in your sweet—"

"Okay! Stop!" She fluttered her hands for a moment, then her shoulders relaxed, and she sighed as if she was releasing the last of her tension.

"Did it work?" He thought it had, but he needed to be sure. It wasn't as if he was a counselor, and he doubted telling Olivia what he planned to do to her once he had her near a bed would have been considered appropriate therapy.

Then again, if it actually did help her, he didn't give two shits what anyone said.

"If your intent was to make me want to smother you in your sleep, then yes. It worked."

"That's just a bonus," he countered. "It'll give me a reason to spank you again. Did it make your anxiety go away?"

She cocked her head to the right and appeared to be considering her answer. "Yes, but maybe you shouldn't do it in front of other people. Can you wait until we're alone?"

Laughing, he let her go and started cleaning up the table. "Where would be the fun in that?"

"Jake!" She spun to face him, hands on her hips as she met his gaze with an angry glare.

"Eyes down." He loved being able to order her to do that —even if it would be a rare occurrence.

Olivia blinked and immediately dropped her head as if surprised she'd been able to look at him. "Sorry."

"Good girl." He finished cleaning the table, then pushed the bus cart toward the kitchen. "We'll finish cleaning up, then you can decide if you want to go into the dungeon."

22

OLIVIA

Jake didn't press her for a decision. Instead, he talked about what was left in the walk-ins and pantry while they finished cleaning up from supper. She should have been planning meals to make sure nothing was wasted, but she couldn't focus on food.

She couldn't focus...period. He was too close...too present to allow her to think about anything but how it had felt when he made her come—and how it had felt to look into his brilliant blue eyes. It was so rare for her to be able to do that, and she couldn't quite understand why she felt no discomfort after looking at his face for so long.

Strangely, his eyes no longer reminded her of radioactive waste.

Then again, she might change her opinion if he tried to embarrass her in public again. It had worked to knock her out of a burgeoning anxiety attack, but there had to be a better way that wouldn't let everyone in the state know she was about to sleep with her boss.

Nothing good ever came from that, yet she wouldn't be able to hold out for long. She wanted him too badly. Aside from that, their relationship had a built-in expiration date.

If...when her conviction was overturned, she'd move on and put her life back together. Despite Kendra's job offer, she didn't think she'd be welcomed as a permanent employee. Thankfully, the brain squirrels had nothing to say about it.

"Olivia?" Without warning, he appeared in front of her, and she almost dropped the bus pan she'd been carrying to the sink. His expression filled with worry, he helped her set it aside, then took her hands. "Hey, are you okay?"

"I'm...yes." To her surprise, she hadn't lied. "I'm sorry. I wasn't paying attention. Did I miss something?"

He cocked his head and studied her for a moment, then nodded. "I wanted to know what you did before prison. I know you were in school, but you mentioned you also had a full-time job."

"Oh." She helped him load the dishwasher, then rinsed out the bus pan. "I was a longshoreman at the Port of San Diego."

"Really? Wow!"

She risked a peek at his face but wasn't sure what she'd

expected to see. His words could have meant too many different things. He might have been impressed or surprised a woman would be doing that job. Maybe he was disbelieving.

As she considered whether she wanted to know what he'd meant, he added, "That's badass! Did you get to operate one of those big cranes?"

"No, mostly I drove a forklift, and sometimes a yard tractor to move shipping containers around."

"That's still badass as fuck."

He smiled, meaning he'd probably meant the compliment. She decided to believe it for the moment. "Um...thanks?"

"And now, I'm curious. Why did you decide on accounting?"

She considered her answer for a moment. "I like numbers. They're quiet and make sense. Sometimes, they can be a mystery too."

"How so?"

In an effort to keep her hands busy, she went to the shelf where her knives were stored, then sat at the prep table and drew a whetstone over the edge of her chef's knife.

She loved her knives. Although she didn't recognize the brand, they fit her hands perfectly and stayed sharp for a long time. After testing the edge with her thumb, she slid it back into its slot and pulled out her boning knife.

"I was going to specialize in forensic accounting. You

know, when accountants look over a company's books to see if there's been any malfeasance. I like finding clues and...anyway. Sorry, most people think accountants are boring."

"Actually, I think it's fascinating." He fetched his own knives, then sat across from her to sharpen them. They were the same brand as hers, but larger to fit his hands.

The sound of stone across steel was measured and comforting. She supposed most people found it grating, but she liked the repetitive noise.

"Like a puzzle, right?"

She looked up at him in surprise, then remembered his eye contact restriction. "Yes. I guess I feel like...I don't know. Scooby Doo?"

He laughed, then said, "I always wanted a Mystery Machine. One of these days, I'll buy an old van and paint it."

"That sounds fun." She slid the last of her knives into their case and closed it. "May I ask you a question?"

"Sure." He put his knives away, then laid hers on the shelf.

"Where do you buy your knives? I want a set of my own for when I...you know."

It was probably silly to ask about them now, considering she wouldn't be able to afford them for a long time, but she didn't want to forget.

"Honey..." He touched her shoulder, then moved so she could look at him if she wanted to. "Those *are* yours."

"I know, but when this mess is over, and my conviction is overturned, I want my own."

She felt his gaze on her like tingly little prickles. It was disconcerting yet wasn't uncomfortable. She glanced at him but didn't like the way his brow furrowed and looked away.

"Olivia, when I said they're yours, I meant it."

"I can't take them with me when I leave though. They're not *mine* mine."

"Yes, they are." He crouched, then tilted her chin to force her to look at his mouth. "I had them made for you. They won't fit anyone else in the kitchen."

She flinched, then dragged her gaze up to his eyes. "But... why? How?"

"Because I wanted to." He eased away to give her some space, but it didn't help. She was too overwhelmed by what he was telling her to register his actions. "As far as how... Do you remember me asking you to squeeze those clay cylinders your second week here?"

"Um...yes?" She'd thought it odd at the time, yet she'd been too frightened and anxious to do anything but obey.

"The bladesmith used them to make a mold for the handles. They literally won't fit anyone else." When her hands fluttered, he covered them with his own to keep them still. "So, yes, they are yours. When...if you leave, you'll be taking them with you."

———

JAKE

He'd had no intention of telling Olivia about those knives, but he wasn't going to lie to her either. And he especially wasn't going to think about her leaving.

What would happen if they didn't catch her cousin? Eventually, her parole would run out. If he was very lucky, she'd take the job Kendra offered and stay, but he couldn't ask her to do that when she'd already made plans—no matter how much he wanted to.

It was possible they wouldn't be able to get her conviction overturned. He didn't want her stuck doing something she didn't like either, but with a criminal record, Kendra's offer might be the only one Olivia got.

He hated himself for almost wishing it was, but at least then she wouldn't be in his kitchen unless she wanted to be.

"I have no idea what to say." She blinked and tipped her chin up to look at him for a split second. "I guess...thank you. It's a very generous gift."

"You're welcome." When she twisted her fingers into knots, he gently untangled them and stroked her hands until she relaxed. "First things first. If you're not feeling the dungeon tonight, or even letting me share your bed, you don't have to. The knives are a gift, and my only expectation is for you to enjoy using them. Okay?"

The last thing he wanted was for her to feel obligated. As

much as he wanted her obedience, it was more important for her to be willing.

"Yes, I understand." She took off her chef's jacket and tossed it into the hamper, leaving her in a plain black tank top. "I think...can we go into the dungeon?"

"Will you tell me why?"

Her golden skin darkened with a flush as she removed her scarf, letting her beautiful curls spring free.

If she had any idea how many times he'd jerked off imagining twisting her hair around his fist while he fucked her from behind...

He shook the thought away and focused. She might never be comfortable enough to look at him, but fuck, he loved looking at her. Although her facial expressions were still challenging to understand, it would come with time.

Assuming he had it.

In a way, their shared inability to read each other's nonverbal cues was good. They were on a level playing field and would have to work harder to communicate. It also helped him understand what made her tick.

He almost wanted to laugh. BUD/S had done jack shit to teach him to control his hair-trigger temper, but he found it easy with Olivia.

Maybe it was because, for once—for her—he wanted to be better.

"I think—no, I hope it controls the squirrels." She wadded her scarf, then straightened it and folded it neatly. "I mean, I'm pretty sure Berto is coming tonight, but... I guess I want to not think about him, you know? I want to pretend he doesn't exist, even if it's for only a night."

"Is that all?"

"No." Her flush deepened, and she peeked at him. "I want more of what we did before, but with less teasing."

He leaned close and inhaled her soft floral scent, liking the way goosebumps pebbled her upper arms. "Baby, I'll give you more, and I can make you forget your own name."

"Promise?"

"Yeah." He offered his hand, staying in front of her where she could see. Too bad her wish for less teasing would go unanswered. "Are you ready?"

She laid her hand in his and squeezed gently, then gave him a rare smile that faded too quickly. "Um... I think so, yes."

"Good girl." He led her from the kitchen and checked the corridor before taking her into the dungeon. When the light on the lock flashed green, he held it open, allowing her to enter first.

Chances were good the resort was secure, but it was better to be safe than sorry.

Her footsteps were silent on the polished concrete, and her only sound was a soft gasp as he brought up the house lights. Instead of turning them on all the way, he left them dimmed as they'd have been if the dungeon was open, with spotlights focused on the stations.

"It's so different when there aren't any people." She stroked the soft velvet drape, reminding him she liked contrasting textures.

"I'd forgotten you'd already been in here a few times."

"Just for a couple of parties as a server."

He let her wander and explore, smiling when she tucked her hands behind her back as she studied Natalie Mercer's paintings. The canvases were thick and textured with ridges of paint making the images appear almost three dimensional under the indirect can lights. Olivia was probably dying to touch them, and he wished he could let her.

In fact, he very nearly went back to the apartment for the fur blanket she loved so much, but it would slide right off the leather padding on most of the bondage furniture and wouldn't be safe or functional. Nothing stopped them from using the outdoor patio for her aftercare though.

Thankfully, there were plenty of other things in his bag of tricks perfect for indulging her. "I'll be right back. While I'm gone, I want you to choose the piece of furniture you like the best."

"The cross."

Her immediate answer shouldn't have surprised him. The custom bondage fixture created by the Vermont artist, Chelsea Barber, was a masterpiece of intricate carvings. He'd bet his favorite cane Olivia wanted to pet it.

With a start, he realized why she mixed dough with her hands instead of the industrial mixer and wanted to kick himself. The noise probably bugged the hell out of her, and she needed the tactile stimulation.

Deciding to give her an out, he said, "You can touch the cross if you want. We don't have to use it for our play. If you prefer to lie down, we can use the bondage table next to it. The leather padding is very thick and well-cushioned."

He kept his voice soft, not giving her any indication of his preferences. To his surprise, he was in no hurry to start their play. It was fun to watch her explore.

"Where are you going?"

"Just into the aftercare rooms to get my play bag. I promise, I'll be right back, but there's no rush. Take your time and pick your favorite, okay?"

"Um..." She glanced at him from under her lashes, then quickly averted her gaze. "Yes, sir."

23

OLIVIA

She'd never once considered finding herself as a participant in the Club Apocalypse dungeon. Granted, the play space wasn't open to the public and wouldn't be for some time, but it was still almost like a dream.

Maybe, someday, she could have joined a place like this. She'd always wanted more than the experimentation she'd tried with past partners and couldn't count the number of times she'd gotten herself off after reading steamy books or watching porn.

The dream wasn't entirely dead though. The Horsemen were trying to help her get her life back. Jake was going even further. He wasn't treating her like she was damaged or wrong or like she should be locked away and hidden. That wasn't entirely true though. He was kind of hiding her, but it was more because he was protecting her.

Maybe she didn't understand him all the time, but she was pretty sure he wanted her as much as she wanted him.

In fact, she was seriously considering stripping off her clothes so she could ride him like a pony. The only thing stopping her was the anticipation of a proper scene. Although she had no idea what Jake had in store for her, she wasn't nervous. Anxiety was the furthest thing from what she was feeling.

She wanted to see him in tight leather pants with a whip in one beautifully veined hand. He'd look just like the man in one of the paintings on the far wall—older, but still compelling. She'd been told he was the artist's husband. With a muse like that, it was no wonder the artist created such amazing work.

Jake had the most amazing hands with long fingers and neatly trimmed nails just long enough to scratch deliciously. His voice could be gentle too, so enticing when he wasn't being shouty or serious. Even his personal scent was mouth-watering without the overwhelming stench of rosemary covering it.

Humming softly, she touched the carvings on the St. Andrew's cross. It was so intricate, and between the feel of the smooth maple under her fingertips and the wealth of visual stimulation, it was no wonder the thing held her entranced.

Olivia was so focused on the design of two women embracing on the upper left crosspiece, she almost missed the sound of Jake's footsteps behind her.

"It's beautiful, isn't it?"

Reluctantly, she backed away from the cross and nodded. "It's hard to imagine someone carved this. I wish I could meet her."

"Have you ever tried making something like that? Maybe an art class?" he asked.

"I'm not very artistic." Despite her words, she couldn't help imagining creating such beauty from a piece of wood.

"Want to know a secret?"

"What?"

"Chelsea, the sculptor who created the cross, used to be a general contractor. She didn't figure out her hobby was more lucrative than renovating kitchens until her husband convinced her to sell something."

"Wow." She kept her hands at her sides, resisting the urge to touch the cross again. "She's so talented."

He moved behind her, making sure she heard him coming, then laid his hands on her shoulders. "Don't say you're not artistic either."

His warm breath tickled the back of her neck. "Why? I can't do—"

"Your food, Olivia. You cook because you enjoy it, and you're willing to experiment. You like creating meals that please people. Is that not art?"

She opened her mouth to disagree, but he put a finger over her lips before she could speak.

"Also, the next time you say you're not artistic, I'm going to beat your ass like a drum. Got it?"

The words shocked her into stillness, yet... She couldn't decide if the warmth in her chest was from fear or anticipation. "I...yes, sir."

"Good girl." He brushed a kiss over her temple, then took a step back. "Undress for me."

Although he'd seen her naked before, her hands shook with nerves as she grasped the hem of her tank top and pulled it over her head. This was different somehow. More serious, or maybe more meaningful.

What did he think about when he looked at her? Did he think she was pretty? After removing her shoes and socks, she unbuttoned her jeans and let them fall to the floor, then stepped free of the heavy fabric.

Olivia was fairly certain her appearance didn't frighten children, but she desperately wanted to know if he found her attractive. Did he want her as badly as she wanted him?

He'd gone down on her though. He'd made her come so many times yet had taken nothing for himself. It was too confusing, and she was too afraid to ask. Then again, she had asked earlier. He'd told her he wanted her, but what if...

Firmly, she shook the thoughts away. There was no way she'd let her insecurities ruin her scene.

"Panties too. Fold everything, set your clothes on a chair, then stand in front of the cross."

She bit her lip and took off her underwear. After folding her clothes, she laid them on one of the chairs surrounding the stage featuring the St. Andrew's cross. Her skin prickled under his perusal, but it felt good—like he was touching her.

"Beautiful. Put your hands behind your head, fingers laced together."

"Yes, sir." She lifted her arms, feeling almost too exposed as the movement forced her spine to arch. To her surprise, the shaking in her hands stopped the minute she put them into the position he'd ordered.

A trickle of liquid arousal dripped from her pussy, and she bit back a whimper. With every command, she fell deeper under his spell until there was nothing left but the anticipation of his next request.

"Now, feet shoulder width apart. Show me what's mine."

She swallowed hard, forcing her suddenly dry throat to work as she positioned her feet as he'd asked. That word *mine*, spoken in his husky baritone... It was a claim she couldn't mistake. He didn't mean it though—at least not forever. Maybe one night would be enough.

"Such a good girl for me. I love how obedient you are." Jake circled her, and the force of his gaze penetrated deep into her skin. "Are you scared?"

"No, sir."

He traced a finger down her spine, then laughed softly when she shivered. "Liar."

———

JAKE

"I'm not afraid of you."

Fuck, Olivia was beautiful. Judging by the stiffness in her spine, she wasn't being entirely truthful, yet the lingering tension quickly melted from her body and her breathing steadied.

He could have watched her for hours—exposed and vulnerable, yet so powerful in her submission. He couldn't believe he'd once thought her too weak to stand up for herself.

Unfortunately, they didn't have all night. Sooner or later, someone would come looking for them, and he was done letting other people see what belonged to him.

Even though he'd thought it entertaining at first, he wanted to find Mark and punch him in the face for seeing Olivia naked and bound in the kitchen. Logically, he knew it was ridiculous, but he couldn't help it.

"Are you sure?" he asked, getting his mind back on the business of making Olivia Rivera come so hard she forgot her own fucking name.

"Nervous, but not afraid."

"Good." Jake smoothed his palm down her back, then cupped her gorgeous ass. "Keep your hands where they are, but I'd like to blindfold you if you're okay with it."

"I thought you were the master. Aren't I supposed to obey everything?"

"No." He wished he was though. "I don't get to be your master unless you consent to be my slave."

"Then what are we doing here?"

"Chasing squirrels?"

She snorted out a giggle. "What time is it?"

"Um..." The musical sound of her laugh nearly threw him off his game. He glanced at his phone and grimaced, wondering how it had gotten so late. "Ten fifteen."

"Why don't we pretend I'm Cinderella. I'll turn back into a pumpkin at midnight."

"I'm not following."

She arched her back and repositioned her feet. "I'll be your slave until midnight, then we go back to...whatever it is we are."

"Hmm." He considered the idea for several seconds and nodded, even though she wasn't looking at him. The Cinderella thing gave him a wonderful, wicked, utterly filthy idea. He just hoped she liked it. "All right... Princess."

"How can a slave be a princess?"

"Easy." He brushed hair off her neck and trailed kisses

over her exposed skin. "I'll be Prince Jake, the Conqueror, and steal you from your palace. You'll be my personal concubine."

"Oh, I... *Dios*." Her breath stuttered and goosebumps formed on her arms as her nipples drew into tight peaks.

She was obviously getting into the game, but he wanted to pull her deeper into the fantasy. "I am now your God, Princess. You'll learn to want nothing aside from obeying my every desire."

He wrapped a hand around her neck and gently guided her to the prop storage room. Loaded with costumes and roleplay accessories, he was sure he'd find what he needed.

"What happens if I don't?"

"Good behavior will be rewarded, Princess."

"And bad behavior?"

"Then I get the reward of punishing you, and sometimes I'll do it anyway because it makes my dick hard."

He opened the door to the prop room, enjoying her gasp of surprise.

"What is all this?" she asked.

Careful to stay in character, he swatted her ass. "You will address me as your highness or master, slave."

She gulped and risked a peek at him. "I...um—"

"Say yellow if you need a time out, and red if you want to stop, sweetheart."

"No." She wrinkled her face, then took her hands from

behind her head and fisted her eyes. "I'm sorry, I'll try harder. Just give me a second."

He pulled a chair from one of the makeup vanities and set it in front of her. "Have a seat and take all the time you need."

To his surprise, she leaned against him and gave him a quick hug. "I'm okay. I just didn't realize we'd started, and I sometimes need time to adjust."

"Are you sure?"

Although he was fucking proud of her for communicating her needs, he wondered if he was doing the right thing. She wasn't going to be his Princess—at least not past midnight. He wondered if he should let her dress and take her to the apartment.

There was just one problem with that. It didn't matter where she went. He was going to follow. The only thing he knew for sure would stop him would be if she rescinded her consent.

He almost wished she would. Fuck knew he couldn't do it, but the minute she appeared to be in any distress, he was going to call a halt to the whole thing.

"Yes...master." Instead of waiting for a reply, she went to a rolling rack of costumes and removed a pink gown with a laced bodice. After checking the size, she slipped it over her head and tied the strings holding the front together.

It was too long and pooled at her feet, but the sight of her in that nearly transparent dress about made him come in his jeans. With some effort, he pulled himself together, determined to make the fantasy good for her.

Then again... He swallowed hard and tried not to look at her pert nipples showing through the gossamer fabric, wondering if he should just take her to an aftercare room and fuck her unconscious. He pushed the thought away and forced himself to focus on their roleplay.

"A princess needs a crown." He went to a shelf and grabbed a tiara laden with pink rhinestones, then placed it on her head and arranged her hair over her shoulders. "Perfect. And don't worry about the dress. Everything is professionally cleaned after it's worn."

"Thank you." She studied herself in the mirror, her head cocked to the side. "Maybe a little lipstick?"

"Look in the top drawer of the vanity to your right."

She retrieved an unopened tube of lipstick and applied the scarlet color to her lush mouth. After capping it, she said, "I look...pretty."

"You do." He hesitated for a split second, wanting nothing more than to have those plump red lips wrapped around his cock, then grabbed a black cape and another, heavier crown and put on his costume. "We'll start our game now. Are you ready?"

She straightened her crown, then turned away from the mirror. "Yes."

"Are you sure?"

She lifted her head, obviously forcing herself to look at his face. "Yes, your highness."

"Naughty girl for daring to meet my eyes." Straightening his shoulders, he peered down his nose at her and tried to look royal. "Run, Princess. I want to chase you before your punishment."

24

OLIVIA

She spun and hiked up her dress, then ran as fast as she could. It was less from fear and more from...

Maybe it was a little bit of fear. Jake's entire persona changed the minute he put on the cape and crown. Although she had a hard time with facial expressions, there was no question about what he was feeling.

He was going to chase, capture, then punish her. And he would enjoy it.

She kind of thought she would too. For once, her brain was focused on only one thing.

Jake.

He'd catch her soon. The dungeon was large, but she could only run so far. Besides, she wanted to be caught. It was like she was living out a historical romance with a hapless heroine and a morally gray prince. They'd always been her favorite because the heroines somehow managed to teach their princes to be decent humans before the end. The best were the ones in which the heroines got to be a little bit gray on the edges too.

Not that Jake needed lessons on being decent. He might be nasty bad in the bedroom, but he was a good person—his earlier treatment of her notwithstanding. Maybe her near fall from the cliff had done her a favor and forced them to listen to each other. If they hadn't... She shook the thought away and focused on their game, refusing to let the brain squirrels take it away.

Hearing his heavy footsteps behind her, she picked up the pace and jumped to the low stage featuring the St. Andrew's cross. His laughter echoed in the cavernous room, sending a thrill of anticipation down her spine.

When she tried to duck behind the cross, he caught her hair and pushed her against the heavy wood, using a hand to protect her face from the impact.

"Gotcha." He tugged her hair almost hard enough to hurt, forcing her head back. "Such a naughty princess to run from a well-earned punishment."

She almost giggled, but it would ruin their game. "Please, no, your highness! I promise I'll be good!"

"It will take many punishments before my spoiled princess becomes a good slave," he husked into her ear, making her shiver with anticipation. Still holding her hair, he led her to the spanking bench he'd indicated earlier, then pushed her down until her chest hit the leather bolster.

After letting go of her hair, he lifted her until her knees rested on the lower cushion, making sure her dress was out of the way. He stroked her back as he moved to the front of the bench to face her.

"Are you still okay?" he asked softly, crouching to peer at her face.

"Yes. Still green."

He leaned toward her and kissed her temple. "I'm proud of you."

Warmth filled her chest, making her heart thump as tears welled. It had been so long since anyone had told her that, and Jake had said it twice. Not only that, he'd interrupted a roleplay to make sure she was okay.

It was almost like two people lived inside him. He was both a sweet, caring dominant, and so filthy he made her blush every time he opened his mouth. Except...she liked it better when he was dirty and raw.

She understood him when he was like that. His words and vocal inflections matched. Even if she couldn't see his face, she...got him.

He tugged her arms out in front of her, then shackled her wrists to rings set into the sides of the bench. The steel was cold against her skin, yet he didn't hurt her or make the cuffs too tight. In fact, they were loose enough she could slip her hands free if she wanted.

His voice deepened, becoming rough and gravelly, almost but not quite threatening. "Are you sorry for misbehaving, Princess?"

"Yes, your highness. I am very sorry."

Slowly, he pulled her dress up to bare her backside, then stroked her bottom with a warm hand. "You're not convincing me. I don't think you're sorry at all."

She swallowed, her suddenly dry throat clicking with the effort. Suddenly, she wasn't Olivia anymore. No longer was she a forklift driver studying to be a forensic accountant.

Or a convicted drug trafficker trying her best to survive in a commercial kitchen.

Her name was Princess, and she'd been captured by a wicked prince intent on her subjugation. Heat pooled in her core, and she whimpered as a trickle of arousal dampened her pussy.

He chuckled with dark amusement as he swiped a finger across her folds and held it in front of her mouth. "No, you're not sorry at all. Suck, slave. Show me how you'll worship my cock in thanks for your punishment."

Closing her eyes, she accepted his wet finger into her mouth, tasting her own essence. She swirled her tongue around his finger, making him hiss out a curse and jerk away.

For a split second, she wondered if she'd made him

angry, but one glance at the rigid cock he tried to hide with his cape made her realize she'd been wrong.

Triumph filled her and she smiled, boldly meeting his eyes. "I will never obey you!"

"Oh, really?" He cupped her chin and tightened his fingers on her jaw, almost but not quite pinching.

"Never! I'll escape and return to my...um..."

His expression lightened and he grinned. "Castle? Palace?"

"Thanks." She cleared her throat and tried not to giggle. "I'll return to my castle and raise an army to defeat you."

"You'll never get away! No army can stop me, and you'll be my concubine slave forever!"

"I will not!"

Their fantasy would never become reality, but she could be brave in their game. She could look into his face without fear or discomfort. She could be a princess, proud and strong —and he could be the dark prince she secretly craved.

He lifted his hand, revealing a thick leather strap that terrified her, yet made her core pulse with desire at the same time. "I'll wager I can make you change your tune, Princess."

———

JAKE

"Do your worst, knave."

He'd never been a fan of roleplay before, but it was different with Olivia. Maybe it was because she seemed to actually enjoy it and was comfortable enough to let herself sink into the character she was playing. Her pleasure in the game enhanced his own.

He'd only intended to show Olivia the strap to increase her tension, yet her reaction was entirely unexpected. Although her facial expressions were still hard to read, he couldn't miss the way she licked her lips and blushed.

Nothing stopped him from using it though. Like many implements, a strap could be both gentle and harsh depending on where and how it was used. Some, like a dragon's tail, stung no matter what, but those would be too much for a novice.

She rattled the cuffs binding her to the bench and glared at him. One of her wrists slipped free and she pushed it back into the restraint without missing a beat. "I'll never obey you no matter what you do to me."

After setting the strap aside, he crouched to see her face. The middle of a scene wasn't the best time to ask about hard limits—especially during a roleplay. He should have thought of it before they started. "Time for a safety check. How are you doing?"

"I'm okay. Thank you."

He pushed a loose curl from her eyes and kissed her temple. "Having fun?"

"Yes, sir."

"Good. I should have found out earlier, but do you have hard limits aside from me shouting at you?" When she didn't immediately reply, he added, "You know, things you won't do."

She nodded, then chewed on her lower lip. "I don't like to be called names."

Understandable, considering how her cousin spoke to her. He pushed the thought away. Now wasn't the time to contemplate murder, and he simply didn't have time to dig a hole for the body. "Okay, what else?"

"Um... I don't know?"

"All right." Jake propped a hip on the edge of the bench and let the strap tickle her spine. He was so intent on watching her back arch to meet the leather, he almost forgot what he wanted to say. "I don't like watersports or diaper play. How are you with anal?"

"The first two sound a little messy. It's not for me, but I'm not going to yuck someone's yum. I've never tried anal."

"Yucking a yum isn't allowed at Club Apocalypse, but it's okay to have preferences." He pulled a steel butt plug from his bag and wiped it with cleanser. Roughly the diameter of his index finger with a flared base, it was the perfect starter toy. After getting himself back into his role of evil prince, he said, "Now, Princess, it's time to make you mine."

"Um... Oh, yes." She lifted her head and glared at him over her shoulder. "I'll never be yours."

"You'll say differently when I'm fucking you after your punishment, but I'm a kind master." He coated the plug with a generous dollop of lube, then showed it to her. "Tell me right away if this hurts or you don't like it, okay?"

"You're out of character."

"Better that than ruining your fun." He dripped more lube on her opening, then swirled it around her puckered rosebud, enjoying how she flinched.

"That's cold!"

"It should be. It's kept refrigerated." It wasn't—not usually anyway—but room temperature could be like ice compared to a normal body temp.

"You're not kind at all. It's no surprise that people call you Prince Jake, the Cruel."

Inexorably, but gently, he pushed a finger into her ass, smiling when she rocked her hips against his hand. "Breathe and push out, Princess. Don't forget I'm offering you a kindness."

"I...oh, goodness!"

"Yes, no, maybe?" he asked.

"Yes, I...oh, fuck."

Delighted with Olivia's response, he added a second finger and scissored them to prepare her for the toy. He loved introducing newbies to things beyond vanilla, yet it was a huge responsibility. He had to make it good for her, but also impress upon her the importance of safe and sane.

"Such a good concubine," he murmured, sliding the toy into her until it was firmly seated. "You're so beautiful when you're obeying your master. Look how well you're doing."

"Jake, please!"

She slipped her hands from the cuffs but grasped them tightly and inched her thighs further apart to give him better access. He wanted nothing more than to drop to his knees and eat her pussy until she came for him but needed to let their fantasy continue.

"Patience is a virtue, and you still haven't gotten your punishment."

She pushed her butt toward him, then reached between her legs to finger her pussy. "Let me show you how good I can be."

"Fuck..." He squeezed his eyes shut and cleaned his hands with antibacterial wipes. Olivia was going to be the death of him, and he had no idea if they were still in the role-play or not.

He grabbed the strap and let it fall to her ass. Not too hard though. A faint pink line blossomed on her generous flesh as she cried out, and he let the thick leather fall again.

All the while, he watched her carefully as he painted her backside with pink splotches. Most importantly, he listened to the music of her pleasured cries and made sure she was still playing with herself. The minute she stopped, so would he.

His cock throbbed against the zipper of his jeans, dampening the fabric with a steady stream of precum. With every movement and every fucking breath, his desire grew. He no longer wanted to fuck Olivia.

He needed it like air.

A shiver worked its way up his spine, and he petted her scorched backside. "What's your color, baby?"

Her eyes shuttered as she turned to look at him. Perspiration dotted her forehead and upper lip, glistening under the indirect illumination. Slowly, she pulled her hand from between her legs and moaned softly as she licked her fingers one by one.

"Green. Now, shut up and fuck me."

25

OLIVIA

Jake stilled, his hand resting on her sore bottom. It was less sore, and more tingly though. The strap might have looked wicked painful, but he hadn't used it that way. It was as if he'd warmed her up for something better.

Although the steel plug wasn't uncomfortably cold anymore, it jostled inside her with every move she made, sparking nerve endings to life. Her fingers hadn't been enough, and her pussy ached with need. She was done being patient.

When he didn't immediately reply, she said, "Or is the cruel prince too—"

"No more roleplay."

He crouched and touched her chin, making her look at him. To her surprise, it was easy to meet his gaze. Maybe with him, she could be more or less normal. Not normal, she corrected herself. He'd beat her ass in earnest if she let that word come out. The thought didn't scare her though. It was more comforting than anything else.

With filthy words and a few salacious threats, he was teaching her to think better about herself. Even though they'd never share a real relationship, the ability to see herself as special and talented was a priceless gift, and she'd never forget what he'd done for her.

He'd also taught her not to accept being treated badly. No more would she let people like her cousin take advantage of her or make her feel unworthy of love. Of course, Jake had bullied her unmercifully, yet it didn't bother her now that she understood his reasoning. He'd also apologized—which Berto had never done—and even at his worst, Jake had never insulted her personally. He'd limited his disrespect to her food and had admitted to lying about it to make her stand up for herself.

It was such an odd thing for him to do when he'd admitted to wanting a willing slave. She wasn't sure how she felt about that, but the small taste he'd given her had been enticing.

Would it be so bad to let him control her to that level? Maybe not, but she was too afraid she'd get used to it and lose herself all over again when it was taken away. It would be better for both of them if she kept her emotional distance —no matter how much she hated the idea.

"I like being a princess."

Laughing softly, he kissed her forehead, then stroked a thumb over her cheekbone. "You can be a princess whenever you want. Are you sure about this?"

She let go of the shackles and climbed from the bench. "I'm sure."

"Good." After taking her hand, he led her to the exit, walking so quickly she had to jog to keep up.

"Where are we going?"

"Your favorite place. I'm going to make love to you under the stars." Fortunately, nobody was around as he dragged her through the apartment.

The scent of roses filled the air when he opened the secret door and held it for her. She picked up the hem of her dress and went down the steps, drawing the sweet fragrance into her lungs. He stood behind her, letting his body heat warm her as he massaged her shoulders until even the lingering ache from her mishap on the cliff disappeared under his touch.

The fountain tickled her ears, adding an extra layer of sensory delight to the experience, and the brilliant full moon cast everything in a silvery glow.

"Last chance, *querida*."

"Last chance for what?"

"If you're not ready for this, rescind your consent."

Before she could reply, the squirrels in her head clamored for attention.

You're not good enough.

He's trying to let you down gently.

You'll never be able to keep a man like Jake McBride.

Closing her eyes, Olivia envisioned herself locking the nasty little fuckers in a soundproof box. Maybe she'd never get rid of them completely, but she didn't have to listen anymore.

She turned to face him and slowly lifted her hands to unlace the bodice of her costume. It slid to the ground in a puddle of fabric, and she kicked it away. Ruddy color decorated his sharp cheekbones, and he wiped a hand across his mouth, but he didn't take his eyes off her.

The way he stared at her... It was both disconcerting and intensely arousing, and he reminded her of a hungry lion.

"I won't if you won't."

He moved into her space, letting his body heat warm her once more. His shadow beard rasped against her neck as he pressed whisper soft kisses to her skin. "I want to make love to you like you deserve."

"And how do I deserve it?" The sound of his voice and those glancing touches had her so close to the edge, and she bit her lip before she begged again.

Then again, Jake liked it when she begged.

"Slow..." He kissed her temple, then eased the tiara from her head and set it aside. "Hard..."

He put his hands on her waist and stroked her sides, then cupped her ass. "And all night long."

His touch sparked the tingle left from his spanking back to life. She gasped when he pushed the butt plug deeper inside her.

"*Dios.* Yes. A million times, yes."

The couch was still laid flat, and he quickly threw a sheet over it, followed by the fur blanket she liked so much along with a couple of pillows. "In you go. It's getting cold."

"This from a man who keeps lube in the fridge?" Instead of obeying, she stroked the hard planes of his chest and tugged his shirt free of his jeans. "It's my turn to see you."

"You think so?" He smiled, his teeth flashing in the dim moonlight.

"Yes." She unbuttoned his jeans, then drew the zipper down, letting her hand brush against the ridge of his cock. It felt hot even through the soft cotton of his boxer briefs, and she licked her lips, wondering if she dared have a taste.

Then again, fortune favored the bold. His clean, masculine fragrance was even more tantalizing than the roses. She kissed her way down his chest and dropped to her knees.

She took him into her mouth and swirled her tongue over the plump crown of his cock, tasting the sweetness of his precum. He was far too big for her to take all of him, but she loved trying.

"What are you doing?" His voice was hoarse and strangled, making her smirk as he tangled his fingers in her hair. He tugged on it, yet it wasn't enough to make her stop.

She licked a path up his shaft, then tightened her hand around him, slowly jacking him. "If you have to ask, I'm doing it wrong."

———

JAKE

He had no idea when he'd lost control, but he was surprisingly okay with letting Olivia take the lead—for the moment. He enjoyed seeing her self-confidence even more than he liked how she met his eyes while he fucked her mouth.

"That's right, baby." He tightened his fist in her hair and held her still, then carefully thrust into her mouth. "Suck my dick like a good girl."

She hummed around his shaft, nearly making his eyes roll back in his head as he tried to keep himself from blowing his load on her face. That could be a game for another time. Keeping her still, he pulled away slowly without allowing her to chase him.

"I wasn't done." She sat back on her heels and pouted, but her beautiful brown eyes sparkled with humor.

Fuck.

He stripped out of his jeans, trying to ignore the shaking

in his hands. He couldn't remember ever wanting a woman as badly as he wanted Olivia, yet he suspected she still thought this was a game.

It wasn't—not to him. For the first time, he allowed himself to consider keeping her. Why couldn't he have what Mark and Ryan had found with Kendra and Carrie?

Because Olivia has a fucking life, asshole. She isn't going to stay.

Yeah, that was why. He'd just have to make everything perfect, so she didn't decide to make him one of her regrets.

"Shit!" He raced up the stairs to Mark's room, then dug through the nightstand drawer. His breath left his body on a harsh exhale when he found what he needed without having to go back to the dungeon.

Talk about leaving her with a regret. That one might have lasted eighteen years minimum. He'd step up to support her financially and coparent their child without a second thought, but...

He was lying to himself. It sounded like the best idea he'd ever had. Getting her knocked up would mean he'd have more time with her, and she'd make beautiful babies. With luck, they'd be smart like their mom, and not a dumbass SEAL with anger-management issues.

Fortunately, he wasn't so far gone he'd consider abusing her trust like that.

Not quite anyway.

"What's wrong?" Olivia stood at the base of the stairs, silhouetted by moonlight. Fuck, she was so beautiful.

"Nothing." Hoping he didn't look like an idiot; he went back outside and held up the box of condoms. "I just forgot we'll need these."

The worried frown left her face and she relaxed. "Me too. I'm glad one of us has a few brain cells left."

"We'll share our functional brain matter, so we don't give anyone food poisoning." After taking her hand, he led her to the bed, meaning to get her tucked in. She looked too gorgeous though, and he couldn't stand the idea of covering her up.

"That would be unfortunate." Her plump lips curved into a smile as she took the box from him and extracted a condom. "Almost as unfortunate as you not lasting all night like you promised."

"So naughty." He squeezed his eyes shut and tried to pull himself together. "On your knees, *querida*. Put that condom on me and make me like it."

She lowered herself to her knees and tore the wrapper open with her teeth but didn't sheathe him right away. Instead, she gazed up at him, still wearing that knowing smile. "Or what?"

It was too much fun watching her play and explore boundaries, but he forced himself to give her a stern frown. He tangled his hand in her hair and tugged gently. "Disobedient slaves will get edged all night and won't be allowed to come."

"The horror." Keeping her eyes on his face, she took him into her mouth, then massaged his balls with her callused hand.

Tingles shot down his spine and he gritted his teeth when she sucked the crown of his dick and took him deeper until he bumped the back of her throat. She coughed once, then hummed as she pressed a wandering fingertip to his asshole.

Make stupid choices, win stupid prizes.

She was fucking ending him. Giving her hair another gentle tug, he pulled her away, and groaned when she gave him one last suck before letting go.

"Condom. Now."

"Yes, master." Her eyes left his face for the few seconds it took her to slide the latex over his aching erection. She stood, then snaked a hand around his neck and kissed him. "Make love to me?"

"I thought you'd never ask."

Enjoying her squeak of surprise, Jake picked her up, then dropped her gently to the faux fur blanket. He gave himself a single moment to look at her before he knelt between her parted thighs.

Surprisingly, the butt plug was still in place. He considered removing it, but it would probably come out when he fucked her. Aside from that, it would increase her pleasure.

He lowered himself to his elbows and kissed her, tracing her lower lip with his tongue until she opened for him. Whimpering softly, she dug her nails into his shoulders and tried to deepen their kiss.

Forcing himself to stop, he asked, "Are you sure?"

"More than." She wrapped her legs around his hips and tried to pull him closer. "Make love to me, please."

The heat of her pussy nearly scalded him as he sank into her wet channel. She cried out and bucked, taking his cock deep. With the last shred of his control, he kept the pace slow, but went deep with every thrust. He needed her to come a million times before he dared let go.

He sat up, grasping the base of the condom so it didn't come off, then moved down her body to lap at her delicious pussy.

Ignoring the faint taste of latex and lube from the condom, he devoured her, sucking her clit into his mouth to lash it with the tip of his tongue.

"Jake! Please!"

"Such a pretty beg." He pushed two fingers into her and curled them, then pressed against her g-spot. "I'm going to tie you down next time. You'll be helpless and so, so delicious when I eat this beautiful cunt."

"*¡Madre de dios!*"

He'd almost forgotten how much she liked when he talked dirty. "I'll bind you to the spanking bench and use that vibe on you. I'm going to edge you until I'm ready to fill that perfect ass with my cum."

With his free hand, he pinched her clit hard and took the fantasy even further. "We'll be up on the main stage so everyone can see how my cum leaks from you."

"Jake!" She screamed his name over and over as her channel tightened on his fingers.

Without warning, she stiffened, then exploded, drenching his face with her sweet essence. Fuck, he loved making her squirt. To his surprise, the butt plug hadn't fallen out, but he pushed it deeper inside her, making her let out a breathless whine.

Olivia was heaven and hell wrapped up in one delicious, golden package. She still reminded him of edible gold leaf, but it wasn't because of her skin color. She was a fucking treasure.

His treasure, and he wanted it to last forever.

No... He wanted *them* to last forever.

26

OLIVIA

Her vision hazy, she watched Jake put on a fresh condom and tried to remember how breathing worked. She felt like she might float away on the air that didn't seem to want to leave her lungs.

He knew just how to send her into the stars. Whispered words drew her attention and she blinked.

"Treasure, treasure, treasure. My precious treasure."

It was less Gollum and more... More the words of someone who cherished her. And it sure as fuck wasn't the brain squirrels. They never said things like that.

Her limbs quivered, but she managed to gather enough muscle control to pull him close. "Make love to me, please."

Although he resisted for a second, he finally let her do

what she wanted. "I still need to make you come another million times."

"Make me come once more," she countered. "I think my heart won't take a million."

He chuckled softly and eased his thick cock inside her, right where she wanted him to be. "Mine either."

Slowly, inexorably, he drew her to the heights of pleasure again, making love to her like he never wanted it to end. She didn't either, but almost too soon, her core tightened, and she crested the wave of delight.

Instead of being tossed in unrelenting surf, this was gentle, lingering, and so damned good that tears pricked her eyes. It was less intense, but somehow more.

Deeper, more consuming. More...everything.

It made her wish for things she had no business wanting. A home. Family. A man who loved her despite her neurodiversity. Laughing to herself, she pushed those fantasies aside. Jake's debauched imaginings were better.

That was what she told herself, at least.

Sweat slicked their bodies and she relished the slide of her hands over his muscular back as he collapsed on top of her with a groan of repletion.

"Are you okay?"

"I should be asking you that." He rolled off her, then pulled up the blanket and wrapped her in his arms. "Fuck, Olivia. I... No words."

She snuggled against his chest and inhaled the perfume

of their love as the faux fur caressed her skin. "Yes. I'm surprised I can breathe."

"Same." He brushed a kiss over her temple. "Rest for a while, but we need to go inside soon."

"Before I turn into a pumpkin."

He laughed softly and tightened his arms around her. "You'll never be a pumpkin, sweetheart. Always a princess."

"Mmmm." She closed her eyes and let herself drift. It wasn't true, but it was nice to think about.

———

A concussive boom of sound brought her from her doze, and she jerked, the surprise making her fall from the couch. "Jake? What's happening?"

He grabbed her arm and jerked her to her feet. "Inside. Now!"

Before she reached the steps, another explosion sounded, this one closer, and to her horror, red flames lit up the night sky. She didn't need to be told Berto had finally made his move.

She tried to remember the boy who had once protected her, but he didn't exist anymore, and hadn't for a long time. He was a thug who threatened to cut out her tongue and had set her up for a felony conviction.

"God dammit, Olivia! I'm going to beat your fucking

ass!" Before she could reply, Jake picked her up and tossed her over his shoulder, then raced inside to his room.

After dropping her to her feet, he cupped her cheeks, then kissed her hard. He went to the closet and tossed something at her. "Get dressed and put this on."

The weight of a Kevlar vest dragged her arm down, and she nodded as she scrambled into clean clothes. "What's happening?"

"Looks like we're under attack." He tugged his jeans over his hips and shoved his feet into boots, then jerked a T-shirt over his head.

"I can help! I—"

Baring his teeth, he spun on her, then gripped her chin hard. "Olivia, I swear to fuck, I will beat your ass bloody if you move from this room!"

The threat should have scared her, but it didn't. Jake was reacting out of a sense of duty...of protectiveness. That didn't mean he had to do it alone—especially since this whole mess was her fault.

"Yes, master."

His eyes softened and he pulled her into a tight hug before kissing her temple. "Stay here and hide if you hear anyone. Be safe. I'll come back soon."

She smiled and returned his hug, then tucked herself in the corner between the bed and wall. "I'll be safe. Promise."

He took a step toward the door, then glanced back at her,

his expression a mix of sadness and resolve. "We'll talk soon."

Without another word, he walked out, closing the door behind him.

No, they wouldn't.

She grabbed her phone from the dresser, wondering if she wanted to see a message or missed call from Berto. Her thumb moved of its own accord, and she tapped his contact.

To her surprise, he picked up and she swallowed hard at the sound of his soft voice.

"*Hola, muñequita.*"

"You know, Berto, it would be really nice if you passed along some of the wealth you're getting," she purred, trying to stifle the urge to throw up.

"Why should I? You did nothing."

"I went to prison and didn't tell anyone who set me up."

"True." He went silent for a moment, but she didn't miss the sound of gunfire in the background. "Because you're family, a hundred grand. Take it and keep your mouth shut."

Crossing her fingers, she prayed nobody was being hurt. "You can do better than that. The man who wanted the English woman offered more."

"You aren't worth that much."

"I might have found one of her computers."

"I should cut your throat for keeping that from me."

"Such a loving cousin," she spat. "Do you want it?"

"*Puta.* You have nothing I—"

"Sure about that?" She went into the bathroom and turned on the shower. "Shall I add bath salts? The water is quite warm."

"Stop! What do you want?"

She wanted her life back. She wanted to not have a cousin willing to destroy her for a few dollars, and she wanted to spend the rest of her life in Jake's arms.

And more than anything, she wanted to protect Jake and what he and his friends had built. If it meant giving up... If it meant losing everything, she'd gladly pay the price for their safety.

"A quarter of a million US dollars, in cash. Safe passage, and a first-class ticket to the destination of my choice." Her throat seized, and she swallowed before she asked for Jake's safety. She couldn't let Berto suspect anything. "You'll get the computer when I get my money. Do what you want with the woman and her computer."

"When did you grow a spine?" Berto almost sounded like he admired her, and she couldn't decide if she wanted to laugh or cry. "Anything else?"

"Yes. You're going to forget I exist. I never want to hear your voice again. I'll meet you by the pool in a few minutes."

She ended the call and let out a sigh of relief, then grabbed a jacket, hoping she had the nerve for what she planned.

"You utter bitch."

The soft words made her flinch, and she spun around. To her horror, Jake stood in the doorway, his fingers tight on the knob.

"I—"

He sneered, his eyes cold as ice. "Go. Get your money. That's what you came for isn't it?"

"Please, Jake, listen. I—"

"As soon as I get rid of your asshole cousin, I'm calling the cops. Enjoy the rest of your sentence in jail."

————

JAKE

Most of the guest wing was ablaze. Detritus littered the pool like paper lanterns floating on the water. It was a small glimpse of beauty in a destroyed landscape.

Six years of his life were gone. Everything he and the rest of the Horsemen had built was lost.

He ignored the lingering tracer fire arcing over Club Apocalypse and stared at his phone. It hadn't been too hard to believe he'd heard only half the conversation when he'd first heard her talk to her cousin, but he didn't have that excuse anymore.

Olivia had always been too good to be true. So submissive, so beautiful and willing. He should have known better.

After all, she'd been placed to do exactly what her cousin wanted. She'd played all of them.

Fuck. It shouldn't have hurt, but it did. He shouldn't have been so angry, but he was. She was iron pyrite. Fool's gold, and he was the dumbass fool.

He closed the audio feed and pocketed his phone. Fuck her. She could go down with her cousin, and he'd be the first in line to put her ass in prison where she belonged.

"Jake." Gabby laid a hand covered in a black leather glove on his arm. "Give her a chance, yeah? I have plenty of footage from the cameras."

He shook her off, resisting the urge to shout. "A chance to do what? She offered the asshole you and your work for money."

She opened her mouth, but Sean laid a finger over her lips, silencing her reply. "Let her draw them out," Sean said. "Once they're in the open..."

His voice trailed off, letting Jake read between the lines.

"Yeah."

"Good." Ignoring Gabby's whispered objections, Sean took her inside, then returned. "I'll try to get behind them. Mark is already running the perimeter."

He shifted his weight and reached for the one thing that had never let him down. The Barrett was heavy and cold in his hands, yet the smell of gun oil and steel comforted him as he crept behind the poolside concession stand and set up for his shot.

He didn't give a good goddamn about his targets. Male, female, whatever... It didn't matter. His job was to make sure they didn't hurt innocents.

The round in his chamber wasn't for Olivia though. He had every intention of letting her regret her choices for a long time. He exhaled and let his anger and disappointment float away, calming his heart rate and respiration as he waited.

Waiting was both the easiest and hardest part of his work. Some jobs had taken only a few days, while he'd spent months waiting for others. This one would be over before dawn.

"Berto, I'm here."

Despite his preparation, he had to forcibly stop himself from leaping to his feet when he saw Olivia walk across the pool deck. She carried a black laptop bag over one shoulder, but nothing else, and ignored the lingering gunshots echoing from the desert.

He snorted and rolled his eyes. What the fuck had he been thinking? There was no way she'd have done that unless she was sure nobody would shoot at her. He thanked God he'd used a rubber. The thought of having a baby with her...

"Fuck this." He settled down and pushed his anger aside, then focused his scope on Olivia. The gunshots quieted and he heard soft footsteps cross the concrete but didn't dare take his attention from her.

Soon enough, a man stepped into view and approached to stand a few feet from Olivia. Taller than her by a few inches, the family resemblance was unmistakable.

"*Hola, prima.*" Berto smirked and stepped closer, but she backed out of reach.

"Where's my money?"

"Is that my computer?"

"Not until I have my money."

"I could take it from you."

"And I can drop it." She held the bag over the pool. "I left it on to make sure everything will short out. Want to test me?"

She lowered the bag, letting it brush the surface of the water.

"Wait!" Berto snapped his fingers and another man trotted to him, carrying a black duffle bag. "I'll double your payout if you give me Sean Franklin."

"Why?"

"I got another bounty. What do you care?"

"Just curious." She nodded at the man carrying the duffle. He dropped it at her feet, then waited. Giving Berto a smile, she picked up the duffle and exchanged it for the computer. "I'd say it was a pleasure, but I hope you rot."

"Oh, it's definitely been a pleasure." The smirk left Berto's face, and he lifted a handgun. "They say blood is thicker than water, but it's not thicker than half a million dollars."

The click of metal echoed from multiple locations, letting Jake know Berto's weapon wasn't the only one trained on her. To his surprise, she didn't move, and simply stared at her cousin as if daring him to shoot.

Jake touched the trigger on his Barrett and gritted his teeth. It didn't matter what he did. Olivia was going to die.

This wasn't what he wanted. Sure, he wanted her punished. He wanted her ass in a cell—not dead. Letting out a breath, he focused his scope on Berto. Olivia would be lost, but he'd take the asshole out.

"I heard you were looking for me!"

Jake cursed at the spoiled shot, then readjusted his aim as Sean, hands in his pockets, walked toward Berto.

"Found you," Berto replied, turning his weapon on Sean.

"What's the going rate for a retired SEAL?" Holding his arms out, Sean walked closer. "And who's paying?"

"Half a million, dead or alive." Berto shrugged, then curled his finger around the trigger. "Sorry, not sorry."

Without warning, Olivia darted in front of Sean as Berto fired, taking the shot meant for his friend. She fell hard, blood spilling from the wound in her upper chest.

"No!" Jake's shout went unanswered, and he dropped to his knees, the Barrett falling from nerveless fingers. She couldn't be... No. Just fucking no.

Hadn't he given her a vest? It would have hurt, but she'd have survived. Why wasn't she wearing a fucking vest? And what the fuck possessed her to take a shot meant for someone else?

"Fuck, you're stupid," Berto snapped as he lifted his gun. "Thank God, you're—"

Another shot rang out, and the blossoming rose in the middle of Berto's forehead cut off his words.

27

OLIVIA

"You're going to be fine. I promise."

She tried to make her brain work around the rapid Italian but couldn't quite catch all the words. It was too hard to breathe, and she needed to see if Jake was okay.

Shouted orders rang, but she ignored them and tried to sit up.

"No, *tesoro*." Nicolo pushed her down, his hands gentle but firm. "Be still."

She wondered if Jake still thought she was a treasure. Probably not since he thought she'd betrayed him. That was okay though. As long as he was alive...

She let out a breath and relaxed. As long as Jake was alive, it was worth it.

"We've got you, sweetie." Sean's concerned face swam in her vision, and she blinked. To someone else, he shouted, "It's an in and out, but blood pressure's dropping and she's losing blood."

There was a prick on her inner elbow, the pain there and gone in a second.

"Find the shooter and bring them to me. I want them alive." Nicolo's voice hurt her ears with its violence. She wanted to feel sorry for whomever he sought but couldn't quite manage it.

"Not...Italian, *por favor*." She coughed and tried to roll to her side, but someone held her down. "Where's Jake?"

There were too many voices and too many unanswered questions, but the pain didn't let her concentrate.

"Ms. Rivera, my name is Linda. Do you know what year it is?"

She blinked and tried to focus on the blonde woman's face. "It's the year I was supposed to graduate college."

———

"That's going to leave a mark," she muttered, pulling up her hospital gown to cover the staples holding her shoulder together. There was a matching set on her back marking an exit wound, along with a broken collarbone.

Everything hurt like crazy, but the pain meds took the edge off. Mostly. Besides, she was still alive—which was more than she'd expected.

She tried to feel sorry about Berto's death, but the emotion wouldn't come. If she was honest with herself, she was glad he was gone. More than that, she was relieved Tia Jozefina hadn't lived long enough to see what he'd become.

Blood wasn't thicker than water. It was as thin as poorly brewed tea. Still, she missed the boy he'd been.

She also missed Jake.

Mark and Kendra had visited, and so had Sean and Gabby, along with the rest of Club Apocalypse's staff. She would forever wonder why Nicolo Bianchi came every day, and she'd lost count of the number of times she'd given her statement to the police.

But Jake hadn't come. Not a single fucking time.

Maybe it was time for her to grab a clue and realize he never meant all the things he'd said. He'd taught her so much though. No longer would she accept abuse from anyone. She knew how to silence the dumb brain squirrels too.

All she needed was her life back, which wouldn't happen because Berto was dead and couldn't give her the exoneration she needed. She rubbed her face, then tried to settle herself in a more comfortable position.

"Ms. Rivera?"

She sat up as a man in a gray suit walked in, followed by

a woman in a cream pantsuit. She had no idea who the woman was, but the man looked vaguely familiar, and she tried to place where she'd seen him. Aside from the expensive suit, he was...bland, with thinning brown hair and brown eyes.

"Yes, what can I do for you?"

"I'm Richard Waters, assistant district attorney for Navajo county. You might not remember me." He gestured at the woman, who gave Olivia a smile. "This is Anne Lindstrom. She'll be representing your interests in this matter."

Richard's name jogged her memory and she nodded. "You were the prosecutor for my trial. Before you ask, I'll return to my work release when the doctors let me go."

She crossed her fingers they'd find her something better than the recycling center. As kind as everyone had been—well, almost everyone—she couldn't go back to Club Apocalypse.

"That's not why we've come." He set a briefcase on the rolling meal cart and opened it, then removed a thick folder. "Your conviction has been overturned. I just need you to—"

"Excuse me?"

"I beg your pardon." He laid the folder on her lap and opened it. "Sign here, and here, please. I'd like to get this matter settled."

"No. Tell me what happened."

Anne held up a hand before he could speak. "Your arrest was handled improperly, meaning your rights were violated.

There was insufficient evidence and what little the prosecution had was the result of entrapment. If the judge and attorneys handling the case had been minimally competent, the case would have never gone to trial in the first place."

Giving Richard a hard glare, she added, "In any case, sign those documents, and we'll get everything taken care of."

"That's it?" she asked. "Just a few signatures and you'll give me my life back?"

"Essentially, yes." Richard peered at her, then pulled a pair of reading glasses from his pocket and put them on. "There are highlights marking where you need to sign."

"And the assets you seized when I was convicted?"

There hadn't been much. Her only possessions had been the contents of her apartment and a used Honda, but she wanted to see what he'd say.

Richard shifted his feet and glanced away. "I'm afraid I—"

"Forget it." She scribbled her signature on the forms, then closed the folder. "God forbid you give back what you stole from me."

"Ms. Rivera," Anne interrupted, "you are entitled to compensation, but it will take some time to organize."

She tried to let go of her anger, but it was so hard. "Thank you for that. I appreciate it."

"Yes, of course." Richard took off his glasses and slipped them into his coat pocket. "For what it's worth, I'm sorry."

When she nodded, they walked out. She almost called

them back though. Who had hired Anne? No attorney was going to review her case out of the kindness of their heart.

At least Richard apologized. That was more than she'd expected. She rolled over and blinked back tears. She'd wished for this. She'd wished for freedom and for her conviction to be gone.

Unfortunately, she hadn't considered the aftermath, and now she was homeless, still recovering from being shot, and...

Useless. Loser. Stupid...

Still had a brain full of squirrels that needed to shut the fuck up.

"Okay." She sat up and unplugged the monitors tracking her vitals, then eased the IV needle from the back of her hand. She couldn't stand the thought of being somewhere she didn't want to be for a single second longer than she had to. "I need out of here."

"You have no idea how much I've longed to hear those words, my *tesoro*." Nicolo strode into her room, carrying a garment bag and a small suitcase.

"I'm not yours."

She was Jake's, but he didn't want her. He never had.

"No." He set the bag on her bed and unzipped it, revealing a gorgeous silk caftan painted with swirls of pink and green. "No one owns you, least of all me, but for my sins, I offer you a...hand up?"

"Um...okay? What's in the suitcase?"

"Additional clothing, which I requested to allow for your injury, along with your passport. I've taken the liberty of including a debit card with enough to cover your expenses until you're on your feet again. I've also arranged your release from the hospital."

"Are you the one who hired Anne? What's in it for you?"

He nodded, then gave her a smile and shrugged. "You guessed my nefarious plans."

"Well, thank you for that. It means a lot, but I don't understand why. What do you want from me?"

"I simply wished to see you receive justice." He went to the window and clasped his hands behind his back. "You are welcome to join me in Italy, of course, but you may go wherever you choose."

Maybe she'd misjudged Nicolo. Oh, she still believed he was dangerous, yet... It was also possible he was the only truly altruistic person she'd ever met aside from Tia Jozefina.

"Thank you." She went to him, then stretched up on her toes to kiss his cheek. "You're very generous, but I just want to go home."

JAKE

Olivia was gone.

Fortunately, she hadn't thrown away her phone,

meaning he could track her position. Although he wondered
how she'd managed to get to Guatemala when she wasn't
allowed to leave the state, it was none of his damned
business.

Hell, if he had any sense, he'd uninstall the tracker on his
phone and forget about her. That would be the smart choice.
He slapped another sandwich together and decided to take
care of it later.

The only thing giving him any satisfaction at all was
knowing she wasn't with that fucking Italian. At least, he
didn't think they were together. There was no way to know
for sure.

Nicolo had vanished without a single word of goodbye.
He hadn't even told Gabby he was bugging out. He'd left
behind several guards, but none of them knew where he
was. Jake didn't think they'd have told him anyway. Like all
reputable mercs, their loyalties went to the person who paid
them.

Privately, he suspected they were there to protect Gabby.
As far as he knew, the bounty on her was still out there.

He finished wrapping the sandwiches and set them in
the cooler. Olivia would have come up with something
better than day old bread and grocery store deli meat, but he
tried not to think about that.

Not that it mattered since he was just feeding the
construction crew rebuilding the guest wing. They wanted
quick and edible over fancy and time-consuming.

In a way, that asshole Berto had done them a favor. The original building hadn't allowed much room to expand, and now they were getting the day spa they'd wanted, a larger fitness center, plus an additional ten suites.

Of course, that meant Gabby was usually shooting flames out her ears since she was the one footing the bill. Everyone had learned to walk the other way when they saw her coming. Even Kendra didn't cross her.

At least Gabby's security system had worked perfectly. Although the fires had ruined her expensive cameras in that wing, they had plenty of crystal-clear video identifying everyone who had taken part in destroying Club Apocalypse.

He liked knowing they were all in jail, held without bond while they waited for their trials, but he wondered if they'd end up murdered in their cells like Carrie's father and uncle.

The door slammed open, and he arched a brow when Gabby stormed across the kitchen, her heavy boots thudding on the tile.

"Can I help you, Dr. Knox?"

Without a word, she slammed a laptop case on the prep table. He frowned, recognizing it as the same one Olivia had intended to give to Berto.

"What's going on?"

"I'm tired of you. Your food is disgusting. It's cold, tasteless, and I swear to God, if you don't give me proper beans with my breakfast, I will ensure you never have a credit rating above a hundred."

"Tell me how you really feel," he muttered. "Eat from the buffet like everyone else. Your short order cook is gone."

"Because you didn't trust her or ask her for an explanation."

"She didn't offer one."

Not that he'd given her a chance. As long as she was okay, she could do whatever the fuck she wanted. Her choices were fairly limited though. She'd have to pick between jail and another work release.

With Berto dead, there was no one to exonerate her. Considering what she'd tried, it wouldn't hurt her to spend another year or two behind bars.

Then again... Would she end up like her cousin if she had to go back to jail? Maybe that was why she'd broken her parole and ran to Guatemala. His gut roiled uncomfortably, but he ignored the disquiet. Olivia Rivera was officially no longer his problem.

"Piss off and open the bag."

"Why?" He pushed the bag aside and sprayed the prep table with sanitizing solution. There was no way he was touching whatever was in there. At best, he'd be contaminating evidence.

"I thought you might want to see what Olivia nearly died for."

"No." He didn't give a shit what it was. It hadn't been worth her life.

"Stubborn git." She huffed irritably, then opened the bag. "Go on, look at it."

He shrugged and put away his cleaning supplies. "It's empty. So what?"

"Yes, Jake. It's empty." She pinched the skin between her brows, then zipped the case closed. "Does that mean anything to you?"

"Should it?"

Rolling her eyes, she grabbed the bag, then walked to the door. Before she left, she said, "God, you're thick."

"Wait!" Something in his chest tightened, stealing his breath. There was one question he hadn't asked, and he wasn't sure he wanted to know the answer. "What was in there when Olivia had it?"

Her face softened and she curved her lips into a smile. "It contained exactly what you saw. No more or less."

"Are you fucking kidding me?"

What the hell had Olivia been thinking?

"I do not kid when I'm this angry. You should probably also ask what was in Berto's bag."

"Are you going to tell me?"

"It was as empty as this computer case. Ask yourself why." She took a few steps closer and narrowed her eyes. "Now, I'll be generous and give you time to think about what you've done, but I want proper beans with my full English at eight sharp the day after tomorrow or you can kiss your credit score goodbye."

"Do you know where she is?"

"You still have the tracker on her phone. Find her yourself since you're the one who lost her in the first place."

She walked out, letting her parting words dig themselves into his gut like knives.

Had he been wrong? He shook his head and snorted. No, Olivia set her cousin up just like she'd done to him. If it hadn't been at his expense, he might have cheered and laughed his ass off when Berto paid for an empty computer bag.

Except... His bag had been empty too. She had to have known Berto would check hers, meaning...

His ass hit the stool and he nearly fell when it slid out from under him. She'd known, all right. She'd been willing to risk her life to draw Berto out and give the Horsemen a chance to catch him.

Had she known her cousin planned to kill her?

He couldn't decide if he wanted to get on his knees and kiss her feet when he begged her to forgive him or beat her butt raw for putting herself in danger like that.

Fuck it. He'd do both. First, he had to find her. Oh, and figure out how to get a convicted felon back across the border.

"Baby girl, running isn't going to save you. I hope you're ready."

28

OLIVIA

Carrie had the right idea when she took off to Scotland to get away from Ryan. When the Horsemen were assholes, it was best to go somewhere nice to decompress. Maybe she should set up an escape fund for women in need of a Horsemen-free environment.

El Paredon was peaceful, with only the sound of sea birds and the low conversation of a pair of surfers catching a few waves as the lowering sun turned the water to gold. The black sand radiated heat, yet the breeze kept things comfortable. In the distance, she caught the tiny specks of fishing boats.

She would have killed to join the surfers, but her

shoulder wouldn't be up to it for several weeks and she still had to wear a sling. At least the incisions were closed, and the pain was more or less gone. As long as she didn't move around too much, it didn't bother her.

This was her birthplace, and held so many fond memories, yet the sea made it easy to forget things too—such as betrayal and men with blue eyes like toxic waste.

It wasn't entirely Jake's fault though. She should have tried harder to explain. Then again, if a gunshot wound didn't make him realize she hadn't been working with her cousin, nothing would.

That was on him. Not her. She was done living her life to please other people. With Berto, it had gotten her a drug conviction and a bullet to her shoulder. With Jake, it was just a broken heart.

When the breeze blew the scent of grilled fish toward her from one of the beachside restaurants, she slid her feet into her sandals and covered up her swimsuit for the short hike to her cottage, deciding to shower and change before supper.

It was better to be inside after dark anyway. The one thing she hadn't missed about her hometown was the mosquitos.

Despite her determination to forget Club Apocalypse altogether, she still had questions—not the least of which was the identity of Berto's killer. It hadn't been one of the Horsemen. None of them had been in the right position according to Mark and Kendra.

Considering none of them had gotten arrested, it was probably true. She'd been fighting to stay conscious at the time and hadn't seen anything.

The bigger question was why, and even Nicolo had no answers for her. She had her suspicions though. Berto hadn't worked alone. His gang hadn't had the contacts or resources to obtain the rocket launchers used to destroy the resort. Hopefully, the police could track down where they'd come from.

Aside from that, Berto's plan to put her in jail and then place her in Club Apocalypse for her work release had taken months. He'd never had the patience for long games, and by his own admission, someone had been paying him. Maybe it was better to ask why that individual wanted him dead.

Fortunately, she'd told the police everything she knew about what Berto had attempted, so there was no reason for her to return to Arizona. With her name cleared, she could go anywhere, and finding a job wouldn't be too difficult. She could finish school, study for her CPA certification, and move on.

It was none of her business what the Horsemen did. Not anymore.

After cleaning up, she went back out. There were several wonderful restaurants in town, and the seafood was plentiful, cheap, and very fresh. She could live comfortably for years on what Nicolo had given her, but she didn't want to take advantage of his generosity any more than she had to.

She chose a place she hadn't yet tried and decided to give herself one more week of vacation before she returned to America.

The server seated her on the patio overlooking the beach, then set a bottle of water on the table. It wasn't cold, but she didn't mind. More quickly than she'd expected, the server returned with her fish, accompanied by a large platter of vegetables, salsa verde, and extra tortillas.

After the first bite, she decided to add the place to her list of favorites. It was beyond wonderful to eat a delicious meal she didn't have to cook.

"Is this seat taken?"

The fork fell from her hand and Olivia stilled at the painfully familiar voice. Just looking at Jake McBride made her heart lurch and slam hard against her ribs. After swallowing, she took a sip of water before she choked on her food.

"How did you find me?"

"The tracker on your phone." He sat across from her, then folded his hands on the table.

"Great." For a moment, she considered tossing the damned thing into the sea, then thought better of it. It was too late to do anything about it now, but she was buying a new phone the minute she got back. She'd throw the old one in the alligator enclosure at the zoo. Well, the trash bin next to the enclosure anyway.

"How did you get out of the country with a felony conviction?"

"Nicolo hired a decent attorney for me. She got my conviction overturned and brought the documents to my hospital room. I signed them, checked myself out, and decided to take a vacation. What do you want?"

"I..." He shifted in his chair, then looked down at his hands. "I owe you an apology. I should have trusted you enough to let you explain what you were doing. And then I should have tied you to the bed so you couldn't do it."

It was strange. He'd dragged her through so many emotions during her time with him. Fear, anger, sadness...

Incredible happiness... And now, he wanted to say he'd have protected her when he wouldn't even look at her? He wasn't the one who had trouble with eye contact.

All she felt was numb. Even the brain squirrels were silent as if they knew she truly didn't care what he thought about her. She didn't like feeling that way about him though. Shouldn't there be something left in her heart for a man she'd slept with?

Unfortunately, there was. His scent, unpolluted with chemical fragrances, teased her senses, reminding her of how he'd changed his soap and shoes for her, and everything else he'd done to accommodate her needs.

He hadn't done it to get her into bed either. She'd made the choice to sleep with him on her own. Maybe he cared, but was it enough?

Would she keep waiting for the next time his anger and mistrust got the better of him? If she stayed with him, would he eventually take things too far? He could no longer threaten her with going back to jail; what would be next?

Her heart wanted her to say yes, but she couldn't. No matter how much she wanted to be in his arms again, she wasn't going to let anyone make her feel like she was one misunderstanding away from abuse. Being with Jake was like falling into a rabbit hole with spikes at the bottom. She'd already been down there once and deserved better.

"Thanks. Apology accepted." She met his eyes, then swallowed a bite of her fish. "Have a safe trip home."

———

JAKE

He didn't know why he'd expected Olivia to fall into his arms like he hadn't been a complete asshole to her. After all, he'd been the one to teach her to stand up for herself. Bitching because she'd learned the lesson wouldn't be the dumbest thing he'd ever done, but it was close.

To his surprise, she gazed at his face without flinching. Unfortunately, her eyes were flat and antagonistic, which didn't bode well for his plans.

Hell, just looking at her in that brightly colored sarong with her hair in a wild tangle of curls barely contained by a scarf almost made him forget what he wanted to say. The sling holding her arm in place was a quick and gut-wrenching reminder of his failures.

"I'll leave, but I'd like to ask you for a favor first."

She took another bite of her food, eating like she didn't have a fucking care in the world. "Depends on the favor."

"I owe you an explanation. Will you listen?"

"That's a big ask from someone who didn't offer me the same courtesy."

Ouch.

Olivia didn't do sarcasm. If she said something like that, it was the truth as she saw it. He had to try though. She deserved honesty—even if it didn't convince her to stay with him.

"Please?"

"You have until I order dessert, then you can leave."

Her fish was almost gone, but she still had a full plate of vegetables and tortillas. "Okay. I...okay."

She drummed her fingers on the table, but not the rapid tattoo he'd come to expect when she was nervous or needed to stim. This was a slow, measured beat that communicated her impatience.

To give himself a few seconds to think, he waved the server over and asked for a bottle of water, then cleared his throat. "I...okay. This probably won't surprise you, but I have anger issues."

Arching a brow, she layered vegetables on a tortilla, then spooned salsa on top. "I'd never have guessed."

Maybe Olivia *did* do sarcasm after all.

"I got into fights all the time when I was a kid, and even through college. I used to see a therapist, but it got better, and I stopped going." When she opened her mouth to speak, he held up a hand. "You're the last person I should have lashed out at. I shouldn't have said all those awful things, and I would do anything for a do-over."

"Would you go back to therapy, Jake?" She folded her tortilla and took a bite. "If you do, will you decide you're cured and do the same things over again?"

"I—"

She dropped the tortilla, wiped her hands on her napkin, and laid it next to her plate. "Who's next on your list of victims? Is there some other woman waiting for your vicious accusations? Is she begging for a little kindness without knowing how nasty you can be?"

He swallowed and quelled the urge to defend himself. She needed to speak her truths without interference, and he needed to listen.

"You make me sound like a predator."

"You fucking groomed me," she spat. "You pushed and pushed until I was strong and happy and believed you when you said I was beautiful and special. You were just waiting for a chance to knock me back down."

"You're right about the first part. I did groom you because you are beautiful and special, and I wanted you to see in yourself the same things I see." When she tried to walk away, he grabbed her hand, pulling her to a stop. "You're wrong about the rest."

She jerked free, but didn't leave, thank fuck. "Then explain it to me. Tell me how it's okay for you to expect me to listen to your sob story when you refused to hear me?"

"I take things out of context, okay?" When the server turned to look at them, he lowered his voice. "I hear things and my brain automatically assumes people are trying to hurt me. It makes me want to hurt them first before they get a chance."

"Okay, I—"

"And then I fell in love with you, and it hurt even worse when I thought you were... You almost died because of my anger issues."

She blinked and cocked her head to the right, but her angry expression didn't change. "I didn't."

"No, but I didn't protect you. You should never have been out there in the first place. Anyway, I'm sorry. I'll leave you alone now."

Without waiting for her to answer, he walked out, pushing his way past other diners in his haste to get as far away as he could before he lost it. Worse, he still needed to find a place to sleep until it was time to catch his flight home.

Fuck. He'd have slept on the beach if the mosquitos

weren't so bad. With his luck, they'd carry his dumb ass out to sea, or he'd contract malaria. Talk about a gift that kept on giving.

Sharing his truths—his innermost secrets and failures—hadn't been enough. She'd barely reacted when he told her he loved her, and it about cracked his heart in two.

Still, the trip hadn't been wasted. Olivia would never know, but he'd already scheduled himself for therapy. He owed it to her, and he never wanted to see another person hurt because of him.

29

OLIVIA

Houston wasn't so bad, but the traffic between Rice and her apartment across town was murder. She couldn't complain though.

When Gabrielle Knox offered a scholarship, a smart person took it and didn't ask questions. Olivia liked to consider herself smart, recent events notwithstanding. She even had a job lined up in Boston, of all places.

Giving the cars behind her a threatening glare, she merged across six lanes and snagged a spot between a semi and a BMW whose driver seemed to care about his fenders.

Did one need snow tires in Boston? She shuddered and gave the car to her right a short burst from her horn for being a dumbass.

"I'm driving here, asshole!"

She didn't remember learning to drive so aggressively. It was almost disconcerting, and she wondered if the Horseman she was trying her best to forget had rubbed off on her.

No, she was just tired of being pushed around. Tired of not taking her own space. Tired of words telling her she was loved and actions saying otherwise.

Shut your mouth and stay sweet. Don't cause trouble.

Fuck that. Without lube.

As she exited the expressway, her phone chimed with the bagpipes she'd programmed for Gabby, and she tapped the button on the steering wheel to accept the call.

Her car was yet another thing to thank Gabby for. It was a lease, but she'd never had one with working air conditioning, much less Bluetooth.

"*Ciamar a tha thu?*"

"You're learning Gaelic. I'm impressed." Gabby was silent for a moment, then said, "Mark and Kendra just announced their engagement."

"Congratulate them for me."

"They're throwing a party and want you to come."

"I'm busy."

"Really? I didn't tell you the date."

Olivia spun the wheel, cutting off a minivan to turn into a fast-food place, then got in line for the drive through.

"You're paying a fortune for my tuition. I have to study so I don't waste the investment."

"You've also finished at least half a master's degree in one semester. Do be a dear and don't bullshit me in public."

"Fair."

"Will you come?"

"I—"

"Welcome! Can I take your order?"

"Large fries, double cheeseburger, small chocolate shake, and extra ketchup packets, please."

"Thank you. Your total is on the screen. Please pull around."

"That's just bougie as fuck," Gabby said.

"Your opinion is duly noted." Blinking back tears, she tried for a smile as she paid the teenager at the window. As much as she loved Gabby, she couldn't go back.

There were too many memories at Club Apocalypse. She couldn't smell roses or even listen to a fish tank pump without feeling a fur blanket against her skin. It was like having a phantom limb.

"Olivia, please. We miss you."

"You miss my beans and black pudding." She collected her food and left the restaurant, then drove to her apartment complex on autopilot.

"That too."

"Okay, I'll come, but it's a two-day drive. When is the party?"

"Squee! Thank you! It's tomorrow night, but don't worry about the drive. I'll have a plane meet you at the airport."

———

The resort didn't look the same. Instead of two identical wings with the main entrance and lobby centered between them, the one on the right was now two stories. The roof over the lobby had been raised to tie in with the new construction, then broke where it met the original, revealing a bank of windows and an outdoor pavilion covered with shade structures. She couldn't quite see, but it looked like there was a rooftop garden up there too.

It was elegant and beautiful, yet still kept to the original vintage look that had made the hotel so charming. She was glad the work had been completed so quickly, and especially happy to see the full parking lot.

She didn't want to be there, and had no intention of staying, but she liked seeing the resort thrive.

Instead of using the valet service, she parked some distance from the entrance. It would be easier to make her escape if she didn't have to wait for her rental car. It wouldn't take her long to give her regards to the happy couple, and she could be back in Houston in time for her date with her textbooks and a pint of ice cream.

"I can't believe I didn't just send a gift," she muttered to herself as she walked inside, carrying the wrapped bottle of whiskey she'd bought for Mark and Kendra at the airport. The old Olivia wouldn't have thought twice about flying across two states for an engagement party, but she'd done it for Gabby more than anything else.

"Olivia!" Sierra, the front desk manager, hurried across the lobby, then swept her into a tight hug that nearly stole her breath. "We're so glad you could make it!"

"Um...thanks." Gently, she wriggled free of the hug, but didn't protest when Sierra led her to the front desk.

"Your suite is ready. I can't wait to see what you think of it. Where's your luggage? I'll have a valet take it up."

"I'm not staying." In truth, she had an overnight bag in her car for emergencies, but there was no point in bringing it inside. She set the whiskey on the counter, then added, "Will you put this with the rest of the engagement gifts?"

Sierra's smile faded, but she nodded. "Sure. I'll keep the suite open if you change your mind."

"I just came to wish Mark and Kendra well. I need to get back to Houston and study for finals."

"That's too bad. We were hoping for a longer visit. Everyone misses you."

"Maybe some other time." Old Olivia would have caved and done what Sierra wanted. New Olivia didn't even apologize for refusing.

"We'll hold you to it." Sierra pointed across the lobby at a wide staircase. "The party hasn't started yet, but everyone is upstairs if you want to say hello."

"Okay, thanks."

Maybe she could get this done and be gone without having to sit through a party. She walked up the stairs and outside. She'd been right about the rooftop garden. It was still in the planting stages but would be spectacular in a few years.

When she heard soft voices from across the garden, she ducked behind a statue of a nymph to give herself time to prepare what she'd say.

All the Horsemen were seated in a circle, including Ryan's wife Carrie, Gabby, Kendra, and a woman Olivia didn't recognize.

"And you, Gabby? What's your unhealthy behavior?" the woman asked.

"I was homeless for most of my childhood, so now I buy houses," Gabby replied. "I think there are around two dozen, some of which I bought sight unseen. It's unhealthy to spend that much money on property I'll probably never visit."

"How about you, Kendra?"

"I take notes constantly." She held up a legal pad, revealing pages filled with her handwriting. "I know I don't have memory issues, and nobody will try to gaslight me again, but it's a crutch."

"Cheaper than real estate though," Gabby said, patting Kendra's hand.

Everyone laughed at the comment, making Olivia crack

a smile. This was obviously a group therapy session, but she wasn't surprised when Jake didn't join the conversation.

At least he was trying.

"Your turn, Jake," the woman said.

Instead of remaining silent, he nodded and rose to his feet. "I hurt people before they can hurt me first. The minute someone gets too close, I start thinking of how they'll betray me, and I lash out when I should listen."

"Have you done that with Mark, Ryan, or Sean?" the woman asked. "You've been friends for years and started a business together."

He smiled, but it was sharp and bitter. "No. Well, not for a long time anyway. They beat the shit out of me and told me to stop being a dumbass."

"Yes, we did," Mark murmured.

"I broke his nose," Ryan added.

"He had it coming," Sean said.

The woman nodded and studied him for a moment. "Jake, do you think pushing people to the point of violence is your unhealthy behavior?"

"Maybe...no, probably." Jake massaged the back of his neck and shrugged. "I guess I figure if people are willing to smack me down for being an idiot, it means they care. I just wish...never mind."

"What do you wish?" the woman asked.

"There's one person..." He smiled and walked to the railing, then looked out over the desert. "I really wish she'd punched me in the face."

———

JAKE

He wasn't telling anyone anything they didn't already know. Well, the women probably weren't aware of his issues, but his friends were. Hell, his nose was still crooked from Ryan's fist.

Except... It felt freeing somehow to say the words out loud. Not for the first time, he wished he'd talked to Doc Laura ages ago. As their on-call counselor, she'd heard it all, and with her help, he was starting to work through the triggers that turned him into a raging asshole.

Too bad the person he most wanted to tell wouldn't listen—not that he blamed her. At least he'd managed to teach her to protect herself. He could be happy knowing that.

The sound of a woman's heels crossed the pavilion, and without turning, he said, "We're sorry, the garden is closed for another hour, but the restaurant patio is open."

"Jake?"

He spun and lost his breath as his heart skipped several beats. "Olivia?"

She walked closer, but he wondered if he was seeing

things. Her curls were bound in a scarf but spilled over to her shoulders. Her purple and blue maxi dress was cut low in front, revealing generous cleavage and a reddened scar from the gunshot wound.

Fuck, she was the most beautiful thing he'd ever seen, but she had to be a mirage. Maybe he'd finally lost his mind completely. Even his nose got in on the hallucination when the breeze blew her floral perfume at him as she moved within reach.

"That's an order I'm delighted to obey," she murmured.

Without warning, she balled up her fist and punched him in the mouth. The force of her blow knocked him backward and he stumbled on a chair, then righted himself before he fell over.

"Um… It's good to see you." Warmth trickled down his chin and he swiped at it, then blinked at the red coating his fingers. Hell, he was so happy she came back, it didn't even hurt.

Much.

She sniffed and shook out her hand, letting him know she'd hurt herself. To Mark and Kendra, she said, "Congratulations on your engagement. I left a gift with Sierra, but I'm afraid I can't stay for the party."

Without another word, she turned and walked away.

"Jake," Laura said, ignoring the snickers of amusement from his so-called friends. "I think you got your wish granted. Are you going to follow through?"

"I...wow." Would Olivia sock him in the face again if he did?

Probably.

He caught a glimpse of the top of her head as she went down the stairs, but before he could chase her, Ryan tapped his shoulder.

"Clean yourself up first," Ryan said, handing him a handkerchief. "You don't have time for ice, so suck it up."

"Yeah." He swiped the white linen across his mouth, then dropped it and took off running. Unfortunately, she was already out the door and walking to an SUV with rental stickers by the time he reached the exit.

"Olivia! Wait!"

The SUV chirped before she reached it, but she stopped and turned to face him. "What do you want?"

"I... You look great."

"Thank you. If you'll excuse me, I need to get to the airport."

"You flew all this way to congratulate Mark and Kendra?"

"Yes. Gabby asked me to. Punching you in the face was just a bonus."

"Wait! Can you stay just a little longer? I thought we could talk."

She huffed out a breath, then opened the driver's side door. "I said everything I cared to say in Guatemala, but I'm glad you're getting help. Good luck, and I wish you the best."

This was what he'd wanted for her from the moment she

walked into his life. He'd prayed for her to advocate for herself—to stand up against bullies and demand the respect she deserved.

He couldn't let her go like this though. Not until he had a chance to tell her everything he should have said and didn't.

"Sorry, that doesn't work for me." Without giving her a chance to reply, he crouched and grabbed her thighs, then tossed her over his shoulder.

"Jake! What the hell are you doing?" She kicked and hammered her fists against his back, making him tighten his grip on her thighs before he dropped her.

"We're going to talk. I have some things to say, and I need you to listen."

"I needed you to listen too!" She caught him with a kidney shot and he winced, hoping he wasn't going to be pissing blood later. "You didn't even visit me after... You didn't give me a chance."

His chest tightened, but he gritted his teeth and carried her down the hall to the apartment, then went straight to his room and shut the door. After setting her gently on her feet, he stood with his back to the door, blocking her escape.

"You're right. I should have listened, and I'm sorry. I..." He pressed the heels of his hands against his eyes, then slumped against the door. "I was afraid."

"Of what?" Frowning, she took a step closer. "Of me?"

"Of what I felt for you." He almost reached for her but

thought better of it. "God, if you knew how much I love you. If you had any idea—"

"I don't because you didn't tell me." She turned away from him and went to the window. "You told me I belonged in jail though."

"Please, let me finish."

"Sorry."

"I love you, and it scared the shit out of me because it meant you could hurt me. I mean, really hurt me, and just the thought of it made me... I don't know, crazed."

"Jake, I—"

"I was so scared I was making a mistake. What if you were like your cousin? What if I was wrong about you?"

He was babbling and didn't give a shit. He couldn't even look at her, but he needed to say everything before she got tired of him and left.

"You didn't tell me you loved me. You let me think you hated me after I gave my heart to you."

"Would it have changed things? Would you have believed me?"

She took a step closer and laid a hand on his face. "I needed to hear it, Jake. I needed the words, because without them, I had nothing but the ugly ones you gave me."

He moved out of reach and blinked, trying to hold himself together. "I understand. For what it's worth, you have them now. I love you, and even if...when you leave, I won't ever stop."

"I—"

"Anyway." He cleared his throat, then opened the door, making sure not to look at her. He didn't think he could meet her eyes again without breaking down. "I'll let you be on your way."

She grabbed his shoulder and spun him around. "I swear to God, if you interrupt me one more time..."

Before he could reply, she grabbed his hair and yanked, then kissed him.

30

OLIVIA

J ake wasn't the only one putting his heart on the line for a chance to let someone carve it out with a chef's knife.

She'd never really considered his point of view, and for that, she owed him an apology. Of course, she relied on his words to tell her what he was feeling, and he hadn't been honest with her.

He was so strong...so self-assured. It hadn't occurred to her that he might be vulnerable, but everyone had a kryptonite. Maybe they owed each other an apology.

Still kissing her, he lifted her into his arms and turned, putting her back against the wall, then slammed the door. She wrapped her legs around his hips, desperate for more contact with his body, needing his touch like she needed to breathe.

She tasted the blood from his split lip but couldn't stand the thought of letting him stop to clean it up.

"I love you," he whispered, kissing a path down her throat as his hands roamed all over her. His touch felt so good, and she couldn't believe she'd lasted so long without it.

"Love you too." She let her head fall against the wall and rocked her hips against him. "Please, I need you."

"Fuck, yes."

Fabric tore as he yanked at her dress and tugged her panties out of the way. He pushed two fingers inside her, making her cry out in delight and struggle with the zipper on his jeans.

"Please, Jake!"

Still kissing her, he brushed her hands out of the way and yanked his zipper down, then thrust inside her. He was almost brutal with her, his kisses rough and hard with desire, but it was exactly what she needed. She'd forgotten how good he smelled too. He still used plain soap, even after being apart for so long.

"*Dios*, yes. Please, harder!"

Her back hit the wall, making her shoulder twinge. The sharp stab of pain was there and forgotten, overwhelmed by the feel of Jake pounding into her.

"Fuck, you feel so damned good." He pressed her harder

against the wall, then snaked his arm under her thigh to open her for deeper thrusts.

Her channel tightened as a cataclysm built inside her as she tried to kiss him everywhere she could reach. Pleas in a mixture of Spanish and English spilled from her mouth, the words breathless with desire.

Before she could tumble over the edge, he jerked free of her hold, but didn't let her fall. Without warning, he grabbed the front of her dress and tore it down the middle. Her panties met the same fate.

He stared at her for several seconds, then wiped a hand over his mouth, smearing the blood from his cut lip. "God, yes. Olivia Rivera without a bra is a wonder of the known universe."

Before she could answer, he grabbed her hair in one fist and marched her to the bed, then pushed her down until her chest hit the mattress. He kicked her feet apart, then thrust into her again.

The change in position made her see stars, and he used her hair to keep her still for him. The sting in her scalp only added to the overwhelming conflagration building inside her, stealing her breath until she couldn't speak.

She sobbed her pleasure, and tried desperately to hang on for the ride, but Jake was fucking her like the world was ending and she was down for every minute.

He pulled her hair until her spine arched, then lowered himself to bite and suck her neck. "Fuck, you feel good.

Gonna fuck us both unconscious. Then I might fuck that beautiful ass. After that, I'll make you breakfast while you're naked on your stool, so I can eat that delicious cunt whenever I want. I'll have to make you another breakfast because the first one will burn while I'm making you come on my face."

"Jake!"

Spurred on by his filthy, wonderful words, her climax blasted her into pieces. Tears fell from her eyes, but she laughed as she tried to make her lungs work. He'd remembered what his dirty talk did to her.

"Shit! God damn it! Fuck!"

Without warning he pulled out, leaving her desperate for more. Hot cum lashed her back as he emptied himself on her skin. It was dirty, and so decadent that she purred and brushed her ass against his groin in invitation, more than ready for another go. She wanted to be on top for the next one.

"Fuck!" Jake climbed on the bed, then bent to look in her eyes as he stroked her back. "Are you okay? I'm so sorry."

"Mmm." She rolled to her side and tried to open her eyes but wasn't able to wipe away the grin of satisfaction. "I hope you're not sorry about fucking me until I forgot how to breathe. Ready for round two?"

———

JAKE

He liked to think he wasn't a complete idiot, but that was a fucking lie.

Olivia's face and neck were covered in blood smears from his split lip. She had marks from his fingers on her arms and thighs, plus a few spots on her butt that would probably bruise, and there were hickeys *everyfuckingwhere*.

Jesus fucking Christ! Was he a goddamned animal?

Worse, he'd made love to her without a condom. Without. A. Fucking. Condom. What the hell was wrong with him?

Of all the irresponsible, stupid things to do...

"Hey, sweetie." His hand shook as he cupped her jaw. "Are you okay?"

She blinked lazily, then kissed the tip of his nose. "I said, mmmm. Can we do it again?"

"I—"

"Again, please." She slid down the bed, then licked the crown of his dick.

"Jesus. Oh, shit. Olivia!" He pulled her up until she was sitting next to him but kept hold of her before she got frisky again. "Honey, I wasn't wearing a condom, and I am so, so sorry. That is the absolute worst violation of your trust, but I promise I'll be with you for whatever you want."

"Oh. Okay. We'll remember for round two."

"Olivia..." He pinched the skin between his eyes and

reminded himself not to shout. "I might have gotten you pregnant."

"Pretty sure you didn't. Wrong time of the month, but I wouldn't push that too far." She wriggled free and tried to reach for his cock again, but he wasn't having it.

"Stop, please." He grabbed her again and held her against his chest, determined to make her listen. "I lost control, and I am so very sorry."

She turned in his arms and cupped his cheeks, her eyes finally losing the haze of arousal. "I'm fine. I was tested recently and haven't been with anyone but you in...well, longer than I want to admit. You are also fine because I know all the Horsemen are tested regularly. I'm not going to get pregnant right now. Are you hearing me?"

"You're covered in bruises too."

"And?" She kissed a path from his jaw to his neck, making him grit his teeth and try to not be a dick. "You're not doing it right if you don't leave bruises."

"And...I bled on you because I didn't get my lip taken care of after you punched me."

She sighed and pouted, then let him go. "You're determined to yuck my yum, but that's a fair point. Shower, then ice for your lip, then round two."

"I tore your dress."

"It was sexy as hell. You can buy me a new dress and tear that one too. I'll send you the link."

Deciding to quit while he was ahead, he fell back to the mattress and sighed. "You win."

"Yay!" She pulled him to his feet, then led him into the shower.

Slowly, she washed him, her fingers massaging every bit of tension from his spine. It almost felt like a dream, yet it was real. Beautifully, vibrantly real. She'd come back to him and heard him. Forgiven him for his many sins against her.

He returned the favor and blessed every god in existence when she let him wash her hair. Once they were both dry, he tucked her into bed, then raced to the kitchen for snacks and a bottle of wine. He was halfway back to the apartment before he remembered she didn't drink.

Fuck it. It wasn't the first time he'd messed up, and it wouldn't be the last.

She smiled at him when he set the tray on the nightstand. "Thank you. I'm starving."

"It's just a charcuterie, plus bread left over from last night's supper service. I brought wine because I'm a dumbass. I'll grab you a bottle of fruit juice from the fridge."

"No, the wine is okay." She ate an olive, then spread mustard on a slice of bread and topped it with ham and cheese. "I'm with you, so it's good."

"I thought you didn't drink."

"With you, it's okay. I trust you."

He rubbed his chest, trying to decide if what he was

feeling was a fucking heart attack or incredible gratitude. "Can you explain that?"

She poured wine into their glasses. "I never drank before because I didn't know if it would make me do something dumb or make me look weird in front of other people. You took all that away and made it okay to let you help me with my sensory issues. With you, I can be dumb and weird because you love me, and you can be dumb and weird because I love you too."

"Jesus, Olivia. I don't deserve that."

She snuggled closer, then devoured the last of the olives. "Probably not. You're sometimes an asshole, but you're my asshole. Everything else will work out, especially if we get to round two soon."

He choked out a laugh, then pulled her into his arms. "I love you, baby. I'll try not to be a dick anymore."

"Round two will grant you much dispensation."

"We'll miss Mark and Kendra's party."

Her eyes glittered with humor as she popped a fig into her mouth. "Pretty sure we already did."

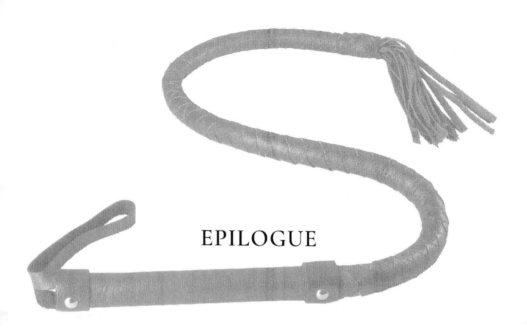

EPILOGUE

Gabby's ass twitched as she walked toward the bathroom, making Sean want to trace the ornate tattoos covering her hip and thigh with his tongue. Rainbow hair trailed down her back, brushing the cute dimple at the base of her spine. The blinding multicolored hair was almost a crime though. According to the neatly trimmed landing strip on her pussy, she was a platinum blonde.

"I trust you'll be gone before I finish," she murmured, giving him one last glance over her shoulder.

"Of course."

When the bathroom door shut behind her, he fell back against the pillows and sighed. They went through this nearly every morning, and he was beginning to feel like a bar hookup she'd chew off her arm to escape.

She'd let him fuck her six ways from Sunday, but the minute he started talking about taking their relationship public and letting her be the little he knew hid inside, she shut him down—and he let it happen.

Every. Single. Fucking. Night.

He'd never met anyone so insular and had no idea why he kept coming back for more. There were other women. He even knew more than a few who needed a Daddy dom.

"I'm an idiot," he muttered to himself. Still grumbling, he got up and dressed in the previous night's clothes, then crept across the apartment to the kitchen for coffee. Fuck, it wasn't even four in the morning. Until Gabby, he'd given up the dawn patrol the minute he left the Navy.

Not even Jake was awake, and he was usually in the restaurant kitchen before five to get the breakfast service going. Then again, Olivia was in town. She was busting her ass studying for finals and didn't have much time to spare, but always flew in on Friday after class to spend the weekend with Jake. Fortunately, she'd accepted Kendra's job offer, meaning she'd be at Club Apocalypse permanently in less than a month. They'd needed a full-time accountant for some time, and even with a third-party vendor, Kendra couldn't keep up with it forever.

Jake wasn't the only one who wanted to keep Olivia close. With her cousin dead and her drug conviction overturned, she was probably safe, but they weren't taking any chances.

That led him to the real reason he spent his nights with Gabby. She'd been specifically targeted with a bounty big enough to tempt a small-time crook. Had they thought she was an easy mark?

Maybe, but easy was the last word he'd use to describe Gabrielle Knox. He'd seen her spar with Sierra. She was vicious and deadly, yet she was just as vulnerable to gunfire as anyone else—like Olivia, who was still getting therapy for her shoulder after taking a bullet meant for him.

Hell, Sean had been targeted too. He sat at the breakfast bar and sipped his coffee. Olivia's cousin Berto had mentioned him by name before someone put a thirty-caliber round in his brain, meaning it was personal, and whoever it was didn't want Berto to talk. Was it just him, or was their mystery adversary going after all the Horsemen?

Worse, whoever was after them was involving innocent people. Maybe the Shepherds of the Coming Peace cult and a small-time gang weren't exactly pillars of the community, but people were dying.

They'd all made enemies during their service. Gun runners, warlords with delusions of grandeur, terrorists... If he included the families of those people, the possibilities were endless, and he had no idea where to start looking. He hated the thought, but he'd almost considered asking Nicolo Bianchi for help.

Unfortunately, or maybe fortunately, the insufferable Italian was gone. He'd disappeared without a word to anyone but had left several guards for Gabby—not that she needed them since she never left the property. No, she spent her days staring at half a dozen computer screens and didn't go to bed until he fucked her unconscious. Even then, she was up after only a few hours and didn't even eat unless he forced her.

What did she see in those lines of code? He wasn't a bad programmer, but the sheer volume of information on those screens staggered him. Sometimes, he thought she worked on the children's games representing her bread and butter, but that wasn't even half. Hell, the woman's sandbox computer for offline testing should have been considered a weapon of war.

If she ever put that thing online... He shuddered, remembering the one time she'd hooked it up to an old laptop he'd intended to donate to the women's shelter in Flagstaff. She'd sent it a single subroutine, and in less than ten minutes, the laptop caught fire.

Of course, Gabby being Gabby, she'd giggled and danced around like a ferret on cocaine while he put the fire out. He'd been right about her the day they met. She was a very dangerous woman, but contrary to what he'd originally thought, she was using her powers for good.

At least, he hoped so.

Sighing, he rested his forehead on the heels of his hands. He'd been an ass to her back then and she hadn't deserved it. At least he'd apologized.

Her bedroom door opened, surprising him from his funk. Instead of the pink plush onesie with cat ears and bunny slippers he'd come to expect as her normal work attire, she wore a tailored black pantsuit and heels Kendra would have salivated over. All her piercings were gone, and she'd covered her hair with an expertly wrapped hijab. Even the visible ink on her hands had been hidden with makeup. Even more strangely, she wore a plain gold band on her left ring finger.

He didn't believe she was married. Not for a single minute. But what if he was wrong?

She looked professional and elegant, yet he hated it. It wasn't her, and he missed the flamboyant color that revealed her personality. "What's the occasion?" he asked.

Instead of answering right away, she poured herself a cup of coffee and drank it without the chocolate milk and sugar she usually took.

"Gabby?"

"I have a videoconference, then I'll be leaving for a few days. It might be as long as a week."

He resisted the urge to tell her no. She wasn't his little, and he had no business stopping her from doing whatever she wanted. "Where to?"

"I have business in Dubai."

His Spidey senses were tingling. Even if he could manage to ignore the clothes, her entire persona had changed right down to her accent. The thick brogue was almost gone, replaced with a softer Oxford drawl.

Even her destination was suspect. Although Dubai was friendly territory, it was very close to places that weren't. Many were downright dangerous for a woman traveling by herself too.

"With whom?"

Her smile was the only thing vaguely familiar. If he hadn't known better, he'd have sworn he was talking to a stranger.

"I'm afraid that's none of your concern, Mr. Franklin. It has nothing to do with you or Club Apocalypse."

"Meeting with your cuckolded husband?"

Frowning, she cocked her head. "I beg your pardon?"

"The wedding ring. That's a new addition to your jewelry."

He fucking hated how jealous he sounded. At best they were frenemies who scratched an itch. She wasn't his, and if she belonged to someone else, he had Sean's sympathies.

"It's from a discount store. I'm not married, but it's easier to do business when I'm thought to be."

"Good point." He finished his coffee and rinsed the cup, wondering how much of what she said was the truth. "I'm going back to bed. Have a safe trip."

"Thank you. It's sure to be...productive."

He nodded and went to his room, then waited until he heard her return to hers. Keeping his footsteps silent, he crept to her door and pressed his ear to the wood. Although he felt like an asshole for invading her privacy, too many things weren't adding up.

Why, after weeks, did she suddenly decide to take a trip to the Middle East? Aside from that, what business was so critical that it required a personal visit? None of it sat well.

She spoke, making him still. Although her accent was atrocious and she stumbled over several words, Gabrielle Knox was speaking Farsi. He kicked himself for not learning more when he'd been in Afghanistan, but there was no help for it.

When the conversation ended, he hurried back to his room, his anger growing with every step. He had no idea what she was doing, but it was going to stop. He didn't care what it took.

And when she came back, she was going to find out what happens to little girls who lie to their Daddies.

———

Sounds like someone is in trouble! Keep reading for a sneak peek of Death's Desire.

For sneak peeks and teasers, sign up for my newsletter. You'll also get a free book delivered right to your inbox!

DEATH'S DESIRE
SNEAK PEEK

GABBY

She plopped into the leather captain's chair and kicked off her shoes before fastening her seatbelt. Sean Franklin was becoming a problem.

More precisely, her reaction to him was inconvenient at best. He was distracting her, and that couldn't happen anymore. Too many pieces were falling into place, and she needed to keep her distance.

Already, she'd gotten too close. She'd allowed herself to feel things neither of them could afford—especially when she was so close to her goal. Worse, he'd been targeted because of his relationship with her, but she couldn't figure out how anyone had found out. She'd been so careful; not even the other Horsemen knew.

At least, she thought she'd been careful.

He'd make someone an amazing Daddy someday. Unfortunately, it wouldn't be her—no matter how much she wanted to crawl into his lap and let him fix everything.

Some things were beyond repair though, and she was one of them. Despite that, she couldn't help a surge of jealousy when she thought of the little girl who would eventually call him Daddy.

It was simply intolerable, and she didn't have time for messy feelings about a man she didn't even like most days.

"May I bring you a cocktail before we take off, Dr. Knox?"

Hiding her flinch of surprise, she smiled at Alfred, her butler and oldest friend. "Just coffee, please."

"Yes, ma'am."

She sighed but didn't protest the formal address. Alfred's name used to be Dennis—back in the day when he wore denim and leather and had more knives in his pockets than she had tattoos. He'd shed it all, along with his old name, because butlers were not named Dennis, nor did they carry knives.

Proper butlers were called Alfred, of course. They wore bespoke suits and starched white shirts with cufflinks and perfectly knotted ties to hide prison tattoos. Their white gloves concealed scarred knuckles. They did not curse, nor did their carefully modulated voices reveal any hint of the streets when they called their employers ma'am and sir.

Perhaps it was unkind to judge him so. He wasn't the

only one who had created a new life. They'd both changed, but sometimes, she missed the scrappy bloke he used to be. At least he'd found himself a wonderful partner. His husband, Peter, was a delight, and it made her heart happy to see the love in their eyes when they looked at each other.

He returned quickly with a silver coffee service and poured for her, but she wished she'd asked for one of the steel travel mugs she'd gotten used to. She'd be less likely to spill it everywhere, but Alfred would have had apoplexy.

She took a sip and nodded. As usual, it was perfect. "I've missed your coffee."

"That's very kind of you to say, ma'am. Will that be all?"

"Yes, thank you."

When he returned to the galley to prepare for departure, she retrieved her laptop from its case and let it connect to the inflight Wi-fi. It was perhaps not the most secure way to browse the internet, but she was running out of time and options.

Club Apocalypse had been bait. Someone had dangled a tasty clue in front of her face, and she'd snapped it up like a fish after a damselfly. She'd put innocent people in danger because of her hubris and utter certainty of her own superiority, and it had cost her a bloody fortune.

Worse, she knew barely a handful of people with the skills and resources necessary to create such a tangle of destruction. It went beyond hacking a small American resort property of no great value into human trafficking, arms deals, and terrorist activity. She counted most of those individuals as friends.

Which of them was it? Ella and Cristian, with their new baby, perhaps? Cristian was a possibility. The Moretti clan had been involved in such things in the past, but Ella had put a stop to the more salubrious aspects of their business.

Maybe it was Adriano and Lauren Costa. They had the wealth and connections but focused more on JoJo's, Lauren's steakhouse in Connecticut.

Nicolo Bianchi was smart enough, but he lacked the assets necessary to compete at that level—unless he was working with someone else. He was quite morally gray at times, yet she doubted he'd risk the fallout if he was caught. If even a hint of scandal attached itself to him... He'd not only lose a very lucrative career as a financial adviser to the world's wealthiest people, he'd likely lose his life as well.

She didn't like to think of any of her closest friends being involved and wasn't sure she could do what would need to be done if they were. Then again, there were no friends on that playing field—only enemies.

Maybe it was someone she didn't know. Some new competitor in the business of international crime and finance—which in her experience, often went hand in hand. Had she stepped on someone's toes?

The thought didn't make her unhappy. There was nothing she liked better, yet she drew the line when it involved innocents. Unfortunately, even her contacts in

Dubai had no information for her, despite their exorbitant retainer. Mogadishu, her next stop, wouldn't be as safe, but her presence might shake someone down into talking.

Pushing the uncomfortable thoughts aside, she slipped into the dark web to check the bounty boards. At least Sean's was gone, but she frowned when she found hers. It wasn't the half million Olivia's cousin Berto had mentioned. He'd rounded down a touch.

"Five hundred two thousand, five hundred and seven dollars? That's oddly specific happy prime number fuckery." It was just a number, albeit a fun one. She often calculated primes in her head when her brain needed something mindless to chew on. It was just something she did when she was bored but had always kept it to herself. People already thought she'd be the one to develop world domination computers. There was no sense giving them more ammunition.

It was silly, really. Computers were ill-suited to the vagaries of human behavior. They'd crash in an instant and beg for people to fix it. The nascent electronic overlords had her deepest sympathies. Humans were aggravating and perplexing on a good day.

There had to be some significance to the number though. She didn't believe it had been chosen randomly.

"All right, friend." She double-checked her IP mask and logged a new bounty using the next closest Fibonacci prime. "Shall we play a game?"

"Dr. Knox?"

She took off her glasses and blinked up at Alfred. "Sorry, what?"

"I'm afraid our departure has been declined. A federal marshal wishes a word with you."

How had she not noticed her plane hadn't taken off? As usual, she'd been too lost in a puzzle to pay attention to her surroundings, but it was one more bit of evidence that she was losing her touch.

"I—"

"Dr. Knox, please exit the aircraft," a woman in a black jacket said, her hand resting on the gun belt at her waist as she stood in front of the exit.

"Of course." Gabby stood, then slipped her shoes back on. "I'm sure we can handle this matter pleasantly."

With a bland smile, she allowed the marshal to cuff her and put her in the back of an unmarked vehicle. They wouldn't be able to hold her for long; her contacts in the State Department would see to that.

It was more an annoyance than anything else, but it proved one thing.

Her adversary was more powerful than she'd thought.

———

SEAN

He wished he knew what Gabby was up to. He didn't want to think about her being involved with whoever was trying to harm the Horsemen, but he had to admit it was a possibility. Then again, if she was, why would she have spent so much on the new security measures?

Nothing about her made a damned bit of sense and it was giving him a headache.

Sierra tapped on the doorframe, surprising him from his thoughts. "Hey, Sean. I just got the weirdest phone call."

"Oh?"

"Yeah. It was from a federal marshal named Tessa Warren. Apparently, Gabby needs a ride home from the county lockup. They want to release her into your custody."

"Excuse me?"

"That's what I said. I thought it was a joke at first, but they let me talk to her, and she's definitely in jail."

"What the hell happened?"

Gabby was a lot of things, but he didn't think she'd have done anything to attract the attention of federal marshals. Of course, she had been on her way to Dubai, and had refused to explain it.

"No idea. I'd offer to spring her, but they mentioned you by name."

"I'll take care of it. Thanks for letting me know."

"No problem. Hope you can get things straightened out."

"Me too." Cursing under his breath, he grabbed his keys, then went to fetch his rainbow haired troublemaker from jail.

When he arrived, he was shown into an office instead of a holding cell. Legs crossed, Gabby glared across a metal desk at a man in a dark suit with a badge on a lanyard around his neck. The man was of late middle age with graying hair and carried himself with the bearing of a career soldier.

"Sweetheart," he purred. "Did you honestly think we were going to let you go to Somalia without a detail?"

Wait. Didn't she say she was going to Dubai? Sean resisted the urge to paddle her ass until she told the truth.

"One could only hope," she muttered. "This really isn't your business, Michael."

"Yeah, about that..." Michael rested his arms on the desk separating him from Gabby. "I'm putting you into protective custody as of now."

She shook her head and stood. "I'm afraid that doesn't work for me. I need to—"

"You need to sit your skinny ass down," Michael barked.

To Sean's surprise, she dropped back into her chair, then crossed her arms over her chest and pouted. "My ass is perfectly round and plump," she muttered. "You can kiss it on my way out."

"Move from that chair and so help me, I will put you in Leavenworth."

Judging by the angry expression on his face, Sean had a feeling Michael wasn't kidding.

"But that's in...Kansas." A fleeting smile crept across her face, then vanished when Michael scowled at her.

"I agreed to let you handle this on your own, but you fucked up." He studied her for a moment, then leaned back in his chair. "A year ago—hell, six months ago—you'd have never let an unfamiliar agent remove you from your plane, take your phone, cuff you, and put you in an unmarked car. Alone. You didn't even demand Alfred stay with you. Aside from that, a legitimate agent would have come with a partner, and would have shown you their badge. What the hell were you thinking?"

"You were...testing me? How dare you!"

"Save it. You literally walked yourself to a shallow grave in the desert, Gabs. Your situational awareness is shot. You're not paying attention and you've lost focus. They're shooting at your friends because you're off your game. Are you willing to risk innocent people for your pride?"

Sean winced. He hadn't heard such a brutal dressing-down in years. Better an ass-chewing than a shallow grave though. It sounded like she had it coming, but Michael wasn't done.

"And you let yourself get baited into coming to Arizona because an adult resort was getting hacked, and you recognized the code signature?" He surrounded the last few words with air quotes. "How's that working out for you?"

Sean tightened his hands and tried to control his fury. If what Michael said was true, they'd been protested, bombed, and finally burned out because of her. Logically, he knew it wasn't her fault, but he'd be a long time calming down.

"That's not fair! I—"

"A fair is a place where grown men throw cow shit for distance and accuracy. Do I look like a fucking carnie?" Michael turned his attention to Sean and inclined his head. "Captain Franklin, I'm Special Agent Michael Lewis, Homeland Security. I've been handling Dr. Knox for about five years now. As you and she are already acquainted, I'm entrusting her to your care."

"No!" Gabby's shout hurt his ears, but Michael ignored it and looked at him expectantly.

He knew he should refuse, yet the thought of having Gabby at his mercy... "I'm retired. Why me?"

"You're qualified, quiet, and most importantly, you're here." His left eye closed in a slow wink. "You're also a reservist, according to your file. Consider yourself called up for duty. You will treat this as classified information. It goes no further than you and the other Horsemen."

"I think she needs a more qualified babysitter, sir."

"I'm sure the Horsemen can handle one woman."

"Don't get your hopes up. Our track record has been abysmal of late."

Gabby sent him an ugly scowl, then turned her attention

back to Michael. "Let me go back to Paris. I promise I'll stay there."

"Gabs..." Michael sighed, then tossed a photo on the desk.

"What's this?" she asked.

"Used to be your La Marais apartment. They got your homes in Gràcia and Bruntsfield too."

"Matilde? Carlos?" She covered her mouth with her hand, but Sean didn't miss her whimper of distress. "Peter?"

"Carlos is dead. Matilde is on life support, but the doctors aren't hopeful. Peter was visiting family in York. All three properties were hit within five minutes of each other. None of the others were touched."

Frozen with shock, she stared at the photo as tears welled and trickled down her cheeks. "They were the ones I've had the longest."

"I'm aware. La Marais was first, then Gràcia. Bruntsfield was last."

"I bought them in that order."

Sean's anger faded at the evidence of her distress. Her choked whisper tugged at his gut, making him want to hold her tight and promise he'd make it better. Unfortunately, he couldn't combat a foe who stayed hidden.

"And they were the only ones in which you had live-in staff." Michael let out a breath and stood, then walked around the desk to crouch in front of her. "This will be hard for you to hear, but you have to consider that it's someone you know. I need you locked down with the Horsemen until we figure this out."

"Why them? Why not my own people?"

Michael rubbed his forehead and gazed at her sadly. "As unpleasant as it is, you can't trust them right now, meaning you're going to send Alfred back to Edinburgh. Aside from that, I'm well aware of how much you've spent on security for Club Apocalypse. It's as safe as I can make you unless you want to have your mail forwarded to Kansas."

"That isn't much of a choice."

Sean resisted the urge to tug on her pouting lower lip. Or better, bite it. Unfortunately, if he was going to be stuck guarding her, he needed to get his mind on protecting what was obviously a government asset, and off how beautiful she looked when she came for him.

Michael squeezed her knee, then returned to his seat. "I want you to keep working too. The identity of the person targeting you is somewhere in that overclocked computer you call a brain. Find them before they hurt anyone else."

Gabby rose to her feet, then reached into her pocket and let one of those damned cock lollipops she always carried slide across the desk. "Suck my lady dick, Michael."

Calmly, Michael unwrapped the candy and sucked on it for a few seconds. "Thanks. I like the grape but ask Rhonda to send you some cherry ones next time. You and Captain Franklin can show yourselves out."

Gabby, I don't think those suckers are going to help anymore. Death's Desire is available on March 10, 2023 wherever ebooks are sold.

For sneak peeks and teasers, sign up for my newsletter. You'll also get a free book delivered right to your inbox!

ACKNOWLEDGMENTS

As always, my undying gratitude and love go to Engineer Hubby. Without your support and faith, I wouldn't be writing at all. Love you to the moon and back, baby.

————

Want to see what I'm up to next? Join my Renegades on Facebook. You can also sign up for my newsletter to receive a free short story delivered right to your inbox!

ABOUT RAISA GREYWOOD

USA Today bestselling author of filthy smut, empty nester, and cat snuggler.

Raisa has worked as a teacher, an actuary (her husband called her a bookie—which isn't too far from the truth), mother, and scout leader. She's happily married to her husband of twenty-eight years, and is now enjoying semi-retirement writing the books she always wanted to read with kick-ass heroines and sexy, sexy men.
www.raisagreywood.com

If paranormal romance is your jam, keep reading for a sneak peek of Wicked Truth by her alter-ego Minette Moreau, available FREE at your favorite retailer.
www.minettemoreau.com

facebook.com/AuthorRaisaGreywood

instagram.com/raisagreywood

bookbub.com/authors/raisa-greywood

goodreads.com/raisa_greywood

tiktok.com/@raisagreywood

ALSO BY RAISA GREYWOOD

Club Apocalypse

Grim's Little Reaper: A Club Apocalypse Novella

War's Peace

Pestilence's Cure

Famine's Feast

Death's Desire

Charon's Chaos

Holiday Daddy Doms

Jennifer's Christmas Daddy

A Valentine for Chelsea

Treats for Lucia

Zinnia's Solstice Daddy

Black Light

Black Light: Roulette Rematch

Black Light: Saved

Dad Bod Doms

Henry

Leave Me Breathless

Breaking Donatella

Bridgewater Brides

Their Wanted Bride

Cocky Hero Club

Sexy Scoundrel

Anthologies

Ladder 54: Five Firefighter Romances

Masters of the Castle: Witness Protection Program

Happily Never After (written with Sinistre Ange)

Demon Lust

Blood Lust

WICKED TRUTH - MINETTE MOREAU
SNEAK PEEK

There was a problem with barricading one's door. When her maid knocked, Lily had to get up and remove the obstacle before the woman could enter without causing a commotion.

"A moment, please, Margaret! I'll be right there!"

"Yes, ma'am. A gentleman has come to call. He says his name is Duke Denforth."

Lily tied the sash of her dressing gown and removed the barricade from the door before opening it. "Did he say what he wanted?"

Whilst Lily rarely asked for her services as a lady's maid, Margaret went straight to Lily's wardrobe, choosing the best of her day dresses. "No, ma'am. He asked to speak with your mother as well. I will try to make her presentable after I dress you."

Lily allowed Margaret to take her dressing gown and assist her into her corset and pink frock. "I don't know him. And the Denforth estate is quite a distance away, if I recall." She bit her lip, wincing when her teeth caught the edge of the scabbed cut Caine had given her. "I don't understand why a duke would call on me."

"I'm sure I don't know, ma'am. Let me do something with your hair before I tend to Mrs. Archer."

"Of course." Lily sat while Margaret brushed her hair, the blonde tresses falling to her waist in a wavy curtain. With deft movements, Margaret soon had the mass pinned into an elegant chignon. Lily's belly growled, and she laid a hand over her abdomen, knowing there would be no time for breakfast while a bloody duke sat in their parlor.

She'd forgotten her stockings, but had no time to bother with them. One didn't keep a duke waiting. Hoping he wouldn't notice, Lily settled for slippers, donning them as Margaret hurried away. Taking a deep breath, she wiped her sweaty palms on her dress and went downstairs.

As she entered the parlor, Jason Martin stood and drew her into his arms. Kissing her cheek, he said, "It's good to see you again. You look beautiful, Lily."

She grinned and hugged him tightly, so glad to see her oldest friend, aside from Elizabeth. "What are you doing here? I thought you were apprenticed to—"

"I came back to see to my brothers and met these gentlemen. They wish to make your acquaintance." Laying a hand on her arm, he kissed her once more and backed away.

A man in a somber gray suit turned away from the window to face her, and she realized he must be Duke Denforth. He looked vaguely familiar, but she couldn't place where she'd seen him. His brown hair was untidy, as if he'd been outside in a gale. His nose was straight and perfect over full lips, and his jaw had just a hint of reddish stubble. He smiled at her, flashing straight, white teeth. He wasn't particularly tall, but his carriage and bulk under the fine wool of his coat lent him quite an imposing appearance.

Two men stood with him; one dark as a midnight sky, and the other fair, with the pale complexion and red hair of an Irishman. Men with dark skin were uncommon in the countryside, and she tried to hide her avid perusal of him. The dark man's bald head and a livid scar across one cheek kept him from being conventionally handsome, but he was the most striking man she'd ever seen. Truly, both Duke Denforth's servants were arresting. The redhead appeared very young until one looked into his blue eyes. They were ancient, hard, and very cool as he caught her peeking.

Both were dressed well in bespoke suits and white shirts. They were most likely Duke Denforth's servants, and she wondered why he'd brought them to meet her.

Yet it was Denforth's eyes that caught most of her attention. She'd never seen such a startling hue before. Pale almost to translucence, the green was otherworldly. She saw dew freshened leaves in his gaze, or perhaps new spring grass. Those eyes held such wisdom, and a bit of mischief.

She dropped into a curtsy, nearly forgetting her manners. "I am very sorry to keep you waiting, Your Grace. Will you all sit? Our maid will be in with tea and scones shortly."

"Don't apologize, please. It is very early, and we have arrived unannounced. It is I who should be giving you an apology."

"Dukes don't apologize." She slapped a hand over her mouth as the redhead snorted out a laugh and her face grew hot. "I do beg your pardon. I have no idea what came over me to say such an impolite thing." Despite her embarrassment, Denforth's laughter charmed her and she smiled as he bowed, then helped her to the low chaise longue. "Will you introduce me to your companions?" she asked.

"Of course, Miss Archer." Pointing first at the mahogany-skinned man, he said, "The bald one is Moses, and the redhead who looks like he's sucked on a lemon is Liam."

They each bowed in turn, making her wonder if they were indeed servants. Both men greeted her with the clipped, modulated speech of educated gentlemen. Moses had an unfamiliar, yet charming accent. Truly, it seemed they had more appropriate manners than their master. She had better sense than to chide Duke Denforth for his poor introduction.

He settled his large body rather too close to her. She relaxed, knowing no impropriety could occur with the parlor door open and Jason in attendance. The situation was so disconcerting. Lily had no idea why he would visit her, nor did she remember ever meeting him. Why, such a man shouldn't have known of her existence, much less visited at such an unseemly hour.

Knowing she had a very short time before her mother appeared, she gathered her nerve and asked, "Why have you come to call on me, Your Grace?"

He smiled softly, his eyes considering and thoughtful. "I will discuss it when your mother arrives. I am led to believe you don't have a male relative, so it is her to whom I will direct my inquiry."

"Yes, Your Grace. My father passed away some time ago." Lily could think of only one reason a man might make such a statement, but couldn't fathom why a duke would ask for the hand of a ruined girl with no title and a miniscule dowry, not to mention the fact that the banns had already been read for her marriage to Caine. As her friend Elizabeth had once said, marriage often involved men of middle age with bad breath and worse habits. All of those things were true of Caine Martin.

Settling back against the cushions, she hid a sigh. Duke Denforth's visit must have something to do with her late father's work. Papa had been a gifted scholar of plants and natural remedies for illness. Many of his experiments still grew in the kitchen garden and in the tiny greenhouse abutting the garden wall. Duke Denforth surely meant to purchase plants, or perhaps one of her father's books.

Truly, she was disappointed that she'd found a reasonable explanation for Denforth's presence. She'd quite liked the idea of a young and attractive duke rescuing her from the distressing fate awaiting her. She looked down at her work-worn hands and short nails. Those fanciful tales never came true except in stories, although Elizabeth seemed happy enough with her handsome earl.

When her mother tottered into the room, leaning heavily on Margaret's arm, Duke Denforth stood and helped her into the overstuffed chair in front of the fire.

Dropping a short curtsy, Margaret said, "I'll return with tea in a moment."

When the door shut behind her, Duke Denforth turned to Lily's mother, and said, "Thank you for accepting my call so early in the morning. I'm sorry to disturb you, but there is a matter I wish to discuss."

"I can't imagine what interest we would hold for you, Your Grace. My late husband had very few debts, and I'm sure they've been paid off." Grimacing, she adjusted the black scarf covering her gray hair. "Did Mr. Archer owe money to you? He did nothing aside from putter in that abysmal garden of his. He kept us fed with his tinctures, I suppose."

"No, he didn't. May I also add my condolences for your

loss." He knelt in front of her chair. "I wish to contract a marriage with your daughter, Lily Archer."

Her mother barked out a laugh, sounding much like a hyena Lily had once seen at the zoo in London. "She's already engaged to the innkeeper. Besides, she's ruined for a decent marriage. As much as I love my daughter, I'm afraid that's the best she's likely to get."

"You would sentence her to a loveless marriage with a man who hits her?"

"She would have better choices had she not..." Lily's mother sighed and dabbed at her eyes with a handkerchief. "I'm afraid the matter is already done, Your Grace. She will be married to Caine Martin next week. It will be a fitting fate for a girl with loose morals."

Lily squeezed her eyes shut to stifle her tears at her mother's words, humiliated beyond anything she'd ever experienced. She'd thought her mother loved her, but Abigail Archer planned to force the marriage to punish Lily for something she hadn't done. She supposed she'd known it, but the proof of her mother's feelings toward her made her heart ache. Was she so unworthy of love and respect that even her own mother believed her to be either losing her wits or a whore? And to say such things in front of guests sent a wave of sick shame through her stomach.

Once again, she wished she'd stood up for herself all those months ago, but looking at her mother's judgmental face, she didn't think it would have helped. To her surprise, Moses and Liam moved to stand behind her, each resting a hand on her shoulders. The gesture was more comforting than she'd expected, and she wondered at their sudden attentiveness.

Duke Denforth got up and shook his head. "I'm afraid you're wrong about that, Mrs. Archer."

"I beg your pardon?"

"I am the man who was in Lily's bedchamber that night. I can also tell you that Lily is as chaste and pure as the day she was born." Turning to Lily, he added, "Even if she's been indiscreet with someone else, which I highly doubt, I don't care. Furthermore, I have enough money and power to prevent that farce of a wedding you have planned."

Her mother's face turned purple with rage and she sputtered. "You have no right to say such things to me! I am Lily's mother, and—"

Duke Denforth held up his hand, cutting off her words. "Someone should have said them to you. Do you not see the bruises on your daughter? What happened to a mother being a safe haven for her child?"

He tossed a piece of parchment into Lily's mother's lap. "The contract with Caine Martin is dissolved, and I have a special license signed by the bishop. Miss Archer will not suffer from abuse, or your vile innuendo any longer. You may keep her damned dowry, and I'll throw in another twenty thousand to cheer your wicked soul."

Lily stood, unsure of what she intended to do. She'd

always wished to see the man who had violated her so thoroughly without ever touching her, and she considered the words she'd wanted to give him.

"Excuse me."

Duke Denforth continued to trade barbs with her mother, but Lily was done listening. She got between them, facing him. "I said, shut your bloody mouths!"

She ought to be ashamed of her appalling language. It had come out almost without her control. Her angry screech brought dead, blessed silence, and she took a deep breath before addressing the rake in front of her. Margaret stood at the door to the parlor, her mouth open in shock as she wisely made herself scarce. Jason sat in his corner, a large grin on his face as he waved an encouraging hand in her direction.

"Did you just say you were the man in my room?" Lily asked.

"Yes, my dear, I will—"

"And you admit in front of witnesses that you didn't touch me?"

Taking her hand, he rubbed her knuckles. "I never laid a hand on you! Please, let me apologize—"

She pulled her hand away. "You let me suffer ruin. You let me get engaged to that foul innkeeper, and you let me debase myself entertaining Caine's filthy customers. Why do you come forth now?"

"I will explain everything after we are—"

Something energized her, a glancing touch of power that

coursed through her veins. She tried to grasp it, but the energy escaped her, and she was too furious to chase it. With a scream of rage, she balled up her fist and planted a facer right to Denforth's nose.

Blood spurted and she backed away before facing her mother. "If he's still here when I return, I will accept Duke Denforth's proposal. We will be married as soon as he cleans up his face, and I will make his life a living hell for the next three hundred and thirty-two days." She stomped her foot and shook out her sore hand. "That is the precise amount of time I have suffered from his carelessness."

Both of Denforth's companions looked as if they were about to burst into laughter, and it made her even more furious, if that was possible. She pushed past them and called for Margaret to fetch Father Reynolds, then went to the kitchen to eat one of Margaret's delicious scones and swallow down a cup of tea.

She shouldn't have punched Duke Denforth. She'd been sorry for it the moment the blood gushed from his nose. And she truly didn't mean to be a shrew. He'd tried to apologize, but she'd been so angry, it was as if something had taken over her voice, making her say all those ugly words without her permission.

Guilt plagued her for her thoughts, but Lily no longer cared about her mother's opinions. It hurt that her mother thought so badly of her when she'd never done a single thing to invite her judgment. It was most likely true she would have gotten no better offer, but that didn't excuse her mother's behavior. What mother purposely pushed her only child into an abusive marriage? Even if she had done what the townspeople accused her of, there was no excuse for such treachery. Why, her mother had even said she should share Caine's bed before their wedding!

As if she would ever do such a thing. She took a deep breath to calm herself and said a prayer of thanks that her father wasn't alive to witness her mother's behavior. He'd been such a kind and gentle soul, and would be horrified by the situation. The thoughts brought a pang of sorrow. Her father would have believed her. He would have protected her.

To her surprise, Jason followed her into the kitchen and poured their tea while she fussed with the plate of scones. Setting jam and cream on the table, she asked, "Did you come to see my humiliation so you could tell your father?"

A flash of hurt darkened his brown eyes. "I followed to make sure you were all right. My father will never trouble you again," Jason replied. "I think between me and your husband-to-be, we've convinced him of the error of his ways."

She felt horrible for her unkind words. Jason wouldn't do such a thing. Laying her hand atop his, she said, "I'm sorry I said that. It was an awful thing to say. But what makes you think I should marry Denforth? By his own admission, he—"

"Came back when you needed him most, Lily." Ignoring

the scones and tea, he squeezed her hand. "He's bought a special license, and left my father in a bleeding heap for you."

"I rather think you did that."

"No, I started it. Duke Denforth finished." Shuddering, he added, "I don't know that I'd have gone that far, but perhaps my father has learned his lesson."

Lily split a scone and spread jam on it. Her appetite had fled, despite her earlier hunger. "I've already said I'll marry him. I suppose we'll just have to wait and see if he stays for the wedding."

"He'll be there when you're ready," Jason said.

Why was Jason so sure of that? She couldn't join him in his faith. But perhaps being known as a termagant would be better than being known as a whore. At least this time, she'd have done what people accused her of.

————

Myrddin wiped the blood from his face. He ignored the shrieking woman in the chair, and grinned. What a magnificent creature his Lily was! Untaught, she'd pulled a thread of his magic away, keeping it for her own to give her enough strength to punch him. And she'd done a bloody fine job of it, to boot.

He held his handkerchief to his face and surreptitiously pushed his broken nose back into place, using a touch of magic to heal the break as Moses and Liam tried to hold back their laughter. Fates, it had been centuries since he'd seen such a powerful familiar. It was no wonder Angeline had wanted her.

"...and I cannot believe my daughter struck you! I swear to you, we brought her up better than that!"

"Do be quiet, Mrs. Archer. I deserve Lily's wrath, but she's given me a bit of a headache."

The older woman scowled, but held her peace. He thanked the heavens for small blessings as he, Moses, and Liam walked outside to wait for his bride to return.

When the door shut behind them, Liam let his laughter burst forth. "I shouldn't laugh, old friend, but the look on your face when that tiny girl punched you..." He sputtered and snorted, his giggles increasing until he had to lean against the side of the house.

"It was a surprise, to be sure," he murmured.

"You're not upset?" Moses asked, looking at him speculatively.

"No, I quite deserved her abuse." He sniffed and rubbed at his sore nose. "Although it is my hope she will keep her fists to herself after we marry."

Nodding, Moses said, "She seems a dutiful and obedient girl under normal circumstances." Wrinkling his nose, he added, "I didn't expect her to have such a sweet disposition, given her mother's appalling behavior."

When he got his laughter under control, Liam said, "I

like her. She has pretty manners, and it was a delight to see her give you your comeuppance."

Myrddin sighed and shook his head. Truly, he'd been shocked at Lily's obviously uncharacteristic fit of temper. Rather than making him leery of marrying her, it only made him more intent upon having her as his wife. Despite her softness, he saw an iron will under the façade of a pale English rose. "We have something to attend to while we wait for my bride to get ready," he said.

"Oh?" Moses asked. "We'll stand with you, and you've got a ring for her. What else do we need?"

"We need to investigate her garden," Myrddin said, gesturing for them to follow as he led the way toward the blackberry bushes. "I found a nasty bit of magic in there last night that seems to siphon its health, and Lily's, too, I believe."

"Whose is it?" Liam asked, his eyes intent upon Myrddin's.

"I think it might be a stray from Angeline. She scattered magic everywhere without considering the consequences, but I didn't have time to investigate it when I was here last. Regardless," he said, walking toward the garden, "I need to make sure it's neutralized so it can't hurt anyone."

"If it was Angeline's, it will fade in good time," Moses said.

"But what if it isn't?" Liam asked.

"Once we have Lily safely in our home, I'll come back

and take care of it." Yet when they reached the wall where the sick plants were, the spell had moved to another section of the garden. The plants had been pruned of blighted leaves, and when he tasted the fruit of the blackberry vine, he found it sweet. Lily's small footprints went back and forth through the beds, and he could see divots where she'd knelt to care for the injured foliage.

"The spell was here before, but now it's moved." As he pointed to the burgeoning blight on a climbing rosebush, he heard conversation from the lane and stood, cutting off his investigation when Lily's maid approached with the reverend.

He had suspicions about the nature of the foul enchant-ment that sickened this garden, but it didn't make sense that one of the dark Sidhe would set a spell in a place inhabited by a young woman, especially one with a small trace of light Sidhe blood. Why would the dark Sidhe bother with Lily Archer, especially when it would likely raise the ire of King Omer? King Teran of the dark Sidhe wouldn't stand for any risk to the fragile peace existing between them.

"You should ask that dragon you're carrying about," Liam whispered as the reverend walked toward the house. "He might know something."

Once Lily's maid had escorted the reverend inside, Myrddin turned to Liam. "Drako sleeps, as he has for almost a thousand years. He has no interest in conversation," Myrddin replied, unwilling to admit that he'd entertained the idea himself. However, it was always the wisest course of action to let sleeping dragons lie, even if the dragon's massive bulk rested across his shoulders.

A quietly shut door and footsteps on the gravel heralded Jason coming to join them. His lips twitched into a smile as he approached, his large hands tucked behind his back. By the time he got to the small group, he'd erased the expression from his face. But then Liam snorted, his face turning pink as he tried to hold the laughter inside.

Myrddin looked on in disgust mixed with amusement as the younger men collapsed to a marble bench next to a blooming rose bush. Leaning against each other, they laughed helplessly.

"Did you see his face?" Liam asked. "She popped his nose like a tomato!"

"We shouldn't be laughing at a duke, you know," Jason whispered.

"You're laughing, too."

"I can't help it," Jason replied, wiping his eyes with a handkerchief. "Lily is so tiny. I never realized she had it in her!" Sobering, he stood and held his hand out to Myrddin. "I believe that Lily made her displeasure quite clear, Your Grace."

"Indeed," Myrddin replied. He'd left the swelling around his nose to avoid raising suspicion. It would fade in a few hours, and he had no interest in explaining why a bloody nose had suddenly repaired itself. "She has a bit of a temper, doesn't she?"

Jason smiled fondly as he looked toward the house. "Yes," he replied. "It's astonishing because it's so rare, but when she finally explodes, it's best to get out of the way."

"I see."

Turning back to face Myrddin, his expression went flat and sober. "Her fury is nothing compared to what mine will be if I ever learn you've hurt her. I will make what we did to my father look like a Sunday stroll, and I don't give a damn if you're a duke or the Crown Prince himself."

"I have no intention of ever hurting her, Mr. Martin." Leaning closer, Myrddin asked in a soft whisper, "Did you love her that much?"

Jason shook his head. "Yes, but not as a husband should love his wife. Lily has been one of my dearest friends since childhood." He rubbed his chin and added, "Elizabeth Stratton as well, I suppose. Lily gave us both a place to hide when our parents became unmanageable."

Myrddin had no fear of the young man, of course. Despite his size, he was no match for a mage. Yet it cost him nothing to reassure Jason, and perhaps it would please his soon-to-be wife. It also gave him some insight into her character, and he wasn't unhappy with what he found. "She has a very good friend in you. I think she would be happy if you write to her, and it would be my honor to have you visit us after we're settled."

"We'll see, Your Grace." He smiled and shook his head. "I'm just a simple cooper, and I doubt I'd fit in a duke's household. But if it will please Lily, I'll visit." Glancing back at the house, his eyes lit up when he saw Lily's maid waving at them. "It looks like it's time for me to give away the bride."

Myrddin and his companions followed him back to the house. It was surprising how quickly a confirmed bachelor would jump into the parson's mousetrap for the right woman. He wondered if the young Countess Shepton would be amused by his choice. More likely, she'd be furious.

Without another word, they walked into the parlor. He stopped, his hand on the doorframe as he stared at his wife-to-be. Her honey blonde hair hung to her waist in loose curls, and was held back with ivory combs. Her blue dress was a perfect match for her spitefully glittering eyes. The capped sleeves and heart shaped bodice revealed several bruises on her pale skin, and he wanted to slit Caine Martin's throat.

Ignoring the stares and sour expressions from everyone in attendance, save himself, Liam, and Moses, he walked toward her and bowed over her hand. "I've never seen a more beautiful bride. I am honored beyond measure to call you my wife."

———

Will Lily forgive her handsome duke? Find out in Wicked Truth available FREE wherever ebooks are sold.

For sneak peeks and teasers, sign up for Minette's newsletter. You'll also get a free book delivered right to your inbox!

Made in the USA
Middletown, DE
05 November 2022

14082042R00229